Greek Island Holiday

Ian Wilfred

Greek Island Holiday
Copyright © 2024 by Ian Wilfred

This is a work of fiction. Names, characters, places and incidents are used fictitiously and any resemblance to persons living or dead, business establishments, events, locations or areas, is entirely coincidental.

No part of this work may be used or reproduced in any manner without written permission of the author, except for brief quotations and segments used for promotion or in reviews.

ISBN: 9798332578090

Cover Design: Avalon Graphics
Editing: Laura McCallen
Proofreading: Maureen Vincent-Northam
Formatting: Rebecca Emin
All rights reserved

Greek Island Holiday is dedicated to Rebecca Emin who has guided and encouraged me through my nineteen books. If it wasn't for her wonderful support, these books would not be out in the world.

Acknowledgements

There are a few people I'd like to thank for getting *Greek Island Holiday* out into the world.

The fabulous Rebecca Emin for organising everything for me and who also produced both kindle and paperback books. Laura McCallen for all the time and effort she spent editing the book, Maureen Vincent-Northam for proofreading, and the very talented Cathy Helms at Avalon Graphics for producing the terrific cover.

For my late mum who is always with me in everything I do.

Finally to Ron who has had to live with me talking about these characters for the last six months.

Chapter 1

'Hi, Mum, I'm back. I've just had a call from Angela... Mum, are you there? Oh, please don't tell me you've gone out somewhere...'

'I'm here,' Jan shouted. 'I've been in the garden throwing the ball for Molly. I promise I haven't been doing anything I shouldn't be. If you weren't monitoring me I would be doing a lot more,' she tacked on with a grumble as she walked into the kitchen. 'What's Angela got to say?'

'You're recovering from a very bad broken leg, Mum, and it's only been a few days since you've had the plaster come off, so you need to be careful. Now, sit down and I'll make us a cup of tea, and then I can tell you all about the phone call from Angela.'

As Carla put the kettle on, she thought to herself that it had been so much easier when her mum couldn't do anything because at least then she wasn't worrying about her getting up and attempting jobs around the house. Now she was more mobile, Carla had to have eyes in the back of her head, especially as it would be only a matter of time before Jan would be itching to get back to her cleaning jobs, which she hadn't been doing for the last six months while her leg was in a plaster cast. Carla had been doing the jobs for her mum and she honestly doesn't know how Jan fitted everything in, what with the dog walking and ironing and cleaning. Every minute of the day was filled with working somewhere or other! Here she was at twenty-four – half her mum's age – and she had struggled to cover all the jobs, always running late and returning home exhausted at the end of every day.

'There you go, Mum,' she said as she handed over the cup of tea. 'And as for you, Molly, I have exciting news – your mummy is coming back to Norfolk!' She turned back to her mum. 'Angela called to say she can't wait to get back to Saltmarch Quay.'

'I can't believe she's been gone for three months already. I take it she's finalised all her late brothers' affairs in London? Or will she have to go back? I hope for her sake it's over as it's a big job for someone in their seventies. Either way, it will be nice to see her. As for Molly, I'll miss her living here. But saying that, I'll still see her all the time as I'll likely be taking her for a walk most days.'

'Angela thinks she's done as his house has been put on the market and she's sorted out all his possessions. Everything else she can do from here, with the help of a lawyer. Now, Mum, as for you walking Molly, it will be a while before you're fit and well enough to do that.'

'I know you're worried, Carla, but I really think we need to talk about me taking back a few of my jobs. You've generously put your life on hold since my fall and I feel really bad that you've had to take on all my work when you were supposed to be having a gap year after university.'

'You know as well as I do that I had nothing planned,' Carla said, trying to placate her mum. 'I probably would have just ended up moping around here, not doing anything, so it's been a blessing to have lots to keep me busy. Speaking of, I need to get over to Angela's and give it a good clean. She told me she'd called Simon to see how he was getting on with the decorating and he's agreed to finish today.'

'I can come with you. The house will be very dusty now Simon has decorated, what is it ... must be three or four rooms? It would also be nice to see him.

Simon is a nice lad. Isn't he about the same age as you, darling?' her mum asked suggestively.

'I'll stop you right there, before your imagination runs away with you. Yes, Simon is the same age as me, but I don't fancy him and he doesn't fancy me.'

'Ok, but you could do a lot worse than a nice young man like him. He's tall, dark and handsome. What is it you youngsters say? He's very "fit".'

Carla rolled her eyes and her mother took the cue to change the subject.

'What day is Angela arriving back?'

'Friday, so that gives me three days, which should be enough time to have her place sparkling. It will be nice to have her back, but I don't think she'll be the Angela we knew. Her brother's death will undoubtedly have really upset her, especially as he was her last living relative. I know they weren't in each other's lives day-to-day, but the loss still must have taken its toll on her, and to have to clear out his home would have been so hard.'

'You know, I was only thinking the very same. But with the help from her friends here in Saltmarsh Quay, I'm confident we can get her through it. Time is a good healer. Well, I used to say that, but after six months in that leg cast after my stupid fall, this leg of mine still isn't back to normal yet.'

'Yes, but it was a nasty break, and so you have to be patient. That means still taking lots of rest, so I suggest you start now, while I go and see Simon. I don't think I'll do the cleaning until he's taken all his decorating stuff out, but once that's done I can start upstairs and work my way down. Can I get you anything before I go?'

'No, I'm fine. You go and get yourself sorted at Angela's.'

As Carla drove over to Angela's she thought about

what her mum had said. She'd actually almost forgotten that this was meant to be her gap year. Six months through already and she hadn't come anywhere close to the slightest bit of fun, but her mum's health was her priority, and she wouldn't have it any other way. Pulling up outside Angela's house she could see Simon's van on the drive. She was excited to see what the house looked like now that the re-decorating was complete. She could remember Angela mentioning that she was having all the dark brown doors and skirting board painted white in hopes of lightening up the house. Being an old fisherman's cottage, it only had small windows, which didn't let in a lot of light.

'Hi, Simon,' she called as she let herself in through the front door.

'I'm in the kitchen,' he shouted back. She headed in that direction.

'I expect after the phone call from Angela you're frantically trying to get everything finished before she gets back,' said Carla.

'Actually, her timing was perfect as I was just about to start on the spare bedroom. She's asked me to leave it for now as the other rooms are all finished. You'll be pleased to know I've cleaned around as well, but I will say it's likely not to your mum's standard!' he joked. 'How is she doing? I expect not being able to get around is driving her mad.'

'Don't get me started on that!' Carla laughed. 'You really didn't need to clean the place. That's my part of the job.'

'Don't be daft. I made the mess while I was working so of course I should clear it up.'

'Thank you, that's very kind. Now you've finished here and Angela's coming back, what's next for you? Have you got another job planned?'

'Yes and no. There's work if I want it, but sadly it

won't be like this job. This has been the perfect project as with an empty house I was able to just get on with things... That sounds terrible, doesn't it? I promise I love my work and I only take on jobs I know I'll enjoy, but there's no denying that it's a treat not having to make conversation every day with other tradesmen or the homeowners.'

'After standing in for my mum the past six months, I know exactly what you mean. Trying to dust and hoover when the owner is following me around is madness.'

As Carla turned around, she noticed a painting on the wall that hadn't been there before.

'Is that one of your paintings? It's really good.'

'Yes, it's a little welcome home present for Angela.'

'That's a really nice thing for you to do. I really like your style. Wait, didn't you have an art exhibition recently?' she asked, the painting conjuring up a memory of an advertisement for the show she'd seen in recent weeks.

'Yes, just around the coast in Cromer.'

'So is that something you want to do more of?'

'Oh yes. If I could swap my two careers around, earning most of my money from the artwork and just topping it up with the decorating, that would be my dream. But I can't see that ever happening.'

'Don't give up on your dreams, Simon, we all need them to keep us motivated.'

'I guess that's true. And what's your dream then?'

'I don't have one.'

'That's rubbish. You must have a dream, something you really want to do?'

'Put it this way, I know what I *don't* want to do, and that's anything to do with the degree in business studies I've just earned. Four years of university wasted, all that money for nothing. Of course I enjoyed the fun aspects of it, but the studying just wasn't for me. I should have given it a lot more thought before I went.'

'But at least you know what you don't want to do. Now you just need to find what you *do* want. Why not write a list? It always works for me. If you're entirely honest with yourself, you might be surprised what inner dreams are revealed. Now, on that prophetic note...' he said, and the two of them shared a laugh. 'I should head off. I'm sure I'll see you around soon though, and next time I want you to tell me what the dream is!'

As Carla drove back home, she couldn't stop thinking about what Simon had said about having a dream, but she hadn't lied to him, she really didn't have one ... did she?

'I'm home!' she called as she stepped into the house, leaning down to greet Molly with a belly rub. 'Just a few more days and your mummy will be back here in Saltmarsh Quay. That will be very exciting for you, won't it.'

'How did you get on, darling, has Simon done a good job of the decorating?' her mum asked as she walked into the kitchen.

'Oh yes. The cottage is so bright and I think Angela is going to be over the moon with everything. Simon also did a bit of a pre-clean so I should be able to get the place spotless in a day or less. What do you fancy for dinner? I'm cooking.'

'I'm one step ahead of you there. I've put a casserole in the oven and before you say anything, I promise it only took me ten minutes to prepare so I wasn't on my feet for very long.'

'I'm sorry, Mum, I honestly don't mean to be so bossy. I'm just so concerned about you, that's all.'

'I know you are, darling, but the worst is over and I'm now on the road to recovery, so you can stop worrying. And once I'm back to full strength, I can take back all the odd jobs and you can have the big adventure you deserve, and take on the world... What's wrong? I didn't mean to make you cry! Please tell me,' said Jan, rushing to embrace her suddenly emotional daughter.

'Oh, what a mess I've made. I've wasted four years at university and still have all that money to pay back, but not a clue as to what I want to do. And to be honest, I think I'm actually going to miss doing all your jobs.'

'No you aren't,' her mum said, dismissing the notion. 'You'll just miss the distraction they provided. I think once you've had a chance to clear your head and maybe even get away from Saltmarsh Quay and have some fun, you'll see things differently, and your next steps will become clearer. Take your time, darling, and decide what you really want out of life. If that takes six months or even a year, then no problem. We'll make it work. Now, why don't you go and open a bottle of wine for us, and over a few glasses we can talk about what sort of fun you could possibly have.'

Carla smiled. How did she get so lucky as to have a mum like hers?

Chapter 2

Sitting on the train heading back to her beloved Norfolk, Angela was feeling numb. Closing the door on her brother's beautiful London house for the last time was hard for so many reasons, primarily because of all the happy memories it conjured of the times she had spent with him there over the years. They had done so much when she visited him – gone to the theatre, museums, and of course visited the gorgeous shops on Sloane Street and in Covent Garden. But now she felt alone, and as though she had no back-up person; no one who had known her her whole life and was always there in a pinch. Ok, she'd never really had to call on him for help very much in the past, but it had meant a lot knowing that if she had a crisis he would be there.

She was also tired and worn out, and was looking forward to the seaside air back in Saltmarsh Quay. Yes, just to get away from all the pollution in London would be lovely. The main thing she was looking forward to was seeing her newly decorated little cottage, and being reunited with her beloved Molly, who always kept her company. What she *wasn't* looking forward to, was all the inevitable questions from the locals. She knew they meant well but she just wasn't ready for all of the 'how are you' queries and sympathetic looks, both of which would likely go on for weeks, flying at her every time she walked out her front door. *How are you coping, Angela? Is there anything we can do to help? You know we are always here if you need to talk to someone...* Oh yes, they cared, but she needed to move on with her life and constantly being reminded of what she'd lost wouldn't help.

She had been relieved when Carla offered to meet her at the station so she wouldn't have to get a taxi. Carla could always be counted on to read the room, and wasn't likely to badger her with one hundred and one questions or shoot her too many sympathetic looks. No, as they drove back to Saltmarsh, Carla would just chat and fill her in on the few months of quayside gossip she'd missed, and that would be nice.

Carla saw Angela get off the train as she patiently waited by the barrier. From a distance, Angela looked the same as always – smartly dressed in a chic, colour-coordinated look. But as Angela got closer to her, Carla could see the face didn't match the outfit. Instead, her friend was looking drawn and tired. In fact, for the first time ever that Carla could recall, Angela looked her age.

'Welcome back! Where is your luggage?' asked Carla, a bit confused as she took in Angela's single, small carry-on bag.

'I have a lot of boxes coming from my brother's house so I put my suitcase with them. It seemed easiest that way. How is your mum?' asked Angela, as Carla took her bag and they headed towards the station exit. 'I have been so worried about her. Is she recovered from the fall?'

'She's on the mend. And how are you? I expect you're excited about seeing Molly and of course your newly decorated home.'

'Yes, of course! I've really missed her and just hope she hasn't been too much trouble. I'm also excited to see what Simon has done with the house. He is *such* a lovely lad and I just know he will have taken so much care.'

'Here we are,' said Carla as they arrived at her car. 'I'll just put your bag in the back while you get in the front, and we'll soon be on our way. Saltmarsh Quay, here we come!' she exclaimed, trying to get a smile out of her friend. Hopefully being back in Saltmarsh and taking a few walks around the harbour would soon see her back to her old self.

Settling into the driver's seat, she smiled at Angela. 'Right, let's get going. I thought I would drop you at the cottage and then go back and fetch Molly. The list of shopping you asked me to get has been procured and put away in the cupboards, so you won't need to do a food shop for a few days. As for the boxes you have arriving tomorrow, would you like a hand with them? I'd be happy to pop by.'

'That's very kind of you to offer but I've asked Simon and he's coming around to help me pack them away in the spare bedroom. It's all of my brother's personal items that I couldn't get rid of, and quite a few boxes that were from my late parents' home. I don't think they've been opened for decades! I will need to go through them at some point, when I'm feeling up to it. I expect most of it will be paperwork and photographs.'

'Don't feel you need to rush to get it all sorted.'

'Yes, I'll take my time,' said Angela, looking out the window in contemplative silence.

The rest of the trip back to Saltmarsh was taken up with Carla explaining about her mum's leg and how she was trying to do things instead of resting, desperate to get back to all her jobs and her old life before she had the fall.

After dropping Angela off and taking her bag inside for her, Carla went to fetch Molly. She decided she wasn't going to rush as Angela would likely appreciate having some time alone to look at the decorating and sort herself out.

She called out a greeting when she arrived home and went about gathering Molly's things.

'I see you've had a nice brush,' she said to the pup. 'Your mummy is very excited to see you and I can see why. We'll miss you being here!'

'We certainly will,' her mum agreed. 'She's been a big help with my recovery, keeping me company. How is Angela?'

'To be honest, she looks dreadful. She's so tired and clearly isn't herself, but hopefully the Norfolk sea air will soon get her back to her old self. Right then, Molly, let's take you home.'

Carla laughed as she drove along the quay, Molly's tag wagging like crazy as she looked out of the window, as if knew exactly where they were going. The dog would be good company for Angela and would hopefully take her mind off of all that had been going on in London. As Carla pulled on to the drive, Molly started barking in excitement.

'We're here!' trilled Carla as they stepped inside the cottage.

'Oh, come to mummy! I've missed you so much! I hope you've been a good girl.'

After a big fuss and a tummy rub Molly was off to investigate the house and Angela and Carla headed into the lounge, where there was a tray of tea and biscuits waiting.

'You shouldn't have gone to all this trouble, Angela.'

'What trouble? All I've done is made a pot of tea and emptied a package of biscuits onto a plate. Now, what do you think of the new look?' she asked, gesturing to the room around them. 'Simon has done such a lovely job with the decorating and I'm over the moon. The rooms seem so much bigger and brighter and I can't help thinking I should have had it done years ago. Of course, then it wouldn't have been Simon who undertook the work. He really is such a lovely young man, isn't he? He'll make someone a lovely boyfriend ... or husband, come to that,' said Angela, thoughtfully.

'Don't you start as well!' Angela groaned. 'Mum is trying her best to convince me that Simon and I would make a perfect couple.'

'Oh no, your mum's wrong there. You two are like chalk and cheese! No, I don't think I can see you two together. You're certainly both very good-looking – Simon being tall, dark, and handsome, and you tall and blonde with those lovely long legs – but I think you're destined to be just good friends. Now tell me, once your mum's back on her feet and working again, what are you going to do with yourself? You're young and the world is your oyster.'

'I haven't got a clue, and if I'm completely honest, I don't know where to even start. I don't regret going to university – I had a good time and a few boyfriends along the way, though nothing serious – but I should have had a long-term plan before I went, so I wouldn't feel as lost as I do now. Mum is encouraging me to take off on an adventure, but if you pressed me to pick a country to visit, I wouldn't know which one to choose.'

'Oh, dear, that's where we differ, as I could name one in seconds – Greece! Well, not mainland Greece, but the Greek islands. Give me the sunshine, the gorgeous beaches, the clear blue seas, and the wonderful food... Yes, that would be heaven for me.'

'Maybe that's what you should do now. It would be good for you to get away and treat yourself after these horrible last few months, and of course you know Molly will be fine staying with Mum and me. A holiday on a Greek island sounds perfect, surely you must be tempted?'

'It *is* very tempting, but I couldn't go on holiday

abroad by myself. It was bad enough getting the train on my own from London! No, the thought of dealing with airports is very scary.'

'But if you went on a package holiday everything would be sorted. I really think you should give it some thought. Like I said, you deserve it. Now, on that note, I need to be going. I have an afternoon of ironing at the Freeman house and between you and me, I cannot get over how many pieces of clothing their family of four uses in a week!'

'Oh, you do make me laugh! You sound just like your mum; she's always said the same thing about that family.'

'I guess the apple didn't fall far from the tree!' joked Carla. 'Is there anything else you need before I go?'

'No, thanks. I think a little nap in my favourite chair with Molly beside me is just the ticket for the rest of the day.'

'Great idea. Talking about tickets, maybe after your nap you could see how much one might cost for a holiday on a sun-kissed Greek island?' Before Angela could respond Carla was up and out of her seat, heading to the door while calling over her shoulder, 'Have a lovely nap and call me if you need anything.'

As Angela settled down with Molly, she thought about what Carla had said. A little holiday *would* be nice, and with the inheritance her brother had left her she could certainly afford a *really* 'nice' holiday. Thinking of her brother instantly pulled her back to reality though, and the fact that without her dear brother she was going to be a lot lonelier from now on. And at her time of life, loneliness was one of the worst things that could happen to someone.

Chapter 3

'Hi, Angela! Sorry I missed your call,' said Carla, having called her right back.

'Not a problem. I was wondering if you're free later today. It's not urgent, I just wanted to chat something over with you.'

'I've got a couple of dog walking jobs, but I'll be free after two-thirty. Would that work?'

'That's perfect. Oh, one other thing, could you please bring your laptop with you? I want you to show me something, if that's ok.'

'Of course! I'll see you this afternoon.'

'Is everything ok?' Carla's mum asked as she came off the phone.

'Yes, she just wants me to pop in this afternoon with my laptop. I think I know what it's about as I was trying to persuade her the other day to consider taking a holiday. Before that though, I need to walk Mrs. Hawkins' spaniels, so I'll head out once I've drunk my coffee. They're great dogs, the spaniels, they're really well trained and never run off.'

'I'm looking forward to being back walking them. Perhaps I could come with you today?'

'If you think you're up to it.'

'It's not if I think I can do it, it's what you think, Carla. You're the boss!'

'Very funny, Mum. I'm beginning to think I'm losing the battle with you and will lose my jobs before long as well. Go on, you might as well join me today.'

'I promise it's a good thing, darling. Without all that responsibility you'll be able to come and go as you like. No more being tied down by cleaning jobs and dog walking duties, not forgetting that nightmare pile of ironing. I somehow don't think you'll miss that one little bit.'

Carla nodded in agreement and they laughed as they finished their coffee and got ready to go.

They drove to Mrs. Hawkins' place and decided not to take the dogs to the beach with the pebbles and sand, as it would be better for Jan to stay on firmer ground, so they headed into the lanes behind the beach.

Carla was anxious to see how her mum was coping with the walking, and keeping a close eye on the time, but to her surprise, Jan was doing really well. It wouldn't be that long before she would literally be handing back the dog leads to her. She smiled to herself, wishing she had the same determination her mum had. She resolved to start seriously thinking of her future from Monday, determined that a new Carla would emerge to start the week.

'Are you ok, darling? You look like you're miles away, so I hope it's somewhere warmer and sunnier than here in a damp Norfolk. Not that I'm complaining – I love Norfolk – it's just that I would like a little sunshine.'

'Sunshine would definitely be nice. You're walking a lot better than I thought you would. Do you think I should start handing back a couple of the jobs to you? Handing them back gradually could be the right way to be going as it would allow you to ease into things.'

'That's a great plan. Why don't we start on Monday as it's cleaning day at the Milles's bungalow and it never really requires much. I'm sure Mrs. Milles pre-cleans before I get there!' said Jan.

'If you're sure you're up to it?'

'I give you my word,' said Jan, solemnly.

'It's a deal then. Right, time to turn around. I think you've done enough for your first day back at work.'

As they headed back in the direction they'd come from, they were both laughing. It had been a lovely walk and a nice change to pass the time with someone else. It made Carla realise that these last few months she'd been spending most of her time by herself, and it probably wasn't a good thing. She needed to be with people, making conversation, and as her mum kept telling her, it was time she started having some fun.

Pulling up behind Simon's van outside Angela's little cottage later that afternoon, Carla realised he must still be moving the boxes that had come from London. Grabbing her bag and laptop, she headed up the drive and knocked on the door.

'You have perfect timing as I've just put the kettle on,' Angela said warmly as she ushered Carla inside. 'Thank you for coming at short notice, it's so kind of you. We're just in the lounge.'

'We don't see each other for years and then it's twice in a couple of days!' said Carla, greeting Simon warmly.

'It's so good that you two know each other. I see you have your computer ready to go so I'll just make the tea and then I can explain why I've asked you both to be here.'

Carla and Simon looked at each other, both evidently a little confused, but as Angela was still in earshot neither said anything.

'There we go. Please dive into the biscuits while I pour the tea. How's your mum today, Carla? Does she know how long it will be before she'll be able to start working again?'

'Strange you've said that as she's actually decided just today that she'll start again on Monday. We're going to do the handover in instalments, a little each week, until she's back to her full strength.'

'Oh that's really good, and just what I was hoping to hear. So it will be a month or so before she'll be back to full steam?'

Carla nodded, thinking it was an odd thing for Angela to say. Was she happier with Jan walking Molly? Had Carla done something wrong?

'Right! Down to business. I don't want to keep you youngsters any longer than needs be; I know you both have busy lives. First of all, a huge thank you for what you've both done for me while I was away in London. Simon, I cannot tell you how happy I am with the decorating. The cottage looks gorgeous and I can't get over how much brighter it feels. You have done such a marvellous job, and I cannot take my eyes off your lovely gift. The painting is very special. And Carla, I could never have gone to London if I didn't have someone I trusted looking after my precious Molly. It gave me such peace of mind knowing she was so well looked after and cared for.'

'She's no trouble at all! Mum and I have loved having her and she's welcome to come and stay anytime. Mum said only this morning that she's missing having Molly to chat to.'

'That's so nice to hear. Just like your mum, I chat to her all day long. Thank goodness she isn't able to repeat anything! Now, no doubt you're both confused and very curious as to why you're here this afternoon.'

'I thought I was here to move the boxes,' said Simon, uncertainly.

'Yes, of course, but there's something else as well. I'm so tired and worn out after the last few months, and Carla and I were talking about the possibility of a little holiday with some sunshine. I agree with you that it would do me a world of good,' she said to Carla.

'I'm so glad! Mum and I will happily look after Molly and it will give Simon the chance to get the last room decorated for you.'

'No, that's not exactly what I was thinking. You see, I don't want to go abroad by myself as I would find it very nerve-racking travelling and being by myself. So, what I was hoping was that you both would agree to come with me!'

Carla and Simon exchanged a shocked glance.

'My thinking was that you could be company for one another, as the last thing you youngsters need would be to have to stay with me twenty-four-seven. And of course none of it would cost you a penny; it's my treat, a thank you for all you've done for me while I've been away.'

Carla didn't know what to say. Of course she would love a holiday in the sunshine, and she knew she would get on well with Angela, but Simon was very reserved, and she couldn't exactly see the two of them going partying.

'It's a lovely idea, and I appreciate the offer, Angela, but I don't think I can take you up on it. I'm sure you and Carla will have a great time without me though, and while you're away I can get your spare bedroom decorated.'

'Are you sure, Simon? Because as I see it, you would still be working for me, just somewhere very sunny. It's inevitable that I'll need your help whilst on holiday.'

Carla knew she had to dive into the conversation quickly before Simon came up with more excuses.

'Let me log into my laptop and we can have a look at where you might want to go. I'd ask which country you're thinking of, but I think I know what you're going to say...'

'You probably do! I'd like to go to the Greek islands – I don't mind which one as they're all so beautiful. As there are three of us I think we'll need a three-bedroom villa with a pool. I know what you're both going to say, and yes, it probably will be expensive, but I have the money my brother left me and I know he'd want me to spend it because, as he always used to say, "it does no good sitting in the bank". It would be great if we could find a villa near a little town so we can all come and go as we please.

'And being a villa with no other guests, you would have the space and quiet you need to be able to do some painting, Simon. The light in Greece will be perfect and while you're doing that, Carla and I can sunbathe and shop. Now, I won't take no for an answer so it's no good you two trying to make excuses. Has your machine fired up, Carla? It's time to find out where we're going!'

'All ready. There are so many places to choose from as you don't mind which island you stay on. Maybe we should start by sorting out dates. When were you thinking of going?'

'That's where you two come in. I'm very flexible, so we just need to fit it around Simon's work commitments and your mum. She needs to be fit and well so she can manage without you, and hopefully also take Molly.'

'I think within a month Mum will quite easily be back to her old routine. So, it's just down to what work you have booked,' she said to Simon.

'To be honest, I haven't got anything booked in after the next two weeks, and I have to say that having time to sit and paint on a Greek island is something I've never even dreamed of.'

'I knew I'd have to have a carrot to tempt you,

Simon. I'm glad I picked a convincing one!' Angela said with a laugh.

'Did you have a carrot for me?' asked Carla.

'No, I knew as long as your mum was ok that you would jump at the idea because – and I mean this in a nice way – anything to put off thinking about your future, am I right?'

'You could be...' said Carla, evasively. 'But moving on, let's look for availability in three to four weeks. Do you think it would help if we sat at the table where we can all see the screen?'

For the next couple of hours the three of them looked at villas, checking to see how far each one was from the nearest town as they all agreed it would be nice to be within walking distance to shops and restaurants. Eventually they whittled it down to eight choices, all of which fitted their needs.

'While I go and pour us each a glass of wine, why don't you two pare it down to just a few choices? We could then give each of them marks out of ten and pick the one with the highest score.'

Wine poured, they each marked the top few villas out of ten, then handed their pieces of paper to Angela who totted up the scores.

'Drumroll please! Here we go ... in third place we have the one on Rhodes, in second place is Mykonos... Though that's more of a young people's island so if you would rather go there instead of the first place one, I don't have a problem.'

'Nope! Rules are rules,' said Carla. She looked very serious, which made Simon and Angela laugh. 'So? Which Greek island are we off to?'

'I think you probably both know. It's the one we all gave ten marks to – the villa on the hill looking out to sea with the gorgeous little harbour town nearby. We're off to the fabulous island of Vekianos!'

Chapter 4

It had been two days since Angela had dropped the holiday surprise on Simon and Carla, and Simon was still in shock. Though he'd been reluctant to accept, it had quickly become apparent that trying to get out of going would be a waste of his breath. Angela wasn't going to take no for an answer! But he had slowly started to come around to the idea and was now almost looking forward to it. The dangling carrot of being able to paint when he was there was hugely attractive and he knew he would get on with Angela and Carla. He suspected Carla would want to go out and socialise, which wasn't really his scene, but that wasn't a problem as he would be more than happy having quiet nights in on the terrace, chatting to Angela or reading his book.

He was now on a mission to research the island of Vekianos. He wanted to get a feel for the area and wanted to look to see if any artists were based there, and if there were any art classes on offer. The island didn't have an airport as it was only very small, so they would have to fly to Corfu and then take a boat over, which in itself would likely be a lovely experience and no doubt very inspiring.

A few hours into his online digging he was really enjoying the videos of visitors walking around the island. The little town's beaches were gorgeous but so far his favourite place had to be the harbour, which was so colourful and vibrant, with many of the restaurants overlooking the sea and the tied up boats. He also looked again at the villa Angela had booked for them. It was very special, with beautiful private rooms, and the outside space with the swimming pool was fabulous. Both he and Carla had offered to pay for a part of the holiday, but Angela was having none of it, insisting that it was her treat and they were the ones doing her a favour by going with her.

For such a small island there was so much information online about everything from beaches to coastal walks, and when it came to the food, people had gone to great depths with reviewing all the restaurants. Simon had also discovered that there were boat trips readily available to other islands, like Paxos and Antipaxos, as well as to beautiful Parga on the mainland. He was looking forward to every little thing.

He had really fallen down a rabbit hole with all the research but before he switched off he needed to look for the one thing he was after in the first place: any artists relevant to the island. He hadn't had any luck so far locating an actual artist living on Vekianos, but he had discovered that there was a craft market down in the harbour every Wednesday, and from the photographs he found, he could see there were many artists displaying their work. It brought a huge smile to his face. What a dream it would be to be living and painting on a Greek island and then selling the work in the market. To his mind it was the perfect job, but more than that, the perfect life.

'Would you like a cup of tea?' asked Jan.

'Yes please.'

Carla had been busy thinking about the holiday. She was so excited – two weeks on a Greek island in a luxury villa, how lucky was she?!

'There you go, darling. Now, where are you at with the clothes situation?'

The fact she was going still hadn't entirely sunk in, but it hadn't stopped Carla from thinking about what clothes she might need to buy for the trip. She'd need day outfits, beachwear, and of course, gorgeous evening wear.

'I've looked online and there are things I quite like but I'm not sure if some of it is a little over the top. I want to look nice, but I don't want to stick out like a sore thumb.'

'Over the top is good. Can't you look online to see what people on holiday on the island are wearing? Surely there's a – what do you call it? – a hashtag for Vekianos? That would help. You need to look good. You can't let Simon down.'

'How many times do I have to say that I'm not interested in Simon, and he's not interested in me? Neither of us is looking for a holiday romance.'

'There is nothing wrong with a holiday romance, and in your case it wouldn't have to end when the holiday was over because both you and Simon live here in Saltmarsh.'

Jan smiled but Carla could only sigh.

As Angela stood at the back door waiting for Molly to come in from the garden, she could see that the last three months she'd been away in London had left everything looking a bit messy and neglected. She couldn't remember the last time her little patch of garden looked so untidy. There was a lot of pruning back to be done to get it back to the look that she liked, but she found that, for once, had no desire to get started on it.

'Molly, come on. It's getting late. Let's snuggle up on the sofa and see what's on the television.'

After flicking through the various channels Angela couldn't find anything that held her attention. It didn't help that she didn't know what she was in the mood to watch beyond the fact that it had to be a happy thing. She couldn't handle anything sad. Eventually she ended up switching the TV off and picking up her book, but six pages in she didn't have a clue what she'd just read. Her head was a mess, just like the garden, and she hoped that the holiday to Greece would help to perk her up. The sunshine would definitely help, and being with Carla and Simon would be fun as there wouldn't be a dull moment. Carla had so much energy it was inevitable that they would be off doing all sorts. As for Simon, Angela knew he would enjoy himself but in a different way, a quieter one. Yes, it would be a lovely break away from Saltmarsh.

But where would her life be after the holiday? What would she have to look forward to? There would be no more going up to London, staying with her brother and going to the theatre, and never again would she get to spend time cooking and baking leading up to one of his much-anticipated visits. No, those days were over. She was on her own now, and that left her life feeling very empty indeed.

Chapter 5

Today was the day! Angela, Carla, and Simon were officially headed off to Greece. The journey from Norfolk to the airport didn't take long and the minibus they had hired dropped them right at the entrance for departures. Simon quickly fetched a trolley for the cases and they were soon on their way to check in.

'It all feels very real now! I've had to keep pinching myself the past few weeks, convinced this is a dream. I'm so excited. How about you, Simon?' asked Carla.

'I always knew it was real, but I have to agree I'm very excited. Are you ok, Angela?' he tacked on, looking at their elderly friend with concern.

'I'm fine, I promise, and so looking forward to some Greek sunshine and gorgeous food.'

They checked the departure board then made their way to the check-in desk, which mercifully had a short line.

'I can't wait to explore the duty-free shops,' said Carla, eagerly.

'I don't think you have room for anything else in your luggage!' Simon laughed. 'Plus, I thought you and Angela were looking forward to all the clothes shops on Vekianos.'

'Oh, Simon, you're a man so you don't understand that there can never be too many shops!' chimed Angela.

'I read that the little shops stay open until midnight. How fabulous is that?' said Carla.

'If that's the case, I'll sit in a nice restaurant

looking out to sea with a glass of wine and wait for both of you to come back with all your shopping bags. Here we go, it's our turn to check in. I think this is where they weigh your case and say it's too heavy, Carla.' Simon laughed again.

'Please don't say that! I'm panicking enough already.'

All checked in and through security, the three friends sought out a cup of coffee and a snack. Simon found them a table and while he sat and looked after the bags Carla and Angela headed off to the bathroom.

'Angela, I have to admit that I was a little apprehensive about coming on holiday with Simon. I knew you and I would get on, but I've always thought he was very quiet and I worried that we might struggle with conversation. I'm glad to say I was wrong! He's very funny.'

'He is, but I suspect it's because we've left Saltmarsh Quay and our lives behind. Everyone is that bit lighter and brighter on holiday, aren't they? I, for one, am! And with two weeks of not having to think about our real lives we can just enjoy holiday mode.'

'You're right there. The last thing I need to be doing is thinking of when I come back before we've even left. That's when I need to decide what I'm doing with my life and at the moment I haven't a clue.'

'You never know, you might find you fall in love with a gorgeous Greek boy and never come back.' Angela winked.

'Now that's something that *won't* be happening, I can assure you of that! And who knows? Maybe you'll be the one that falls in love with someone.'

'Ha! As you said, that's not going to happen. Who is going to want a seventy-year-old woman?'

'Perhaps a seventy-year-old man, or come to, maybe a much *younger* man.' Carla grinned as two pink spots appeared high on Angela's cheeks. The colour looked good on her.

'I think we should stop this conversation now and head back to Simon so we can enjoy a nice coffee.'

'Ok, ok. But I have to ask, wouldn't you like a little romance in your life?'

'No, just a coffee and some cake.'

They laughed as they walked back, and it crossed Carla's mind that a little holiday romance might actually be quite nice. Nothing serious, just a bit of fun for a couple of weeks. Something to take her mind off of her future and having to figure out what she was going to do with her life. Yes, a kind, good looking Greek man could be just the distraction she needed, and would keep her from just lying by a pool with a head full of ideas.

Coffee and cake consumed, they saw from the departure board that they still had just over two hours before they would be taking off. They agreed that would give Carla and Angela time to look in a few shops, and Simon said he was very happy to sit with the hand luggage.

'What are you smiling about, Angela? You seem in your own little world, have you told yourself a joke?' asked Simon.

'Sorry, I was just laughing remembering what Carla said when we were coming back from the bathroom. She suggested I should consider having a holiday romance in Greece, and I was just picturing myself on the back of one of the scooters everyone has, hair blowing in the wind, or on a deserted beach with a nice chap who lays out a picnic before we head into the sea. The reality will likely be that I'll be asking you both to help me off the sun lounger as I won't be able to get up because they are too low down!' She laughed heartily. 'No, I think I'll leave the holiday romance to you youngsters, thank you very much. I will happily spend my time with my head in a book instead.'

'No holiday romances for me either,' Simon said supportively. 'The only love I'm hoping to find on the island is for a paint brush and a blank canvas, and I'm very excited about that because it will be a completely different experience from what I paint in Norfolk.'

'So that's the three of us sorted then, me with my book, Simon with his paints, and Carla with a passionate Greek young man.'

'No, I don't want passion, just a little fun. Now, before all that, let's hit the duty-free!'

Simon smiled as Angela and Carla headed for the shops. Any doubts he might have felt about coming on holidays with those two had gone right out of his head. He just knew they would have a lovely time. They all wanted something very different from this trip and when they did meet up together they would no doubt have lots to talk about!

After the four-hour flight, and then the boat ride from Corfu over to Vekianos, they were finally in the taxi on the way to the holiday accommodation. All three of them were in the holiday spirit, though Angela had shared that she was feeling the effects of the tiring day, and would soon be ready for her bed. But first they needed to go and get something to eat.

The taxi pulled up and there was a lady there to greet them. Simon insisted on taking the cases and the bags in while Angela and Carla talked to their host, who explained about the pool and where all the outside cushions were stored. As Simon went through to the big, open plan living, dining, and kitchen area, he couldn't get over everything; it was all very modern and posh. He decided to stack the luggage in one place so that when she came inside, Angela could choose which bedroom they would each have.

'This is gorgeous!' exclaimed Carla as the two women stepped through the door from the patio. 'I know it looked good in the photos, but my goodness, did you see that pool area? We're going to go home with fabulous tans.'

'I certainly hope so, but please don't talk about going home just yet.' Angela laughed.

Once their host had showed them around the villa and said goodbye, Angela and Carla chose which bedrooms they wanted and Simon took the luggage to the right rooms. By the time that was done it was eight-thirty at night and all three were very hungry. They decided not to unpack or even change their clothes, they would just walk down into the harbour and get something to eat. The holiday would start properly tomorrow.

'From what I've read online over the last few weeks, it's only a ten-minute walk down to the town. Will you be ok with that, Angela?' asked Simon.

'Of course! That's no further than I walk around Saltmarsh Quay. I think I might just change my shoes first though, if you don't mind.'

'Take your time. There's no rush as the restaurants don't close until after midnight. We'll wait here,' reassured Carla. Turning to Simon, she whispered, 'I can't believe any of this. First, to be coming on a holiday at all, and secondly, look where we're staying! I really do appreciate what Angela has done for us.'

'Me too. We're both so lucky.'

'I'm ready! It's time to party so lead the way,' said Angela as she stepped back outside.

'Five minutes ago you were telling Simon and I you were tired and ready for your bed, but now you've changed your shoes you're ready to paint the town red!' Carla laughed.

'Come on, you youngsters, keep up! Where's your get up and go? Actually, it's only food and then bed I need tonight, but tomorrow ... who knows what's possible after a good night's sleep.'

It was only a short walk down into the town, their path winding through the little narrow streets with the most gorgeous small shops either side. As they got nearer their destination they started to pass restaurants, but they'd agreed in advance that their first meal on Vekianos would be down in the harbour with a view of the boats as they wanted that real Greek island experience to kick start the holiday. They cut down between a couple of buildings and suddenly there it was, right in front of them: the sea.

'Oh this is what the holiday is all about! Can you both see now why I wanted to come to Greece? The smells, the view, all the colours ... and as for the atmosphere, it's just so perfect. Now, let's find somewhere to eat where we can take in the views. Should we turn left or right?'

'You decide, Angela.'

'Right, this way then, and remember – it's all about the view, not how good the waiters look, Carla,' teased Angela.

'Very funny, but I really do think you have the wrong impression of me. But saying that, he's nice...' she joked, eyeing up a waiter as they passed one of the many restaurants. 'I'm only joking, I promise. Lead the way, Angela!'

They had only been walking for a few minutes when they passed a restaurant where four people were just getting up to leave from a table. Angela said it would be perfect as they'd have nothing blocking the view of the boats, so she walked over to speak to the waiter.

'Excuse me, do you think we could have that table?'

'Yes of course, just let me clear the glasses off and put a clean tablecloth on. I won't be a minute.'

'He's friendly.' Angela nudged Carla.

'What are you like?' Carla laughed. 'Judging by the way he was looking at Simon, I don't stand a chance.'

'There you go. Is it your first time to Vekianos? Either way, welcome to Restaurant Alina. I'm Sakis and I'll be taking care of you tonight,' the waiter said in a rush.

As they sat down Carla was relieved to see how relaxed Angela was chatting to the waiter.

'Thank you, and yes, it's our first evening. We only arrived an hour or so ago.'

'Well I hope you all have a lovely holiday. I'll get the menus but would you like a drink first?'

'Oh, yes please. Wine for me. Simon, Carla?'

They both said that was fine by them, so they ordered a carafe of white to enjoy while they looked at the menu. For the first time since Carla had picked Angela up at the train station all those weeks ago, the worn out and worried look had been lifted away. She was so pleased she and Simon had agreed to come with her because if they hadn't, she was sure Angela would never have come by herself. The three of them all ended up ordering moussaka with a salad, and while they were enjoying the wine and waiting for the food, they took in the view.

'I enjoy people watching so this is the perfect view for me. I know you'll be looking for scenery to paint, Simon, but I could sit here all day. Ooh, don't look all at once but there's a young woman crying over there. It looks like she's saying goodbye to the waiter and ... that's sweet, he's wiping her tears away...' Angela's whispered play-by-play was interrupted by the arrival of their meal.

Catching the direction of Angela's gaze, their waiter Sakis said, 'That's the owner's son Nectarios, and I assure you it's not quite what you think. That young lady will fly home after her two weeks holiday and then another plane will arrive and the whole thing will start again. Different girl, same outcome, over and over, right up until the end of the season.'

'The poor girl! She obviously thinks she's his one and only. That would never happen to me,' said Carla, offended on the other young woman's behalf.

'It's a good job you're here with your boyfriend or you could be his next victim,' said Sakis.

'We aren't a couple, just friends,' supplied Simon.

'I don't think you should tell Nectarios that because he'll insist on serving you instead of me, and I can guarantee that wouldn't be as much fun. Look, just as I predicted, he's going over to that table in the corner, the one with the two girls. Just watch, he'll start to charm them and before long he'll be getting their numbers.'

'To think the other girl hasn't even been gone five minutes! That's terrible. I'm saying it again, that *definitely* won't happen to me,' huffed Carla.

Famous last words, Angela thought quietly to herself.

Chapter 6

Holiday day 1

Simon was the first one up so he made a coffee and took it out onto the patio that looked down to the pool. The sun was just coming up and he could see a few boats way out at sea. Taking in the view he realised he hadn't bothered to look at his phone yet this morning. In fact, he had left it in his bedroom. He smiled to himself, deciding that he liked being disconnected and so that was exactly where his phone would stay for as much of the holiday as possible. He also couldn't get over how chilled and relaxed he felt after being on the island for just a few short hours.

Thinking back to last night in the restaurant made him smile again. It had been fun and the three of them had really gelled, which was a relief as the situation could have been so different. The food and wine were so lovely and they'd agreed that it would be a place they would go back to again. He was still laughing at how mad Carla was with the Casanova waiter, but like Angela had said, the girls he seduced were on holiday to have fun and likely knew the score, not expecting a holiday romance to be anything more than just that.

'Good morning! You're up early,' Angela greeted him.

'Take a seat and I'll make you a drink. Would you prefer tea or coffee?'

'No, you stay there. I'm capable of doing it.'

'I know that, but I was just about to make myself

another drink anyway. I promise I won't fuss around you the whole holiday. Now, pick your chair. I think that one there might be good as it gives a great view right out to sea,' he said, pointing.

'Thank you. A white coffee, no sugar, would be very much appreciated.'

'It's on the way. You just take a seat, breathe in the fresh air, and soak up the fabulous view.'

Simon was right, the air was so clear and the view was to die for. Even though Angela lived in a little harbour town where she could see the sea every day, this was a completely different experience. She could see little boats crossing in the distance and then there were the gorgeous yachts that had moored up for the night. Oh yes she was going to be very content staying here for two weeks.

'There you go,' said Simon, handing her a mug. 'Did you sleep ok? My bed was really comfortable.'

'I did sleep well, thank you. I think the lovely meal and the walk back last night helped. The waiter was so nice and very funny. And as for the other waiter...' she laughed, 'he really wound Carla up! I'm glad he didn't come to our table because I'm sure she would have said something to him.'

'Do you have a plan of action for today? I'm happy to pop into the town to do some food shopping. I was thinking that if we got into a routine of bringing a few things back every time we're down there, we wouldn't have to do big shops.'

'That's a really good idea. I think I'll spend the day by the pool in the sunshine and then we can all head out to dinner together tonight. To be honest, before we came here I did think we could cook in, but now we've seen all those gorgeous restaurants on our doorstep, it seems a waste of an evening not going out, don't you think?'

'I'm happy with whatever suits you.' Simon shrugged good-naturedly. 'The only thing I have planned for the next few days is popping down to the craft market in the harbour tomorrow, so it's a pool day today. Once Carla is up we can put a shopping list together and I'll nip down and get the food first.'

'Did I hear my name? Good morning to you both. Oh my goodness, look at that view, it's spectacular! You should have woken me up earlier. I don't want to miss a thing!'

'We were just talking about the day ahead. Have you any plans?' asked Angela.

'Yes, I have a date with the swimming pool and one of those sun loungers.'

'So, you haven't made a date with the lothario waiter then?' joked Simon.

'Very funny. It took a lot last night to stop me going over to those girls in the restaurant and pointing out what type of chap he really is. I still can't get over how blatantly obvious he was.'

'Oh, he was fine. The girls are on holiday and they were all just having fun. And isn't that what you wanted on this holiday, a bit of fun?'

'Yes, but I can assure you that my fun won't be happening with that waiter.'

Angela and Simon both laughed.

Simon explained to Carla that if they put a little shopping list together, he would go down into the town and fetch everything.

'I'll come with you and then the bags won't be so heavy. It'll also be nice to see the place in daylight. Do you think it would be good to go now, before it gets too hot?'

'That's fine by me. I'll go and fetch a pen and paper and we can make a list.'

After a quick drink and a change of clothes, Carla

was ready. They decided they were going to get just enough shopping to see them though the day, and then tonight, on the way back from dinner, they would buy a few bits for the following day. It was a lovely walk down and she and Simon ambled along in silence, both taking everything in. Once in the supermarket, they each picked up a basket. It was only a small shop, so they knew there wouldn't be a lot of choice, but they only needed basics like bread, milk, cheese, and crisps, and of course bottled water and a couple bottles of wine.

'I think that's it. Can you think of anything else we need?' asked Simon.

'No, we're sorted for now.'

As they placed the baskets down at the till, Carla turned around to find the flirty waiter from last night was stood behind her. He seemed a lot taller now he was closer to her, and he had a smile that she had to admit was to die for. She could see why all those silly girls went all googly-eyed over him; he was very handsome.

'Good morning! Weren't you and your boyfriend in my restaurant last night? Did you enjoy your meal?'

'We aren't a couple, just friends, but yes we were. The food was delicious and Sakis entertained us throughout. We had a lovely time.'

What had she just said? And why was suddenly feeling flustered? She was as bad as all the other girls that fell for his charm!

At her mention of just being friends with Simon, Nectarios's face had lit up.

'I'm glad you had a good time. We'd love you to come back again,' he said, somehow making the invitation sound provocative.

'Could you pass your basket up?'

Simon's request flummoxed her and when she

turned to find he was laughing she got annoyed. Of course he had to witness her embarrassment! No doubt he would mention it – and tease her mercilessly – while walking back to the villa.

The shopping was soon bagged up and paid for and when they stepped outside Nectarios was right behind them. She was determined to play it cool this time if he spoke to her again again.

'Like I said, I hope to see you in the restaurant again before you leave.'

'Something tells me you will, isn't that right, Carla?' Simon nudged her and she shot daggers at him before turning back to Nectarios.

'Yes, I expect so,' she said with a nonchalant shrug.

'Ok then, have a nice day!'

That had gone better. She hoped she'd managed to come across normal and unaffected by him. As Nectarios walked away she fiddled with the two shopping bags she was carrying, just waiting for Simon to make a comment. Surprisingly, he didn't, and they headed to the little bakery for a selection of treats before going back to the villa.

Walking through the gate they found Angela was on the sun lounger by the pool.

'We're back with all the goodies! Have you been in the pool yet?' asked Simon.

'No I thought I would sunbathe first and let the sun heat the water a little. Did everything go ok at the market?'

This was it, Carla just knew Simon would say something, but then ... he didn't, apart from telling Angela that they would pack everything away in the villa. Perhaps he wasn't going to say anything after all? But why not? If it had been the other way around, she would have been teasing him ... wouldn't she? She stopped in her tracks. In just the short time they had started to get to know one another better, she and Simon had started to bond, and she found that, even if pushed, she wouldn't say anything that might upset him.

After all the shopping was put away, Carla made up a tray of coffees and pastries then headed down to the pool to join the others.

'I could get used to this waitress service!' Angela smiled her thanks.

'Me too,' Simon agreed before turning to Angela. 'I also could get used to being on this beautiful island. I know I keep saying it but thank you again for this holiday.'

'You really don't have to keep thanking me. Now, what is the plan for the rest of the day? Neither of you need to be here babysitting me. If you want to go out and explore and have fun, please do! I'm more than happy to stay here by the pool with my book.'

'I'm not sure about Simon, but I plan to do the same. Rotating between sunbed and pool will be my perfect day.'

'That sounds good to me as well. We have some nice things for lunch and plenty of snacks so there's no need for us to go anywhere until tonight.'

'Thank you both again for doing the shopping. As for tonight, would you like to eat where we did last night?'

'I thought perhaps we could find somewhere else, unless you and Carla wanted to go back there?' asked Simon

'Somewhere else would be nice, I think,' said Carla, suddenly blushing. She was surprised to find she was slightly disappointed they weren't going to Nectarios's restaurant again.

'Great! Now I think it's time for me to take my old bones into the pool. Is anyone joining me?'

Simon jumped up off the lounger, ready to dive

in.

'Are we competing with lengths or would you sooner have a game with a ball?' he asked.

'Neither, thank you. I'm just going to bob up and down.'

It was nearly seven-thirty and Angela was ready to join Carla and Simon for the walk down into the harbour. She was a little tired but she put that down to the number of times she had been in the pool. One last look in the mirror and she could see she had caught the sun and had a lovely glow. It had been such a nice day. Carla and Simon were great company, and it was lovely how the three of them got along so well.

'Don't you look lovely! That's a gorgeous dress.'

'Thank you, Carla. The three of us have scrubbed up well. I admit I'm not that hungry after all the snacks we've eaten today.'

'Perhaps we could have a little walk around the harbour first?'

'That's a good idea, Simon, but I think while you two do that I would quite like to sit and people watch. Now, lead the way.'

The short walk down didn't take very long and this time they cut through a different little alleyway. There was so much to see and Angela was looking forward to exploring all the unique nooks and crannies that made up this little harbour town in the coming days.

'Oh, look at this! What a gorgeous little square. The colours from the plants are beautiful and just look at that bougainvillaea, how magnificent. Would you both mind if I sit here? There's no need to rush back as this is the perfect place for me to watch the world go by.'

'If you're sure? We can be back here for nine

o'clock and we can make our way to a restaurant at that point,' said Simon.

'And remember, don't talk to any strangers. We saw last night how these gorgeous Greek men flirt with the single woman that are here on holiday,' joked Carla.

'I think you can be reassured that won't happen to me. Now get out of here, both of you.'

As they left Angela laughed to herself. They'd had a lovely start to their holiday and this was just what she needed to take her mind off of everything that had happened over the last few months. She wandered over to a bench in one of the corners that gave her a view of both the visitors walking in and out of the square, and up behind the buildings to one of the hills, which had little houses all painted white with beautiful blue shutters. They looked spectacular in the last of the day's sunshine and she could happily have sat there for hours, taking it all in.

'Excuse me, would it be ok to sit here?'

Angela turned to find a distinguished looking Greek gentleman. Of course she said yes as she didn't need the whole seat to herself. She shuffled over and he sat down, and then she returned to her people watching. It was so lovely to see all families together enjoying themselves, some of them made up of multiple generations.

'Are you on holiday?' the man asked.

'Yes, it's my first time here.'

'We are very proud of our island and it's always so nice to see visitors looking happy and enjoying being here. So many come back year after year.'

'I can see why. It's very beautiful and populated by such friendly people. Have you lived here all your life?'

'Yes, for many years I had a restaurant down overlooking the harbour, but now my daughter and grandson run it. I try to stay away because I tend to interfere and, well ... it doesn't go down very well. By the way, my name is Lambros.'

'Lovely to meet you, Lambros. I'm Angela. How are you coping with having to let go?'

'My daughter would tell you "not very well".' He laughed. 'If I can't see the restaurant, I'm happy, but if I'm sat there eating or having a drink, I do miss being involved with everything. But times move on and things change.'

'Yes, they do. Hopefully the beauty of the island is some consolation. This is a particularly lovely little square to sit and watch the world go by. A great place to watch the sun go down and to take in those little houses on the hill, all crisp and freshly painted ... apart from that one in the middle, which spoils the view. It's a shame the owners haven't painted it to match and fall in place with all the others as it really sticks out like a sore thumb.'

'But why should it look like the others? If it's habitable and the owner is comfortable and happy living there, why should they feel forced to paint it just to please everyone else?'

'I suppose you're right, but don't you think it stands out for all the wrong reasons? Surely all it would take is a pot of paint and a few hours' work.'

Lambros didn't answer and she wondered if she had offended him. Perhaps he knew who lived there? She needed to change the subject.

'So, tell me, what was it like growing up here on Vekianos? I know it's small, but did it have a school?'

'Oh yes. Things were very different, of course, as very few visitors – if any – came, but in the past few decades the tourism industry has grown exponentially. We suddenly had people coming over on the boats from Corfu, and then locals started to rent their houses out and more building work took place to increase the number of hotels and rental villas. In the early days visitors were happy to just be here; it wasn't like now where they demand ... no, sorry, that's the wrong word, they ... *need* different things. Hot water to start with.'

They both laughed as Lambros explained that hot water to shower was one of the biggest issues on all the islands back in the sixties and seventies, when five or six people expecting to shower one after the other was a major issue.

'I remember those days. Spain and Italy were just the same. These days it's not hot water but the internet that people don't seem to be able to survive without. How times have changed.' Angela sighed.

'They certainly have. Along with the internet, all the accommodations now have to have these posh coffee machines. I have seen a few that you appear to need engineering qualifications just to use!'

'For me it's the simple things that mean the most. For instance, just sitting here, talking and enjoying the view, is everything I need from a holiday.'

'Yes, but you would be happier if that house on the hill looked a little smarter.'

'Perhaps. Not everything is perfect in the world, and you're right, it shouldn't need to be if the owners like it as it is. Oh, here come my friends. It must be time to get some food. It's been lovely talking to you, Lambros.'

'I've enjoyed our chat as well. Before you go, though, I need to apologise.'

'What do you mean?'

'I'm sorry the old scruffy house on the hill spoilt your view. You aren't the first person to tell me I need to do something about it.'

'Oh dear. Lambros, I have well and truly put my foot in it, haven't I? Please ignore what I said. If you're happy, that's all that matters, because to be happy and content is a very special thing.'

Chapter 7

Holiday day 2

Simon was the first one up again and he was buzzing. He had two things on his to-do list today: one was to visit the craft market down in the harbour, and the other was to find a spot for later in the week where he could go and paint.

'You're up first again! I can't remember when I've laid in so long. You made the coffee yesterday so it's my turn today,' said Angela.

'That would be great. Better make three as I think I can hear Carla moving around. Still feeling bad about accidentally insulting the local man about his scruffy house?' asked Simon as Angela bustled about in the kitchen.

'Absolutely awful, but I said it and there was no way I could cover it up. But he did say I wasn't the first to make a comment on it, and even he had to admit it does stick out amongst all the others. Morning, Carla, I'm just putting the kettle on so coffee will be on the way shortly.'

Still half asleep, Carla simply gave Angela a thumbs up, then followed Simon out to the patio. 'Another lovely day in paradise!' she said, the sunshine waking her properly. 'Is it today you're off to the craft market?'

'Yes and I'm excited. They hold it outdoors, which will be a nice change as in the UK these kinds of things are always in church or village halls because of the unpredictable weather.'

Angela emerged with the drinks and they all took a moment to savour the first burst of caffeine. 'Any plans today, Carla?' she asked.

'Yes, and the best bit is that it won't take me long to get there. In fact, I can see them from here!' she said, pointing to the sun lounger and the pool. 'I'm ready for day two of getting a tan. Will you be joining me or are you off to upset some more locals? I'm only joking,' she rushed to reassure her friend, who looked stricken. 'He seemed fine when you said goodbye, and it was such a nice evening after that. The food was top-notch and the staff friendly, but I have to admit that I did miss the waiter from the night before – Sakis.'

'He was really funny. We must go back there to see him again, and also to see if the other waiter is charming another innocent young woman.'

'I don't mind where we eat,' said Simon, amiably. 'I suspect the food will be fantastic in all the restaurants so you two can choose and I'll happily go along with it. Now, you're sure you both don't mind me going out for the day?'

'Not at all! Go and have a nice time but please don't do what Angela did and tell someone you don't like their house.'

'My lips are sealed, I promise. I'll just nip and get changed before I head out.'

It didn't take him long to get ready as he was eager and excited to see what art the island had to offer.

'You look very smart! I hope there will be a few nice female artists there that will appreciate the effort you've put in,' said Carla, supportively.

'Thank you, but it's all about the art, not my shorts and t-shirt. Have a lovely day, both of you, and don't tire yourself out swimming, Angela.'

'No, I promise it's just going to be a lazy day on the sun lounger. Ta-ta!'

As Simon headed down the hill, he looked at the

time. It was just nine-fifteen so he had plenty of time before the fair closed at one-thirty, when the afternoon sun became too hot for the stall holders and their wares. Working his way through the little streets to the harbour it was a completely different vibe from that of the evenings. Everyone had beach bags with them, ready to head off for a day on the sand and in the sea. Thinking he could perhaps spend a couple of hours on the beach this afternoon, he had brought a towel with him.

Once down by the harbour wall he turned right and walked about fifteen minutes to the old pier. He could see more people were going in his direction than the other way, but the reviews he'd read online had warned him it got very busy. As he got nearer, he could see there were stalls not just on the pier but at the side of the harbour wall as well. As he didn't want to miss any of it, he decided to walk along and look at the crafters by the wall first.

The first stall had the brightest and cheeriest pottery – little bowls and small, decorated plates that were all different, but with an overall theme running through them when you saw them displayed together. Next to that there were three stalls with lace, the most delicate work you've ever seen. Reaching the entrance to the pier, he passed it to go across to the other side of the wall and see what else was there. He was glad he had as it was more his thing, with two people in a row selling paintings that were stunning with incredible detail. He was just beginning to think that the pieces were far better than anything he could ever do, but he stopped himself. All art was beautiful and just because his work was a lot more abstract – usually landscapes composed of bold colours – it didn't mean it was somehow less than the delicate detail these artists favoured.

The pier was very busy, and he couldn't get close to many of the stalls. There were a couple of jewellery ones with modern rings and bracelets, and another with potter's crafts, fabulous modern jugs in every colour you could imagine. Next to that was a lady with miniature paintings, each one no more than ten centimetres square. It was incredible how she managed to paint all the details on each one.

As he got to the end of the pier and turned around to look at the stalls on the other side, he was instantly stopped in his tracks by a group of paintings that reminded him of his own work as they were painted in the same modern, abstract style. But where his were darker to show the Norfolk light, these were bright and showed off the beautiful Greek sunshine. As he walked over the girl standing at the stall smiled shyly at him. She looked almost nervous, not at all like the other stall holders who were actively engaging with the milling crowds, trying to sell their work.

'These paintings are gorgeous, so fresh and vibrant! I really like that one with the path leading from the beach over the little hill. It's so clever the way the artist leaves you to imagine what might be at the end of it. You can tell a lot of thought went into it.'

'Thank you, that's very kind, but I have to admit that I'm the artist and when I painted it that never crossed my mind. But now you've pointed it out, I see what you mean.'

'You are very talented. Have you been painting long?'

'Practically my whole life! I was given some paints and a brush as a young child and it's very addictive. Once you start, you're hooked and there's no stopping.'

'I know exactly what you mean. I'm also a

painter, though for me it's more of a hobby than a career. I'm here on holiday and I've been so looking forward to visiting this market, and I'm glad to say it's even better than I anticipated. I'm hoping to get some painting of my own done while I'm here. The weather, especially the light, excites me. Back in England, if it's not pouring down it's windy, which is not the best conditions for being outside with an easel and canvas. Sorry, I didn't ask your name. I'm Simon.'

'It's nice to meet you, Simon, I'm Polina. I'm very lucky living here as there aren't many days between March and October where I can't get outside to paint.'

'That's wonderful. Do you display your work anywhere else? It definitely deserves to be in a gallery.'

'No, just here in the market. My dream would be to show in a gallery one day, and earn a living from painting.'

'I'm the same. To paint creatively as a job instead of just a hobby would be wonderful. You probably know all the best places to paint around here. Do you have any suggestions? I'm here for just under two weeks so I'd love to paint in more than one place, though I will have to buy or borrow an easel.'

'I can help you with both of those things! One of my favourite places to paint is on the other side of the island in the little town of Thagistri. It's just a short bus journey, and if you like, I can lend you an easel while you're here.'

'That's very kind of you.' Simon was touched by the generosity of her offer.

'Will you excuse me? That couple there are coming back to choose a painting and judging by my previous interactions with them, it might take a while. Here's my card with my phone number and email address on. Send me a message and we can arrange for you to borrow the easel,' she said, before turning to the approaching couple. 'So nice to see you again! Have you made up your minds yet which painting you want?'

Simon couldn't believe his luck, he was going to be able to paint while he was here on the island! He was so pleased he had met Polina, and to find that they had shared interests. It had been a long time since that had happened. She was also very attractive and he wondered if he should invite her to go with him to Thagistri so they could paint together. Perhaps when he took her up on the offer of borrowing the easel, he could ask?

Looking at the time he decided that instead of going to the beach he would head back to the villa for a swim and some lunch.

'I return bearing gifts, both sweet and savoury,' he announced grandly upon his return, having stopped to buy some pastries as a surprise for Angela and Carla.

'You are the best! Any man that turns up with gorgeous food is a star in my eyes.' Carla climbed out of her lounger to see what Simon had procured.

'Have you had a nice time? Was the market all you were hoping it would be?' asked Angela.

'It was and I even met an artist who said I can borrow an easel off them for the time I'm here. They also suggested a good place to go and paint.'

'Wonderful!' exclaimed Angela. 'He's come back very excited, don't you think?' she asked Carla once Simon had popped inside to change into his swimsuit.

'It just shows how much he loves his art. To be able to paint here on Vekianos must be such a treat for him.'

After a swim the three of them went back up onto the patio and had lunch. Simon was lost in thought, contemplating how to go about seeing Polina again. Should he phone, text, or email? And should he ask her if she might want to spend some time with him painting?

'Simon... Simon?'

'Sorry, Angela, you were saying?'

'I was just wondering if you had any idea where you wanted to eat tonight.'

'No, wherever you both want is ok with me.'

'I'd like to go back to where we ate the first night. Sakis was funny, the food was great, and we might be entertained by Nectarios and his flirting. Would that be ok with you?' asked Carla.

Angela and Simon said they were happy with that and to make an evening of it they could all go down into the harbour a little earlier to find somewhere to have pre-dinner drinks.

The rest of the day was spent happily in the sunshine with their books and a few dips in the pool.

Carla was the first one to be ready that evening and sipping her wine on the terrace she was feeling good. These first couple days of their holiday had been exactly what she needed. Her tan was coming along nicely, she loved her new dress, and she was ready for a nice night out. She was also looking forward to seeing Nectarios, but she wouldn't be like all the other girls who threw themselves at him. No, she was going to play it cool and have a bit of fun teasing him.

'You look lovely, Angela. I was only thinking to myself that just a few days of sun on my skin has really made me feel better. Would you like a glass of wine while we wait for Simon? We're a little early.'

'I don't think I will, thank you. And yes, the sun

really does help.'

Simon was typing on his phone as he stepped outside. He had settled for a text to Polina, short and to the point.

It was nice meeting you today and your work is really lovely. Thank you again for offering me the use of an easel. I was wondering when and where I could pick it up from you? Simon

'Don't we all look very smart?' he asked as he looked up from his mobile.

'Carla and I were just marvelling at what a little sunshine can do for a person. I don't think Vekianos will know what's hit them when we arrive down there. Are we ready to go and "hit the town", as you youngsters say?'

That made them all laugh and off they went, but unlike the first night they weren't in any hurry as they cut through alleyways and little squares. The shops were gorgeous, if tiny, and Carla pointed some out to Angela.

'Would you like to look in them? The evening is still young and after all the pastries today I don't think any of us are ready to eat just yet,' said Angela.

'No, we can do that when Simon isn't with us. We don't want to bore him.'

'It really isn't a problem. I don't mind waiting,' Simon offered.

'No, that's ok, we'll go another time.'

Simon was surprised to hear Carla turn down the chance of shopping. She must be eager to get to the restaurant to see Nectarios.

It didn't take long to get down into the harbour and they could soon see the sea, which once again looked different. He loved that the boats were always coming and going and the way the light hit the water was ever changing.

Searching for somewhere for a drink before

heading to the restaurant, he suggested, 'How about over there? Those sofas outside that bar look comfortable.'

'They do, but the two of you might have to pull me up when we're done as they look very low.'

'Not a problem. We're at your service,' said Simon, saluting Angela in jest.

They headed over so they could quickly nab the table before anyone else, and once there they ordered a carafe of white wine, sipping and taking everything in until Simon's phone rang and interrupted the contented silence. He saw it was Polina calling and his heart started to race. He wasn't entirely uncomfortable taking the call in front of Angela and Carla, but he had to.

'Hello.'

'Hi, is that Simon? I hope I'm not disturbing you.'

'Not at all! Thank you for calling me back.'

'I was wondering if tomorrow was ok to give you the easel. If you'd like, I can also show you the place I mentioned over at Thagistri?'

'That would be great.'

'Good. Would ten-thirty be ok? We could meet by the old pier where the market was. It's near the bus stop we need.'

'That would be perfect, thanks.'

'Ok then, I'll see you tomorrow. Have a nice evening!'

'Yes, and you.'

Simon could feel he was blushing as he came off the phone and now he had to explain to Carla and Angela what the call was all about.

'You seem pleased about something. Was it good news?' asked Angela.

'Yes, it was the person who's going to lend me the easel. I'm meeting them in the harbour tomorrow morning and then we're catching the bus to Thagistri for a day's painting. Now, are we having another drink here or heading to the restaurant?'

Angela had clearly picked up on Simon not wanting to say any more about his day out tomorrow, but before she could say anything Carla was on her feet and ready to get going to the restaurant.

'Welcome back,' Sakis greeted them warmly. 'Just let me clear this table off and you can sit here. You're all looking fabulous, I can tell you've been enjoying the Vekianos sunshine.'

Angela noticed Carla seemed to be a bit disappointed that Sakis would be their waiter, but she settled into the table anyway. Sakis brought the menus and they ordered some wine, before getting stuck into looking at what they wanted to eat. They had all chosen and closed their menus when Nectarios started walking towards the table.

'Welcome back! Have you decided what you would like to eat?'

Simon could see Carla's face lit up and he gave Angela a secret smile.

'I thought Sakis was looking after us tonight,' said Angela, acting the picture of innocent confusion.

'He's just gone on his break, so you have me for now, if that's ok with you all?'

'I'm sure it will be fine. What do you think, Carla?' replied Angela.

Before Carla could speak someone else appeared.

'No, it's ok, Nectarios, you look after your own tables. I will see to these lovely people until Sakis comes back.'

'It's ok, Granddad, I can manage.'

'No, I insist. Good evening, Angela, I hope the

view is better tonight,' said Lambros, mirth evident in his tone.

'Hello, Lambros, the view is perfect in so many ways, don't you think, Carla? We all have something to look at.'

Simon couldn't stop the bark of laughter that escaped him. They were certainly in for an evening they wouldn't soon forget!

Chapter 8
Holiday day 3

Today was the day. Simon was excited to be painting outdoors, something that very rarely happened for him. He was also looking forward to spending the day with Polina. He still had a few more hours before he met her down in the harbour so he was sat on the patio drinking his second coffee and reflecting on last night, especially the scene at the restaurant, which was so funny he was still laughing about it.

'I'm determined to be up before you at least once on this holiday,' said Angela as she stepped into the sunshine.

'Would it help if I stayed in my room until you were up?' he teased. 'Did you sleep well?'

'I did, thank you. I see you're still smiling about last night.'

'It was just so funny to see Carla and Nectarios flirting with each other and then Lambros trying to impress you.'

'You neglected to note that both Carla and I didn't fall for their charm. I'm still shocked Lambros was even willing to talk to me after what I said about his house, and I did feel sorry for Sakis who was having to do all the work serving everyone else while those two were giving our table all the attention.'

'Somehow I think he's used to it.'

'Are you suggesting that I'm not the only one Lambros flirts with?' she asked, pretending to look insulted. 'I will say that I was impressed by Carla. She hasn't fallen for Nectarios's charm.'

'That's because she can see right through him,

but I will say I don't think he'll give up without a fight.'

'He'll have to work hard to win her attention. Back to you, are you ready for your day of artistic creation?'

'I am. Just to be outdoors painting will be a real treat. You know better than anyone that there are very few opportunities in Saltmarsh Quay to do so. What have you planned for today?'

'I thought I might stay by the pool this morning and after lunch I need to go down to Lambros's restaurant as I left my cardigan there last night. Then I will have a little walk around and take everything in during the day rather than the evening. Perhaps I'll grab a drink and watch the world go by.'

'Sounds ideal.'

It didn't take Simon long to get ready and pack his paints, brushes, and water in his backpack. With one last look in the mirror and a squirt of aftershave he was ready to head down to the harbour to meet Polina.

'Right, I'm off. I'm not sure what time I'll be back so don't feel you have to wait for me for dinner.'

'Enjoy yourself! I'm looking forward to seeing what you paint.' Angela smiled and waved as he headed out.

As he was closing the gate behind him his phone beeped with a text from his mum.

Hi darling, I hope you're having a good time and getting some painting done. Your dad and I miss you but hope it's the perfect holiday. love you lots, mum xx.

As he put his phone back into his bag, he felt so lucky he had such supportive parents. Not everyone did. He was also aware that if he turned around one day and said he was giving up his decorating business to become a full-time artist, they would be happy for him. But he knew he had to be sensible, and making a living with his art would be nearly impossible.

He knew the little streets would be busy with everyone off to the beaches or on boat trips so after stopping at the bakery for some treats for himself and Polina, he headed down to the pier, taking a haphazard route that avoided most of the crowds. He was half an hour early when he arrived, so he found a little wall in the shade to sit on and wait. It was very different here now without the craft fair, very quiet. It actually looked like quite a nice place to sit and paint so he thought perhaps one day he might do just that.

As he sat looking at the boats passing, heading off for the day to different islands, it crossed his mind how comfortable he was feeling. Vekianos didn't seem a new or strange place, in fact he felt as if he belonged here, which was very odd as he had only been on the island for barely three days. Twenty minutes later he saw Polina walking towards him with a couple of big bags. He felt his stomach flutter with excitement to see her, but was it because he was going to be painting or was it simply because he was spending time with her?

'Hi, Simon.'

'Hello! I feel really bad now seeing all you've had to carry. It's bad enough just your things but to add an extra easel as well... Here, let me carry some of it.'

'Thank you, but I'm used to it. I take these bags all over the island and on boats to other islands. It's a way of life.'

'A lovely life. I'm very envious.'

Polina smiled. 'Shall we go to the bus stop?'

Simon nodded and picked up one of Polina's big bags, following her away from the harbour. They arrived at the bus stop a couple of minutes later.

'We shouldn't have to wait long and the journey to Thagistri will be quick. Are you looking forward to the painting?'

'I am but I'm also nervous. I've not actually painted beside someone else since I was at school. Normally I'm in a little room next to my dad's garage, away from everything and everybody. But today, to be next to someone who earns their living from their paintings, will be a whole new experience for me.'

'Not sure "earning a living" are the right words. Oh look, here's the bus.'

As they got on Polina chatted to the driver who she obviously knew. They laughed about something Simon couldn't understand, but he found he hoped it wasn't about him. Once in their seats with all the bags on their laps, Polina started to point things out to him along the way. There were lots of stops letting locals on and off, but eventually they pulled up at Thagistri and after dividing all the bags between them they headed towards the sea, which Simon could see in the distance.

'I should probably first explain that if we go to the right it's all very rocky with a wide, open beach, but if we head over to the left the beach is smaller and you have all the hills looking down on it, so you would get a completely different composition. What sort of thing would you like to paint?'

'I'm not sure, what would you suggest? Perhaps I might be better at the spot that's the quietest, with fewer people popping their heads around to see what I'm painting?'

'Ok, then let's head to the left. From there you can also just about see another little island in the far distance. Of course you could bring it closer in your painting if you wanted. That's the beauty of paintings

– they can be whatever we want them to be.'

'You're right there. Now, lead the way. And are you sure you're ok with that bag?'

'I'm fine, thank you, and it will only be about ten minutes' walk as we can cut through a little patch of olive trees.'

They walked in silence, having to take care where they were placing their feet as it wasn't a straightforward path. Eventually the trees thinned out and there was the sea in front of them. Simon almost couldn't take it all in. It was breathtaking.

'Oh my goodness, Polina, this is just so stunning and unbelievably special. I can see why you feel so inspired to paint here. Is this where you tell me that this is only one of dozens of places like this on Vekianos?'

'I won't lie to you, there *are* a lot of gorgeous places. It's a good thing you're here for a while!'

'Where do we go from here to set up our easels?'

'This way I think.'

Polina led the way again and pointed to a spot back from the beach. When Simon stood sideways he had the sea to the right of him, the hills in front, and the perfect landscape to the left to paint. As they put the bags down Simon took the pastries out of his bag and Polina laughed because as she opened up her bag she revealed she had stopped and bought some as well.

'Great minds think alike!'

As they got stuck into them, Polina unzipped the big bag and took out a very compact folded easel, which she quickly put together. Simon was very impressed with it and thought it made perfect sense considering the number of places Polina must go to paint.

'That is so impressive. Can I put the next one together?'

'Sorry, I only have the one.'

'Oh, I thought when you said I could borrow one that meant you had a spare,' Simon said, momentarily disappointed. 'You use it, I can put my canvas on my knees.'

'No, I insist. I wouldn't have offered if I didn't want to.'

Simon felt really awkward. Why would have Polina have said he could use it if she didn't have a spare? He knew that there was nothing he could do to change her mind so he simply went about getting set up, pulling everything out of his bag for a productive day and then figuring out what his composition should consist of.

'I'm really not sure how I go about this,' he finally admitted. 'Should it be more hills and less sky, or the other way around? It's nerve-racking trying to get it "right".'

'I know exactly how you feel. I was the same a few years ago when I went over to Corfu on a painting retreat. I had been looking forward to it for so long and then when I got there I was overwhelmed by everything. It was as if I *had* to paint the perfect picture and everything had to be just right. It took a day or two there for my heart to stop racing and for me to realise that it wasn't about getting everything right.'

'So you promise you won't laugh when I mess up?' he joked.

'Don't be silly! There's no such thing as messing up. A painting is what it is. Now, with that, I am going to move away so you're more relaxed. Enjoy your day, Simon. Make the most of it.'

He threw himself right into it and escaped into his own little world. He struggled a bit with the heat, but he could put up with it to be painting outside in the sunshine, which itself was pure joy. Stretching into his bag for his bottle of water he looked at the time on his phone and was shocked to find that they had been there for nearly four hours! The time, as they say, had flown by. Standing back and looking at his work, he was happy. He had captured the bones and he could add to it and refine it back at the villa, blending the colours more.

He heard a phone ring but it wasn't his. Polina answered and though he couldn't understand what she was saying, as it was in Greek, he could see that she seemed a little bit panicky once off the phone.

'Are you ok? Is something wrong?'

'No, not really ... well, yes... I don't know how to put it and I should have said something earlier ... and now it seems too late.'

'Slow down and tell me what's wrong.'

'I didn't tell my mum I was coming with you today.' At Simon's confused look, she continued. 'It's a long story but she wouldn't be happy if she knew I was here with you. Yes, I know I'm twenty-five and my mother's opinion shouldn't matter, but it does. And now she's insisted on coming to meet me and she'll see us together.'

Simon was confused, to say the least. Why would Polina's mother be upset? All they were doing was painting and they were outdoors amongst other people. What was so wrong with that?

'It's not a problem,' he said, sliding into problem solving mode. 'How long before she gets here?'

'Fifteen or twenty minutes.'

'Ok, then let's pack up all our stuff and while you wait for her, I'll catch the bus back to the harbour. She'll never know I was here so there will be no problem at all.'

'I'm so sorry for spoiling your day.'

'You haven't spoiled anything. It's been lovely. Please don't worry, everything will be ok.'

With that he turned around and started to help pack the bags. Looking over at her he could see the abrupt end to their day had upset her, but there was nothing he could do if she didn't want him to try and explain to her mum that nothing had happened other than painting. Once everything was packed away, they walked a few hundred yards without speaking before Polina stopped.

'I'm so sorry. I've had a really lovely day and I wish I had explained this to you before so that you could understand. Have a lovely rest of your holiday.'

With that, Polina walked away and Simon was left in a daze wondering what this was all about. One thing he knew for sure was that this wasn't the end for him and Polina. He had enjoyed his day painting but more than that he had really enjoyed being with her, and he wanted to spend a lot more time with her before going back to England.

Chapter 9
Holiday day 3

'Morning! Did you sleep well? You've just missed Simon as he's left for his painting day.'

'I did, thanks, and I woke up smiling thinking about last night. Nectarios's grandfather was really out to woo you!'

'Woo is an odd word for someone your age to use, but you aren't wrong. I was just going to make myself some toast, would you like some?'

'I don't think so, thanks, but I won't say no to a coffee. I'm looking forward to another day by the pool.'

'Me too, though I have to go down into the harbour this afternoon as I left my cardigan on the chair in the restaurant.'

'You don't have to walk all that way. I could nip down before the restaurant opens for lunch and fetch it. I could also stop at the bakery for some of those gorgeous cheese pies for our lunch.'

Angela agreed and laughed to herself as she walked into the kitchen. No doubt Carla would be hoping to see Nectarios. Oh, to be young again! But saying that, she wouldn't want all the pressures young people had on them these days.

'Here you go,' she said, stepping onto the patio a moment later. 'I know we have the lovely harbour and everything else here on the island, but I think the view from here on the patio is my favourite.'

'Yes, I can see now why you love the Greek islands so much.'

'They bring back happy memories going back

many years.'

'Are any of them romantic memories?' Carla waggled her eyebrows suggestively.

'Oh course! And I don't mind talking about them either. Back in my thirties, when I was living with my brother in London, I worked for an insurance company, just doing admin work, and I met a lad called Mark. He was the same age as me and we used to go on dates to the cinema or the theatre, or just out for dinner. Then we started going on holidays together, and that's when I discovered Greece and its beautiful islands. And that was it, there was nowhere else in the world I wanted to go on holiday.'

Angela paused and Carla fought the urge to ask what had happened.

Seeming to read her mind, Angela said, 'Come on, ask me what happened to Mark.'

'No, it's none of my business. It's private.'

'Don't be silly! The bit I didn't mention was that Mark was the nephew of the owners of the company we worked for, and they didn't think I was a "suitable" partner for him. As I didn't come from a rich or successful family, I wasn't "well bred". His parents put a stop to the relationship, telling him he needed to find a young lady of proper breeding.'

'That's so sad. But he didn't have to do what his parents said.'

'You're right, but he did, and so that was the end of the relationship. It's why I've never married; I never found anyone else I loved as much. But enough of the doom and gloom. The past is in the past, and here in the present I'm here on beautiful Vekianos, and I'm determined to enjoy myself, not waste time looking back on what could have been. I think I'm ready for a swim. You?'

There was so much Carla wanted to say but it was very clear that Angela wanted to move on, so that was the end of the conversation.

After another couple of coffees and a little yogurt, Carla grabbed a shower and picked out an outfit that was smart but casual, to give the impression she had just thrown it on. The last thing she wanted was for Nectarios to think she had dressed up to see him.

'Right then, Angela, I'm off.'

'You look lovely. Thank you again for doing this.'

'It's not a problem. Other than something for lunch, was there anything else we needed while I'm out?

'I don't think so, but remember that there's no rush to get back. Take your time and have fun.'

Carla was feeling excited as she made her way through the little streets. The town wasn't that busy, probably because all the boats had gone out on their day trips, and it was too early for the visiting day trippers to have arrived.

She wanted to plan her entrance just right so she'd check from a distance to see if Nectarios was there before going into the restaurant. If she cut through one of the little alleys the other side of the harbour she could possibly see from there.

Sadly, she wasn't in luck. She could see the restaurant but only the first few outside tables. She would just have to risk it.

She stopped to look into one of the little shop windows, not to see what they sold but to check her reflection in the glass. It crossed her mind that she was being silly, just like a teenager who fancied a boy at school, but no, she was cleverer than that. She could see right through Nectarios and that would ensure she stayed in control. After all, she was only taking Angela's suggestion to have some fun. Continuing on her way, she saw that the front row of tables had menus on them, but there was still no sign of Sakis or Nectarios.

'Good morning, Carla, can't you keep way from the place, can we?' Nectarios's smile was as wide as a crocodile's. 'I know we serve the best food on the island, but you ate here only a few hours ago. Or perhaps you have another reason for being here?'

'Yes, I have another reason to be here—'

'To see me?' he interrupted.

He really was so good looking, especially when he smiled, but she had to play it cool.

'You're right, I have popped down to see you,' she said, purposefully making her tone suggestive and laughing inside when his smile grew. 'No, I've actually come to pick up Angela's cardigan. She left it here by accident last night.'

He momentarily looked deflated but quickly rallied. 'Are you sure there wasn't just a *little* bit of you that wanted to see me at the same time?'

'Nope, just the cardigan. Sorry to disappoint you.'

'You aren't disappointing me. I quite like to see the way you're playing this game, Carla, all very cool. It's my turn to disappoint you now though. My granddad found the cardigan and said he'd take it up to the villa himself. It's a wasted journey for you, I'm afraid, unless you'd like to join me for a drink? I was just going to make coffee.'

She nodded, trying not to look as triumphant as she felt inside. The main point of coming down here was to see Nectarios, so she considered it mission very much accomplished. And his announcement that he liked the way she was playing the so-called game was the icing on the cake.

'Why don't you come through to the back? We can chat while the coffee machine is doing its job and maybe we could talk about spending some time together. I could show you the island or we could go on one of the famous boat trips.'

As she followed him through the doorway, she heard someone behind her. Recognising the voice, she turned, and called out, 'Morning, Sakis!'

'What brings you down here so early?'

'Angela left her cardigan here last night and I nipped down to fetch it, but apparently Lambros has it and is going to take it up to the villa later on.'

'I've started on the prep for today. Could you carry on with the outside tables? I'm just taking a break and having a coffee with Carla,' said Nectarios.

'I don't think laying a grand total of two tables counts as starting anything, but go on, I'll get all the others done. Just like I usually do.'

Carla could sense the resentment in Sakis's voice and she felt bad for distracting Nectarios.

'Before I get stuck into doing *all* the work, I have a question for you, Carla. I've been invited to a party tomorrow night, would you like to come with? It won't start until after eleven, when all the restaurants start to close, as the birthday girl is a waitress and most of her guests work in the food industry, but it will be fun with lots of dancing, and I would really love for you to be my guest.'

'Sorry, Sakis, but I was actually going to ask Carla if she would be *my* guest.'

'Sakis asked me first so it's only right I accompany him. It's a date, Sakis, something I never thought would happen when I came here on holiday.' She laughed.

'What, going to a party?' asked Nectarios, looking confused.

'No, being asked out on a date. Thank you, Sakis, I'm excited. I'd best get going now.'

Carla could see Sakis smiling about getting one over on Nectarios. Of course she knew her night out would be fun in a completely different way than if she had gone with the other offer, but like Nectarios had said, she was playing a game, and it was one she was determined to win.

Angela had just tidied up in the kitchen and got her things together to go down to the pool when she heard a knock on the patio door. Turning around she could see Lambros stood there with her cardigan in his hand. Her first thought was *thank goodness he wasn't ten minutes later* as she would have been in her swimsuit on the sun lounger.

'Hello there, I see you have my cardigan. Carla has actually gone down to the restaurant to fetch it so I'm sorry you've gone to all the trouble.'

'It's not a problem. We spotted it last night and as you had told me the other day where you were staying, I thought I would drop it by.'

'Thank you, that's very kind. Can I get you a drink?'

'If it's no trouble that would be lovely, thank you.'

'You take a seat out on the patio. I'll just be a few minutes.'

As Lambros turned around and headed over to the table and chairs, she went to put the kettle on. While she was waiting for it to boil she nipped into the bathroom to check her hair. Thankfully she looked ok. Back in the kitchen she made a pot of coffee and put it on a tray with some biscuits Simon and Carla had bought the other day. As she was walking back out she hoped Lambros wouldn't mention what she'd said about his house. She still cringed at how severely she'd put her foot in her mouth.

'Here we are.'

'Thank you. Have you had a chance to explore

much of the island beyond the harbour? There are some stunning little coves and pretty villages all the way around. Perhaps one day I could show you parts that the tourists don't venture to? We could have lunch in one of the lovely beach restaurants. Only if you want, of course. No pressure.'

'I would like that, thank you. It's a date... Well, not a date, but a ... you know what I mean.' She realised she was blushing.

'You're funny. The last one of those I was on was with my late wife Angelina, many years ago.'

'To be honest, Lambros, I can't even remember when or whom I last had a date with as it was far too many years ago. Please help yourself to some biscuits.'

There was a long silence as they both got lost in their thoughts, thinking about the past. Angela could see Lambros looked very sad and wondered if she should change the subject, or perhaps it would be helpful to ask him about his wife so that he had the chance to talk about her, if he wanted. After all, apart from him owning the restaurant and the house on the hill, there wasn't much she knew about him, in the same way he knew nothing about her. Perhaps she should tell him...

'I feel a little awkward. I want to ask you about your life here on Vekianos, but I don't want to upset you. So maybe I could start by telling you a bit more about myself? To be honest, I've not really been in a good place recently. My brother died about four months ago and I've had his property and belongings to sort out, which meant I had to leave where I live and stay in London and ... cutting a long story short, I went back home a few weeks ago and I felt I needed a break from reality. I would never have come on holiday by myself so I invited Simon and Carla to come with me for company.'

'I'm sorry for your loss, and I really hope your stay helps even in a small way. I'm sure just being with those two youngsters is a tonic. Carla, in particular, is very lively and full of fun. I had to laugh last evening as she really is a match for my grandson. He's so used to the women just falling at his feet, all goggled eyed, but not her. She is making him fight to get her attention, and I say good for her.'

'Yes, Simon and I have been laughing about it. She's loving every bit of it. Young people have so many more opportunities than we had at their age, certainly where travel is concerned.'

'Definitely. You know, when I was young, no one on this island ever thought of leaving. Sure, they'd visit Paxos or Corfu, but certainly not another country altogether.'

'I can't say I'm surprised. Why would anyone want to leave here? It's paradise!'

'Oh yes, I agree. I've had a very happy and fruitful life here. Of course I have had to work hard, but there are an awful lot of people that have had it so much harder. No. I'm sort of content with my lot. I can't complain.'

'Sort of? What do you mean?'

'It's just that ... sometimes I get lonely, which is silly as I have my family and all my friends around me, and I keep very busy. It's late at night and first thing in the mornings that I feel it most keenly. It would be lovely to have someone there to chat to and share things with.'

'I understand that. It's the companionship. I think these last few months, since my brother died, I've realised more than ever that I'm on my own. A good thing that's come out of this holiday is that I no longer think I'll mind travelling alone. It's wonderful to have Simon and Carla with me, but I'm coming to see that I *can* do things on my own when pressed.'

'I understand what you mean, and of course now you have got to know Vekianos, and you've seen for yourself that it's paradise, so there is nothing stopping you coming back by yourself.'

'You're right. I think it's a matter of embracing the fun where you find it, stepping outside your comfort zone and connecting with others. Like last night in your restaurant when we were all laughing and joking. That was incredibly fun.'

'It was. I suspect you're onto something here. Enjoying life for what it is and jumping on unexpected opportunities. Like me bringing your cardigan back. If I hadn't done that we wouldn't have had this nice chat and the chance to enjoy the morning sunshine together.'

'Exactly! Oh look, here comes Carla.' She waved.

'Hello, you two, what are you up to?' called Carla.

Angela and Lambros exchanged a look then said 'we're having fun!' in unison before bursting out laughing, which left Carla with a very confused expression on her face.

Chapter 10
Holiday day 4

Simon looked at the time on his phone as he woke up. It was only seven-fifteen in the morning but he could hear someone else up before him. That was a first! Before he went out into the living room he needed to get his story right in his head, because he knew there would be several questions about his day out yesterday. In a way, he wished after leaving Polina he had come straight back here to the villa, instead of waiting to return until Carla and Angela had gone out to eat, and making sure he had gone to bed before they got back. It was all a bit silly, really. He could have just said he had a nice time, which was the truth, and not mentioned anything about Polina or her mother's interruption.

Still, what was done was done, so he would put on a happy face to cover up his disappointment at not being able to spend more time with Polina, and hopefully they could quickly move on to a new topic.

Taking a breath, he thought, *here goes.*

Five, four, three, two, one...

'You've beaten me to it today, Angela, couldn't you sleep?'

'I had a bit of a restless night but I'm not sure why. How was your painting day? Do you have a new masterpiece to show me?'

'Not just yet.' Simon laughed and headed out onto the patio. The sun was coming up and it already looked as though it was going to be another lovely day on Vekianos. Perhaps he would have a day by the pool with his book.

One thing he wouldn't be doing was painting. He needed a break after the intensity of yesterday.

'I brought you a coffee,' Angela said as she joined him. 'Now tell me, did you have fun yesterday? Was it lovely to paint outside for once?'

'It was a great day. I thought I would be conscious of people walking around and perhaps coming and looking at what I was doing, but I went into a little world of my own with just the view and the canvas, and the time flew by.'

'That's wonderful. Are you off out again today?'

'No, I think I'll have a day by the pool with my book. How was your day? Did you have a nice meal last night? I expect Carla was on form flirting with Nectarios.'

'We did have a nice meal, but we went somewhere different on the other side of the harbour, a little fish restaurant. It was very out of the way so the evening was a lot quieter than usual.'

'What did you get up to during the day?'

'Lambros brought my cardigan back and we chatted for quite a while, just two old people putting the world to rights. We're going to have a day out together soon. He's going to show me around the island and take me to the parts he says the holiday makers never see. I'm looking forward to it. Speaking of going out, Carla's been invited to a party tonight.'

'So, she's fallen for Nectarios's charm? I have to say, I thought she would hold out a lot longer before agreeing to a date.'

'That's where you're wrong, she's going to the party with Sakis.'

'Did I hear my name?' asked Carla as she joined them.

'Yes, you did. I was just saying you're off partying with Sakis tonight.'

'I'm excited because Sakis is so over the top and

full of energy. It's sure to be a good night. Nectarios will be there as well and I think he's a little disappointed I'm not going with him. A little bit of me wishes I was going with him instead, but it will do him good to have to work a bit harder than usual.'

'You might be going with Sakis, but I think the big question is who you'll be going home with!' Simon laughed.

'Stop that! Of course I will end the evening with Sakis. Now enough about me, how was your art day?'

'It was a very nice day. As for today, are we all staying by the pool? If so, I'll go down to the shops and get us some treats. We also need milk and wine I think.'

'Would you like me to come down with you?' offered Carla.

'No, it's fine, you need to conserve your energies for Nectarios – oh, sorry, I mean Sakis.'

This caused all three of them to laugh. After finishing his coffee, Simon went to get changed for the walk down into the town. He was grateful he hadn't had to answer too many questions about the day before.

'So, we need milk, wine, and treats. Can you think of anything else?'

Both Angela and Carla said they couldn't and off he went.

'Since we started planning this holiday, and all the time we've been here, Simon was so excited about working on his art, but today he seems different. Do you think something happened yesterday to knock the shine off it? I get the impression everything didn't live up to his expectations,' said Carla, concerned for her new friend.

'I was thinking the same. I also thought it was strange that when we got back for dinner last night he had already gone to bed. We weren't that late, it was only just gone eleven. Do you think he was disappointed in the work he produced? Perhaps he was hoping it would be a lot better than it actually was.'

Carla could only shrug and hope that Simon would open up to them when he was ready.

As he got down into the town Simon decided to go to the bakery first so that he wouldn't have to carry the heavy things from the supermarket for longer than necessary. As he crossed the little road to the bakery, he spotted Polina, who was with a woman he suspected was her mother, and they were also heading into the bakery. This could be an opportunity to get into conversation without letting her mum know they knew each other. He was nervous but as long as her mum didn't know who he was, everything should be ok. He got to the door of the bakery, and found a queue inside. It would give him a moment or two to say something.

'Excuse me, is this the end of the queue?' he began.

Polina recognized his voice and turned around sharply. She looked a little flummoxed, but Simon could tell by the shy smile on her face that she was pleased to see him. But this opportunity he had created wasn't to see Polina, he needed to ingratiate himself to her mum. He hoped that if she could see he was a nice lad he could possibly be in with a chance to spend time with Polina.

'I'm here on holiday and this bakery is one of my favourite places on the island. I've also enjoyed sitting in the harbour wall and watching the world go by. Are you both on holiday as well?' he asked innocently.

Simon purposely turned away from Polina, so

her mum had to answer.

'No, we live here.'

She turned her back to him and Polina gave him an apologetic look before doing the same.

He decided to try again.

'Can I ask, knowing what you know about the island, if you were a holiday maker here for a week, what would be on your list of things to see and do?'

He could see she wasn't in the mood for this but before he could retreat, Polina spoke.

'It all depends on what you like doing. The buses are great for taking you to the quieter towns and beaches, and then of course there are boat trips over to Paxos, Parga, and Corfu. We also have a lovely craft market here in the harbour once a week.'

With that it was their turn at the counter and Polina's mum interrupted.

'Have a nice holiday.'

She was scarier than Simon had anticipated, and it was so strange how she was controlling her daughter's life. As she paid, another assistant asked Simon what he wanted, and by the time he had told her, Polina and her mum were gone.

As he walked out of the bakery and towards the supermarket he looked to see if Polina and her mum were still around, but they had disappeared. He was intrigued, but couldn't quite pinpoint why he felt the need to get to the bottom of the situation between the two women. It would be better if he could forget all about Polina and just enjoy his holiday here on Vekianos.

'I'm back! Can I tempt either of you with a pastry?' he called once he'd returned to the villa.

'Yes, please! Who says no to the offer of pastries?' asked Carla, aghast at the thought.

'Pastry for you, Angela?' asked Simon.

'Oh, go on then. I am on holiday after all.'

As the three of them sat drinking their drinks and eating their sweet treats in silence, they retreated into their own little worlds. Angela found the silence was comfortable, the kind of comfortable you only found with really good friends. The thought warmed her.

Pastries demolished, it was time to go down to the pool. They each got their things together – suntan lotion, books, towels, bottles of water – and laughed because it looked as though they were packing for a hike rather than a ten-yard walk to the bottom of the garden.

'I'm having a swim first, how about you ladies?'

'Oh, please don't call me a lady. It makes me sound old.' Carla groaned.

'Are you saying *I'm* old?' Angela cocked an eyebrow.

'Sorry, but you know what I mean.'

'I do. I'm only teasing you.'

The joking around had set the tone for the rest of the day and there was a lot of laughter and taking the mickey out of each other. Carla went into the pool room to fetch a Lilo and she also found a beach ball, which she thought could be fun.

'Anyone up for a little game of catch?'

'Excuse me, this *lady* hasn't done any sport since the nineteen sixties. I will stay here on the sun lounger and keep score.'

After a rather energetic and exhausting game of catch with Simon, Carla insisted on preparing a lunch of ham and cheese baguettes with some olive flavoured crisps and glasses of wine. Happily full, the afternoon was a lot quieter, all three of them dipping in and out of their books, the pool, and naps, settling into a routine which suited all three of them nicely.

'I think I'll just have a bowl of pasta here at the

villa tonight before I go to meet Sakis, if that's fine with you two?' Carla checked.

'To be honest, pasta sounds good for me as well, unless you wanted to go down into the harbour area to eat?' Simon asked Angela.

'No, that sounds perfect. That way I can see what you look like before you go out on your date,' she said, smiling at Carla.

'It's not a date, just Sakis and I going to a party together.'

'Well, like we said earlier, you might be going with Sakis but—'

'I get the message loud and clear,' Carla interrupted. 'I can assure you I will not be like all those other girls that fall at Nectarios's feet.'

'Quite right! Anyway, it should be the other way around; he should be falling at *your* feet. Now, I see it's five o'clock. Who's ready for a glass of wine?'

'Not for me, thank you,' said Carla. 'I need to keep a clear head for tonight.'

Simon insisted on cooking so when it got to seven o'clock he prepared a tasty chicken and pesto pasta and they sat on the patio while they ate, watching the sun go down. As Carla filled the dishwasher before going to get ready, Simon and Angela moved from the table into the comfy chairs with their wine, ready for Carla's big entrance ... or should that be exit?

'Drumroll please,' joked Carla as she stepped outside. 'Please be honest, does this dress look ok, or do you think it's too dressy? Should I wear one of my plainer ones?'

'I think you look gorgeous. It's very sexy,' said Angela, supportively.

'It's lovely,' Simon agreed.

'Hmm, sexy wasn't the look I was going for. I think I'll go and change.'

'Don't be silly, it's perfect for a warm summer night out here in Greece.'

'Angela's right. As long as you feel comfortable in it, you should wear it.'

'If you both think? Ok, thanks. I just need to get my bag and I'll be off. I'm not sure what time I'll be back but I presume it will be quite late.' Carla bit her lip.

'I expect we'll be here watching the sun come up with our morning coffees as you come through the gate.'

'Very funny, Simon. I'm sure I'll be back hours before that.'

After one more look in the mirror and another squirt of perfume, Carla was ready. She gave Angela and Simon each a hug, and then she was off out through the gate.

'I'm not sure who's more excited, Carla or myself!' said Angela. 'I know she'll have a nice time and in that dress Nectarios will take one look at her and his jaw will drop to the floor. She looks gorgeous.'

'You're right. The holiday is doing her loads of good. It's helping all of us. I have to say you're looking much better – more rested and more yourself – after just these few days here.'

'I admit I'm feeling a lot better. There's something very special about Vekianos. So, that's Carla and I sorted, how about you? Of the three of us you're the only one who didn't need to come on holiday to get over anything or sort your life out as you have everything going for you back in Norfolk.'

'I suppose you're right,' said Simon, looking dejected. 'I have no complaints.'

His demeanour said otherwise, but Angela knew she needed to give him space if she wanted him to feel comfortable enough to open up to her.

Simon got lost in his thoughts for a moment. It was true, he had a steady job and could pick and choose the projects he liked, but he wasn't ... happy.

'What are you thinking?' Angela gently probed.

'Nothing much, just how lucky I am. My life is ok and though I would love to be doing my art more than the decorating, it's still a work in progress, as they say.'

'Talking about your art, you haven't said much about your painting day yesterday. I get the impression it didn't live up to your expectations?'

'Oh. The day itself was lovely, and the location was out of this world – an artist's dream come true – but something odd happened and I got a bit screwed up about it. I think I overreacted to something that was quite silly and simple and certainly none of my business.'

'I don't understand. You enjoyed the painting, so did something happen with the people you were with?'

'Person. I was with Polina, a girl I met down at the craft market. She's about the same age as me and we both paint in a similar style, but she's a lot better than me. I could really learn a lot from her, but...'

'But? Did you fall out? Is that what you're saying?'

'Oh no, nothing like that. Like I said, it's all very odd. You see, she didn't tell her mum that she was spending the day with me because apparently she wouldn't approve.'

'That is odd. If she's around your age then she's an adult capable of making her own choices, and all you were doing was painting.'

'Exactly! I could tell Polina liked being with me but she seemed scared out of her skin for her mum to see us together. I bumped into her and her mum in the bakery this morning and I sensed her mum was

'... shall I say, not the friendliest of people. I'm sure if she knew I spent the day with her daughter she wouldn't be happy at all, but then, their complicated relationship is none of my business. I'm only here for just over a week, and the last thing I want to do is upset anyone or get involved in something that doesn't concern me.'

'That's such a shame though, as this holiday for you was all about the painting, and if this Polina could be helping you with your art but won't because of her mother, it's a wasted opportunity. Surely there must be a way around it? The last thing you want to happen is to go back to the UK with regrets.'

As Angela went off to bed a while later, Simon found himself replaying her words in his mind. Because he *would* have regrets if he didn't say anything, and not just about the painting. He really liked Polina, far more than any other girls he had ever met. It had been over three years since he'd had a girlfriend and that relationship had ended because of his art, with his ex, Catherine, telling him he would have to choose between her or his passion. In the end, it had been easier than he'd expected to choose his passion for the paints and brushes.

Polina was a completely different scenario because they shared a special artistic connection and a love for their work. He was also just really attracted to her; the way she looked at him, and how, when she was talking, she had such a beautiful smile. It made it hard to focus on anything beyond her lips and he wanted to kiss them so much. He had never felt like this about a girl before. Coming here to Vekianos and meeting Polina had been such a high, but her mother's control over her life felt like an insurmountable obstacle. He didn't know what to do.

Chapter 11
Holiday day 4

As Carla walked down to the harbour to meet Sakis she was excited. A party on a Greek island – how great was this?! She was feeling good with the little bit of tan she had acquired over the last few days, and loved her new dress. Yes, she had scrubbed up well, and she just knew a night out with Sakis would be full of laughs and excitement. Checking the time, she saw she had fifteen minutes before she needed to meet him. One last look in a shop window to check her reflection in the glass and she was ready. She was really looking forward to seeing Nectarios's reaction to her all dressed up and looking her best.

As she got closer to the restaurant, she could see Sakis had spotted her. He smiled and put his arms in the air, offering up a hello hug.

'Well look at you, Carla, you look stunning! I'm going to feel so underdressed next to you. Go and take a seat, I've just got to change out of my work clothes and I'll be ready to go. I won't be long. First though, can I get you a drink? What would you like?'

Before she could answer, she spotted Nectarios walking towards her with a glass on a tray.

'Hi, Carla, you look lovely. I thought while you were waiting for Sakis and I to change you might like a glass of wine.'

'I was just going to get her a drink.' Sakis almost pouted.

'That's very kind of you both,' she said, taking the drink from the tray. 'I'm looking forward to the party.'

As Sakis and Nectarios walked away to get ready, she thought about the night ahead, realising she had no idea where the party was being held or how many people would be there.

Feeling suddenly nervous, she drank her glass of wine too fast, and before she knew it, the glass was empty.

An older woman came over to check on her and introduced herself as Alina.

'I'm Carla. Wait, Alina as in, the Alina the restaurant is named after?' asked Carla.

Alina laughed. 'The very one. My father is the one who gave us both the name.'

'Your father, but that would make you...' Carla's eyes widened as she realised she was speaking with Nectarios's mother.

'You look lovely tonight.'

'Thanks, that's very kind of you to say,' she said, feeling even more nervous than she had before.

'The boys are both very excited about the party, though obviously my son is disappointed he isn't escorting you. I think it's a shock to his system that he has been turned down. It's certainly something he isn't used to.'

'No, I didn't turn him down, it was just that Sakis asked me first.'

'Ah, that explains why Sakis has been making remarks all day to annoy Nectarios. The chefs quickly joined in so it's been quite the day.'

'Poor Nectarios. I feel bad now.'

'No, it's good for him to have some knockbacks. Now, can I get you another drink? I think they could be a while getting ready. They take longer than any woman I know!'

'No, I'm fine, thank you,' said Carla, already regretting having necked the last glass.

'Please have another. It will give me an excuse to

have one and to sit down. My feet are killing me.'

'Ok then, but just a small glass, please.'

Carla noticed the dark rings around Alina's eyes and how she was really dragging her feet as she stepped away to get the wine bottle. She felt bad for the older woman and wished she didn't need to work as hard as she did. The constant heat here on Vekianos couldn't help either.

'There you go. I can imagine the two of them in there fighting over the mirror.' Alina laughed. 'Should we have a little guess as to which one comes out first?'

Carla found she was hoping it was Sakis, or else she would have to make conversation with Nectarios and his mum, which might quickly start to feel uncomfortable.

'My father tells me he is having a day out with Angela soon, and showing her around the island. He's very excited to spend more time with her, though he did mention she'd had several thoughts about his house.'

'She feels really bad about that.'

'She shouldn't! The whole town has been going on at him for years about it as the place sticks right out for all the wrong reasons. He has largely given up on things like that since my mum died, probably because she was always the one who would encourage him to do things. Given that he has more time on his hands since he handed the restaurant over to me, I was hoping he would keep himself busy, but I'm afraid he sort of just goes through the motions day by day. It's as though a bit of him died the day my mum passed over.'

'I understand that. It's actually one of the reasons my friends and I have come here. You see, Angela's brother recently died – he was her only relative – and she has just spent months away from her home sorting out all of his things. The process has taken a lot out of her, and so I encouraged her to have a holiday, but she wouldn't go by herself, hence why Simon and I are here with her.'

'That's so sad, but from what I've seen of her she seems to be having a nice holiday.'

'Oh yes, we all are. The three of us just gel and we have a laugh. Angela's been encouraging us to "go and have fun" and embrace the opportunity to make the most of our time here.'

'Well, fun is something you will definitely have tonight with Sakis and his group of friends! I've been out with them for an impromptu drink from time to time, which always turns out to be a blast, with so much laughter and fun. Between you and me, I have more fun with him and his gay friends than I ever do when I'm out with a group of girlfriends who inevitably just want to moan and groan.' Alina laughed.

Carla smiled and turned as the opening door caught her eye. 'Looks like Nectarios is the first one ready, here he comes.'

'Oof! You can smell him before you see him, can't you. My son does like his cologne,' said Alina with a shake of her head.

Carla took a deep breath. Nectarios looked gorgeous, and it was clear he was very aware of it. He picked up the bottle of wine Alina had left on the bar and then grabbed up a glass for himself and came and sat down with them.

'No more wine for me, thank you,' she said, covering her glass with her hand.

'You sure? I think we have a long wait as it's not a five-minute job for Sakis to get ready. He probably has at least half a dozen outfits in there and that's before he starts on the hair.'

'Don't listen to him, Carla. That is very cruel,

Nectarios. Sakis just likes to look nice,' Alina admonished.

'Mum, are you saying that because I was quick, I don't look nice?'

'You know I'm not. Now, I have things to be getting on with. Have a fabulous time at the party, you two.'

'I think we will, don't you?' Nectarios asked Carla.

Oh dear. She could feel herself going red and she mentally urged Sakis to hurry up. Thankfully, her prayer was answered and he joined them almost immediately.

'I'm here! Are we ready to party?'

'You look fabulous,' said Carla, admiring Sakis's outfit.

'Thank you, I know I do. It's bespoke and all the way from Athens so no one at the party will be wearing this outfit other than little old me. Sadly, we can't say the same about Nectarios's shirt, can we, as last week twelve of them arrived in a gorgeous shop here on the island and so I expect all twelve will be at the party.'

Carla didn't know whether to say something in Nectarios's defence or to laugh.

'Of course, I'm only joking. You look very hot in it, Nectarios, and I'm sure every female – and come to that a lot of the men – will be itching to rip it off of you.'

'Thank you for those kind words, Sakis,' Nectarios said dryly. 'Are we ready to go?'

'Oh yes, let's get the party started.'

With that they all stood up and shouted their goodbyes to Alina.

As they walked, Carla started to feel more at ease. Of course she still hadn't a clue where they were going, but it seemed to be along by the harbour wall. Sakis entertained them with his singing as they walked, and once they got to the end of the harbour wall the road turned in and Carla started to hear music. They must be close to the party.

As they rounded the corner a building with lots of lights and people stood outside came into view. Sakis stopped in his tracks and gave himself a look over, making Carla smile.

'This is it! Are you ready? It's time for the most fabulous guests to arrive.'

'Sorry, Sakis, I can only see you and Carla. Where are the fabulous people you're on about?'

'Very funny, Nectarios. And actually you should be thanking me as I included you in the fabulous, despite the fact that that suggestion requires a stretch of my imagination. Here we go, big smiles...' And with that, Sakis led the way.

'Don't worry, Carla, no one will be looking at us. All of that is in his head and as you know by now, he does love a drama. I promise the party will be very laid back, just a group of restaurant staff after a busy night working, and Zeta, whose party it is, is really nice.'

Once in the courtyard, which Carla realised was a restaurant, she found that a lot of people weren't as dressed up as they were, but she had spotted someone with the same shirt as Nectarios, so Sakis had been right about that.

A little group of lads came over to them and made a fuss of Sakis, and Nectarios soon drifted away, which Carla was disappointed about. But saying that, it had been her choice to attend with Sakis.

'Carla, this is my crew! We're the five young, hip gays on the island. Crew, this is Carla, my new friend. She's on holiday and as you can guess, Nectarios is jealous as she's here with me not him.'

'Hi, it's nice to meet you all.'

Lots of hugs and kisses were showered on Carla but as the music was very loud she largely couldn't hear what the others were saying. She felt a tap on her shoulder and turned to find Nectarios with three drinks. So he hadn't gone off and left her after all.

'Thank you, it's very loud in here,' she shouted, trying to be heard over the music.

A girl came over to join their group and Sakis hugged and kissed her before turning towards Carla.

'Carla, this is Zeta, whose party it is.'

'Hi, Zeta, it's nice to meet you! Thanks for letting me tag along.'

'It's nice to meet you, too! I hope you have a good evening. I'm sure it won't be a boring one if you're here with Sakis. He's known to be the life and soul of any party.'

Sakis pointed to the dance floor and Carla faced a dilemma. Did she go off and dance with the crew or stay with Nectarios? The decision was made for her when two other girls came over and started to hug Nectarios. Clearly, it was time to dance.

The music was good, and the atmosphere was exciting, everyone having fun and letting their hair down. After about half an hour Sakis led them off the dance floor to the side wall and one of the crew went to fetch some bottles of water. They were all hot and Carla appreciated the water. As she was getting her breath back and cooling down a little, she spotted Zeta coming towards them with a very handsome young man behind her. He looked like a model, he was so stunning. Zeta headed right for Sakis and although Carla couldn't understand what they were saying, she got the impression the birthday girl was introducing him to Sakis. Then one of the crew came over to her.

'I somehow think that's the last we'll see of Sakis

tonight.'

'Sorry? What do you mean?'

'Zeta has just introduced her cousin to him, and something tells me they will be glued to each other for the rest of the night. But don't worry, Carla, we will take care of you. Are you ready to get back on the dance floor?'

'Ready when you are! I'll do my best to make up for the missing crew member.'

'Great! Don't tell Sakis, but you are far more glamorous than him and a lot less maintenance, I expect.'

'No maintenance required,' she said with a laugh. 'Lead the way!'

For the next hour Carla danced and laughed with Sakis's friends, her nerves now completely gone. She was so happy and every now and again she spotted Sakis, who was looking well into Zeta's cousin. It was nice to see as he was such a hard-working lad and he deserved to have some fun. She also caught Nectarios's eyes a few time, but it seemed like he was sad, and no wonder – for someone who was very popular on the island, every time she spotted him he was stood by himself.

Carla couldn't remember being so hot and she decided she would take her water outside.

'I'm just going out on deck for some fresh air and to cool down,' she shouted to one of Sakis's friends.

He nodded. 'When you're ready to get back on the dance floor, come and look for us.'

Carla waved and grabbed a water before stepping out onto the little path where she could see the sea, a few boats and yachts bobbing in the water with their twinkly lights on. This really was a very special island. She felt comfortable here, like she was home, something that had never happened before outside Saltmarsh Quay.

'I thought you might like a wine,' said Nectarios, strolling towards her.

'Thank you. I had to come out for some fresh air; it's so hot in there!'

'That's probably because of all the dancing. You haven't stopped.'

'I suppose I haven't. Sakis's friends are fun and the music is great.'

'So you're enjoying the party even though your date has ditched you? I'm only joking. I'm pleased Sakis has met someone, even if it turns out to be just a little fling. I know sometimes in the restaurant it comes across as if we don't get on or like each other, but we do. He brings a lot of joy to the restaurant, and both my mum and I are aware that lots of the customers who keep coming back night after night are down to him.' He paused for a moment then looked at her intensely. 'I'm also happy he's met someone tonight because it means I can spend time with you.'

There was a loaded silence. As much as she wanted to say she felt the same, she knew exactly how he operated and she wasn't looking to be just another holiday romance.

'The island you live on is so beautiful,' she said, clearly throwing him off with her subject change.

'Yes, it is. I know I'm lucky, but I have only begun to think like that in the last few years. If you get a chance, you should explore the rest of the island, beyond the harbour and town. It's beautiful and there are fabulous beaches that are hidden away from the tourists, so secluded most people would never even know they were there.'

'I understand your grandfather is taking Angela out for the day tomorrow and giving her the full Vekianos experience.'

'He is, and he's very excited. My mum and I

haven't seen him like this for years. He even went and bought a new shirt for the occasion.'

'I'm sure Angela will be impressed. Did he opt for the same shirt as you?' she teased. 'By the way, Sakis was wrong. I only spotted two guys in the same shirt, and it's a very nice shirt, so it doesn't matter.'

'Yes, but I suspect you think what's under the shirt isn't as nice. I've given you a bad impression of myself, haven't I? There's no point in lying to you and saying I'm not like that because I am. But in my defence, it's just what happens on these islands. Holiday makers arrive and want a romance for two weeks and, well, we waiters ... oblige.'

'I understand. As long as no one gets hurt, and everyone has a good time, there's nothing wrong with it. And if the girls think they're the only ones the waiters will take a shine to throughout the summer, they're either naive or silly.'

'It still doesn't excuse my behaviour.'

'Don't be so serious, Nectarios, we're at a party! Come on, follow me and let the dance floor see your moves – and more importantly, that shirt. It's time to have some fun.'

Chapter 12
Holiday day 5

Looking at the time Carla saw it was nearly half past ten. She had only just woken up, but that wasn't all that surprising as it was three in the morning before she got back from the party. She could hear Angela leave her room, probably all ready to leave for her day out with Lambros, so she hauled herself out of bed, thinking she had best go out and wish her friend a good day.

'You look fabulous, Angela!' said Carla as she greeted her friends. 'Sorry I'm late getting up.'

'That's the sign of a great night! I want to hear all about the party when I get back later on.'

'The party was lovely and we had a great time. Everyone was so friendly and welcoming.'

They all turned at the sound of the gate opening and spotted Lambros.

'I'm glad I did make an effort,' said Angela, suddenly sounding a bit nervous. 'He looks very smart. Have a lovely day, whatever you're up to,' she called over her shoulder as she rushed to the door.

Simon and Carla watched as the two said hello and Lambros held the gate open for Angela to walk through.

'That was very sweet of him, he's a real gentleman.'

'Believe it or not there still are a few of us around,' Simon said wryly. 'Now take a seat and tell me all about the party.'

'Do you mind if we sit in the shade? My head isn't feeling its best today...'

'Oh dear, sorry to hear that.'

'Don't be sorry, it was well worth it. I had a fabulous night. Honestly, everything about it was great.'

As Simon poured them each some fresh orange juice, he glanced at his phone and noticed there was a text from Polina about an hour ago that he had missed. She said she was going to be out painting at Thagistri tomorrow and that her mum would be dropping her off about ten-thirty and picking her up at five o'clock. He didn't know what to think. She obviously wanted him to go with her, but he wasn't sure. The whole secret thing seemed very childish and stupid. He would reply but first he would give it some thought.

'You obviously had a good time, but was that time with Sakis or Nectarios?' asked Simon as he set their glasses down on the side table.

'Actually, my date dumped me for someone else. No, I'm only joking. The girl whose party it was introduced her cousin to Sakis, and they hit it off. I had a lot of fun with his friends though, and we danced and laughed for hours as the music was so great. The vibe in the place was electric. And I did spend time talking to Nectarios, who of course was his normal charming self, but I also found him to be surprisingly honest about the life he leads here on the island.' She shrugged. 'We had fun.'

'Fun? Please explain,' Simon encouraged her.

'You're funny, you sound like Angela. Well ... not quite, as she would have gone around the subject a bit first, whereas you've dived right in. What I meant was we danced and chatted a lot and then he walked me back here. Oh! He also held the gate open for me, just like another gentleman.'

'So are you going to see him again? And I don't mean just down in the restaurant.'

'Yes, tomorrow. We're going out on his bike for the day.'

'That'll be fun.'

'You surprise me, Simon, you didn't go for the killer question.'

'What do you mean?'

'You didn't ask if I kissed Nectarios... Why are you laughing?'

'Because I don't need to ask you – your face says it all! Of course you kissed him.'

Carla didn't reply. Was it that obvious she had? She wondered if her happiness was what had given it away. As for the kiss, it didn't last long, just enough time to say good night, but it was special, something she would look back on when she was home in Saltmarsh as a highlight of her holiday here on Vekianos.

She went for a shower then and as they had agreed to stay at the villa for the day Simon said he would nip down to the bakery for a delicious and authentic lunch of Greek dishes, and to the shop for milk and crisps.

As Simon walked down the hill, he thought back to the text from Polina. A day of painting would certainly be nice, but perhaps it would also be pointless as the whole time they were together, they would be separate, both in their own concentrated painting bubbles. What he actually wanted was to spend time chatting and getting to know her better, and finding out more about the situation she was in with her mum. That seemed impossible though, so he decided he would text her back and say he couldn't make it.

As he came out of the supermarket and headed to the bakery, he saw Nectarios coming out of the bakery with a big box of bread. He wondered if he should say hello and ask if he'd had a nice night at the party, but before he could decide, Nectarios spotted him and walked over.

'Have you been sent down from the villa to get headache tablets? I expect Carla is feeling a little under the weather today.'

'Not at all. If anything, Carla is in a very good place, almost floating in the sky. I think her night out was a huge success in more ways than one.'

Simon knew Nectarios would take his words in all good humour and wouldn't be offended.

'That's good,' he said, trying and failing to come across as nonchalant. 'It was a nice party. I'd best get back to the restaurant with this bread. Perhaps we'll see you there tonight to eat?'

'Something tells me you might. I don't think any of the other restaurants in the harbour have the same attraction as Alina's. See you later.'

He laughed all the way back up the hill with the shopping, and walking through the gate he could see Carla floating around in the pool.

'It looks lovely in there. Just give me five minutes to put the food away and get changed and I'll join you.'

After having a swim, they chatted about the island and how they hoped Angela and Lambros were having a lovely time. They agreed she was looking so much better than the day she had arrived back to Saltmarsh Quay, for which they were both very glad. After some time on the sun loungers, they headed back up onto the patio and into the shade for lunch.

'Coming here has really given me time to sort my head out, emptying it of all the rubbish from years gone by, and creating space to fill it with new things,' Carla admitted.

'Would one of those new things be a certain

waiter?'

'I can't say I'm not enjoying having fun with Nectarios, but once the holiday is over and I get back to my real life, he'll just be a very sweet memory.'

'But you don't have a real life to go back to. I'm sorry, that sounded really horrible, didn't it?' he rushed to add. 'What I'm trying to say is that your university days are over and your mum is back on her feet, so the world is your oyster. What's to stop you from staying here on Vekianos a while longer?'

'No, I need to start a career and there would be no opportunities here. For a start, I don't speak the language, and everything is based around the tourist industry. I worked in hotels and bars when I was in university and I know that life isn't for me long-term. Moving on, did you want to go out tonight? I get the impression Angela won't be back until late so we could find somewhere to eat down in the harbour.'

'That would be nice. Shall we head back to the pool?'

It was obvious to Simon that Carla didn't want to talk about her future, and he couldn't blame her. What he couldn't understand was why she was being so flippant about Nectarios. Carla was turning down the chance to have the exact type of fun she deserved, whereas he really wanted something more with Polina and couldn't have it.

The rest of the afternoon was laid back, the two of them hopping in and out of the pool and taking it in turns fetching water and cups of tea.

'Six o'clock, Simon,' Carla announced after checking the time. 'I think that means it's time for wine. Red or white?'

'White, I think, but I will get it as I just remembered I need to text someone, and my phone is in my bedroom. I won't be a minute. Would you like some crisps or nuts to go with the wine?'

'Why not. Let's push the boat out.'

As he grabbed his phone to text Polina and say he couldn't meet her tomorrow, he noticed another text from her had come through.

If you do decide to come tomorrow, we don't necessarily have to paint. It might be nice just to chat

Well, that changed everything, didn't it?

Chapter 13
Holiday day 5

Stepping out through the gate Angela looked around for a car, but the only vehicle in sight was a rusty old van. Looking at it a bit more closely, she realised it sort of matched the scruffy house Lambros lived in. She decided immediately that this time she wouldn't make a comment. Lambros walked ahead and opened the van door for her and she saw that there was a nice blanket that looked very clean on the seat. So he had given it some thought after all. Lambros took Angela's bag and placed it in the back before helping her to get in.

'There you go. Be careful with the seatbelt as it can be a bit sticky. I keep meaning to have it sorted but to be honest it's not very often anyone ever sits in the passenger seat as both my daughter and grandson refuse to get into this old van.'

'As long as it takes you from A to B that's all you need. I'm looking forward to seeing your island, Lambros. Where will we be heading first?'

'It all depends how hungry you are. Have you had breakfast?'

'Yes, but that was a few hours ago.'

'Does that mean you could eat a gorgeously light and fluffy omelette?'

'I think it does. Lead the way – or should I say, drive away! Take me to the food.'

As he turned the van around the sound it was making went perfectly with the look – old and clunky – and she did wonder if they would even make it to the food, or if they'd break down on the side of the road and have to wait for someone to rescue them. This had the potential to turn out to be a completely different day than she was expecting! Thankfully, the noises calmed down once they were on the road, and they headed away from the town on a main road.

'This is the road that goes all around the island,' Lambros explained. 'If we just stayed on it without turning anywhere, we would end up back here at this spot within an hour or so. But before that I have lots of surprises for you.'

'I'm looking forward to it, especially the omelette, which sounds lovely.'

'The omelette is only the start of our day of wonderful scenery and food.'

'And with you as my tour guide, Lambros, I think it will also be a day of marvellous conversation.'

As they drove along Lambros pointed out little turnings that he said went to a nice beach or a little village. Angela was still doubtful they would make it to their final destination – Lambros's favourite beach – as every time he had to slow down or stop she was very fearful the van would not get started again. Thankfully, the van chugged on and he soon slowed right down and turned down a little lane.

'This leads to a small cove with a little shack – that's where the omelettes are made – and the place is only used by locals who come for a swim and then head to the shack for a beer or two. My wife Angelina always joked that it was where all the old men of Vekianos came to put the world to rights. She was right, of course, and you'd be surprised how many major decisions for the island have been talked about and debated in this shack. But I can promise you there will be none of that today as we are far too early in the day. No, this morning is all about the food.'

The lane was very bumpy, but it wasn't long

before it fanned out into a big open space with the sea in front of them. To the left Angela spotted a wooden hut that looked like a puff of wind could knock it over. This must be where they were going to eat.

'Now you can probably understand why my wife never came here to eat. But looks can be very deceiving. Just look at this old van! You would never think it could get anywhere but today it has. As for tomorrow ... well, it's hard to say. It might decide it doesn't want to go anywhere.' Lambros laughed as he parked the van under a tree so it wasn't baking in the full sun. He then got out and came around to open the door for Angela, which she thought was very sweet. She noticed the ground beneath her feet was very dry, with lots of soiled old leaves and sand mixed together.

'Are you ready? Like I said, this place is nothing to look at but wait until you taste the food. It will make up for it.'

'I'm sure it will, and the building doesn't put me off one little bit. I would always rather have rustic than modern any day.'

'Yes but there is rustic and then there is crumbling down rustic, if you know what I mean. There is a big difference.'

'You have a point there!' Angela laughed.

Lambros led the way around to the front of the shack, which was very quaint and not as much of a shock as Angela thought it would be. After hugs and hellos from the owner and people Lambros knew, it was time for the food. They both ordered a coffee and the tomato and cheese omelette. There was a lot of chat and banter in Greek and Lambros kindly translated it into English for her as they waited.

Angela could see the food being prepared on a two-ring gas camping stove and she started to smell the cheese. It reminded her of a memory from years ago when she was a child, which made her happy. She and her brother had been so lucky and had had a wonderful childhood, so all her memories were good ones.

The owner appeared within minutes from behind the stove with the omelettes. They were huge, and she worried she wouldn't be able to manage all of it.

'I know it looks a lot,' Lambos reassured her, 'but once you cut into it and see how light and fluffy it is, the worry about finishing it will come off your face. I promise.'

'Was I that obvious?'

As she used her fork to cut into it she saw exactly what he meant. It was like air and the taste was unbelievable; she had never had anything like it and there was no way she would leave a single morsel on the plate. She had died and gone to heaven.

They ate in contented silence and when the owner came to clear their plates he just smiled, knowing without even asking that they had both enjoyed the food.

'Wasn't that a good start to our day? Hopefully it won't go downhill from here,' joked Lambros.

'It was beautiful! I could eat that over and over again.'

'I'm pleased to hear it. Now, I would suggest another coffee but there is so much to pack into our day I think we need to be on our way.'

Angela offered to pay but Lambros said no money changed hands, explaining that when the owner of the shack visited Lambros's restaurant in the harbour he didn't pay either. It was a form of bartering.

As they walked back to the van Angela worried about it starting again, but at least if it didn't they would be somewhere with coffee, water, and food. Her worries came to nothing though, and they were soon back on the main road. Angela was feeling full. She certainly wouldn't need anything else to eat for a while!

'Our next stop will be for a little bit of relaxation on a gorgeous beach. We are heading to Zagandros, which is a little bit of paradise here on Vekianos.'

'That sounds lovely.'

They drove for another twenty minutes and Angela spent the time looking out the window. She could see how barren this part of the island was, though every now and again they drove by the odd house or a patch of land with greenhouses full of tomatoes. Eventually Lambros turned off the main road and suddenly there were a lot more houses. Eventually she began to see the sea in the distance. Pulling off to the side of the road, onto a bit of rough land with four cars parked on it, Lambros again parked in the shade.

'Here we are! I really hope you will like it here.'

'I'm sure I will. You didn't disappoint with the food, and I get the feeling this will be a delight for the eyes.'

Lambros went to the back of the van and got Angela's beach bag for her along with two sun loungers and a sun umbrella.

'You've thought of everything! Please let me help and carry something.'

'If you take the umbrella that would be a help. I also have a couple bottles of water if you would like one.'

He handed her a bottle and then locked the van and they headed towards the sea. It was starting to get quite warm and Angela was grateful Lambros had thought to bring the umbrella for them to get some shade under. It was only a couple of minutes walk down to the beach and as they stepped onto the sand Angela paused. It was picture perfect and deserted apart from three couples. She couldn't get over the colour of the sea; it was so blue and clear. Just perfection.

'Do you have a preference where you would like to sit?'

'Not at all. You choose. You'll know best as you've been here before.'

'Ok then, shall we go to the right, away from the other people and close to the rocks?' Angela nodded and as they set out across the sand, Lambros continued, 'I really can't remember when I was last here. Many years ago, I think, probably when Nectarios was little. So at least fifteen or twenty years ago.'

Once near the rocks, Lambros moved a few stones with his foot before opening up the loungers and then taking the umbrella off Angela and setting it up. They both got their towels out of their bags and then settled on the loungers for the day.

'This is so beautiful. It's just like you see on the holiday adverts. It's a very special place.'

'I was hoping you would like it.' Lambros smiled.

'Oh I do. Is it possible to get here by bus?'

'Yes, it stops right where we turned off the main road, but you wouldn't have to catch a bus. I could bring you.'

'I wasn't thinking of me but rather Simon. I'm sure he would love to come here and paint.'

'Yes, there are gorgeous spots like this all over the island for artists and photographers. Simon must be enjoying his time here with so much to see and paint.'

'Actually, it's a little odd. Before we came he was so excited about the prospect of spending his days painting, and once we arrived he met someone, a nice girl about the same age as him who paints in a similar style. They ended up spending a day together, catching the bus to some spot to paint, and he was rather taken with the young lady, but the day came to an abrupt end because the girl's mother didn't approve. I could understand the mother intervening if they were young but they're both adults.'

'That is odd. Does the girl live on the island or is she just visiting?'

'She lives here. Apparently she displays her work at the weekly craft fair on the pier. Maybe you've met her?'

'Polina. Now it all makes sense. Yes, her mum Calliope is very protective – too protective, if you ask me, as it's almost controlling. It all goes back to when Polina was very young, around five or six, and Calliope's husband went off with a waitress to Corfu ... or it could have been Athens? I'm not quite sure, but the point is they were never to be seen again.'

'That's so sad. I suspect that because she's been hurt she's trying to protect her daughter from the same fate.'

'Exactly. Calliope changed once the husband left, she cut herself off from her friends and she's held Polina close ever since. My wife used to say it was like she felt guilty for what had happened, or thought that people were pointing the finger at her, which of course wasn't the case. If she had only let her friends help her, her life and Polina's would be so much better. But enough of all that, we are here to enjoy ourselves. Are you hungry?'

'No, not at all.'

'When you are, just say. I have snacks in a cool box in the van.'

'You've really given this day out a lot of thought, Lambros, and I appreciate it, I really do.'

Lambros smiled and Angela could tell he was pleased with himself. He had planned the perfect outing.

Laying in the sunshine with no sounds aside from the water lapping at the shore, Angela's mind went to Polina and Simon. She felt for Calliope and thought it was such a shame the woman hadn't moved on, especially as it wasn't just her life it was impacting, it was Polina's as well. But at least now she could explain to Simon it was nothing to do with him and reassure him he hadn't done anything wrong.

'Angela? Can you hear me, Angela?' Lambros called.

'Oh dear, I must have fallen asleep. I hope I wasn't snoring.'

'No we both had a little nap. That's what we do when we get to our age.'

'I'm putting it down to the peace and quiet of this beautiful place. Have we been asleep long?'

'About an hour and a half.'

They both burst out laughing and decided they needed a little swim to wake them up and to cool down as even though they had been under the umbrella they were both hot and sweaty. They each had some water before getting up off the loungers and walking the few metres down to the sea. Lambros was first in, which pleased Angela as she wasn't the most graceful of people and she could do without him seeing her stumble in the waves.

'It's so warm!' she said, surprised. 'Why didn't we get in earlier?'

They floated happily for about half an hour before getting out and walking back to the loungers.

'Are you ready for a little late lunch? Believe it or not it's nearly four o'clock. Where has the day gone?'

'A snack would be nice.'

'I will walk back to the van and fetch the cool box. I should only be a few minutes.'

Once Lambros had gone she wondered what there would be to eat. No doubt he had been to the bakery before coming to pick her up. After she had dried herself off and checked her hair in the little mirror in her bag, she settled back on the lounger looking out to sea. There was a yacht passing by that looked so glamorous and she wondered who was on it. One thing was for sure, whoever it was, they would have to be rich! Until today she hadn't given a lot of thought to the rest of the island of Vekianos as her head had been full of the harbour and the villa they were staying in, but she was now keen to see more of it, especially places like this.

As she turned around, she spotted Lambros walking back towards her carrying lots of things. It looked like a lot more than a paper bag with a few pastries in.

'You are loaded up, Lambros! How many people are joining us?' she joked.

'I promise it just looks a lot as I brought this little table. Give me a moment to open it and then we can begin.'

Once the fold-out table was set up, Lambros opened one of the bags and out came plates, bowls, cutlery, and two wine glasses.

'I was going to just bring a selection of sweet and savoury things from the bakery, but I thought why not go to town, as they say.'

'You shouldn't have gone to all this trouble. A pastry would have been sufficient.'

'I wanted to do things properly. Now, help yourself to the salad,' he said, opening the container. There is salt, pepper, and oil on the side... Why are you smiling? Is something funny?' Lambros suddenly looked a bit nervous.

'I've just ... never been treated like this before. My brother and I used to take a picnic into Regent's Park when I visited him in London, but that was just sandwiches wrapped in tin foil. This is rather special in comparison, so thank you so much.'

'You must miss your brother. It's still very early days for you.'

'I do, but I think it will be worse once I'm back in England. Here I've had Carla and Simon for company, and everything is new – not the normal everyday routine – and with days like this there is plenty to take my mind off everything.'

'Routine is the bit I struggled with after my wife died. In the end I had to create an entirely new one. At first, I threw myself into the restaurant, but that was the same as it had been for the last forty plus years: open it in April, work seven days a week, then close in October. I hate the winter because I don't have the restaurant to fiddle with. Those months are long and very lonely.'

Seeing the depth of sadness in his eyes, Angela didn't know what to say. She needed to change the subject and lighten the mood.

'This salad is gorgeous. The feta is heavenly and after the delicious omelette earlier I really don't think I'll need to eat anything else again today.'

She smiled at Lambros and was surprised to see his face had fallen.

'I've put my foot in it again, haven't I?'
'Not at all. This can be the dinner.'
'If you're sure? We can take a raincheck on any dinner you'd planned and do it another day. But that time it's on me.'

'That would be nice but it's my treat.'
'My treat or there will be no date.'
With that they both burst out laughing.
'Ok you win, Angela, but on one condition – I

want to learn more about you. What you did for work, where you've lived, what hobbies you have, and also did you or do you have a man in your life.'

'We don't need to wait until next time for that. I can tell you know I haven't had a man in my life for over thirty years, so this dating game is very new to me. I'm not sure what the rules are but I am really enjoying myself, so thank you, Lambros.'

Chapter 14
Holiday day 5

After re-reading the text from Polina yet again, Simon put his phone down. It was obvious she wanted to spend time with him, but what would the point be? Even if they could get past her mother's disapproval, he was only here for another week. What if they became closer and then he had to go? No, he was being stupid imagining a lot more to the situation than there really was.

Come on, Simon, snap out of it!

'There you go,' he said to Carla, handing over a glass of wine and a selection of nibbles. 'Just the thing for the perfect end to a day by the pool.'

'And the perfect start to the evening out. I was thinking, do you think we could eat down at Alina's? I promise it's not because I want to see Nectarios, but because I want to hear how Sakis got on with the lad from Corfu.'

'That's fine by me. Why don't we go down earlier and have a walk around, and a drink or two in one of the bars? We can people watch.'

'It's a date! Let's leave here around eight o'clock. That'll give us time to enjoy the last of this gorgeous sunshine first.'

Simon smiled. 'Can you believe how well the two of us are getting on? I knew we would but it's like we're just so ... relaxed with each other, with no pressure because neither of us want anything more than a friendship together. I really like that.'

'Me too. It's the same with Angela, isn't it? We're all just so comfortable with each other. Why do you think it's working so well?'

'Perhaps because we're all in a similar place at this time in our lives.'

'What do you mean?'

'We're all at a moment of change, starting new chapters. With Angela's brother's passing she knows now that she's by herself and as she's in the twilight of her life, she's realising that she needs to make the most of these years. For you, your university years are over and now it's time to dive into the big bad world. And as for me, I've realised that the longer I carry on with the decorating jobs the harder it will be to stop doing them. It's time for me to decide: do I take the bull by the horns and follow my dreams and try to become a full-time artist, or do I give it up for good? This holiday is a stopping and also a starting point for the three of us.'

'That was all a bit deep,' Carla said after a pause, causing them both to laugh. 'I think we're going to need another glass of wine. Actually, you know what? I'll just fetch the whole bottle.'

As Carla popped to the kitchen Simon thought back to Polina's text. He needed to reply and he knew now what that reply would be. The simple fact was that if he didn't meet up with her, it would likely be something he would regret in years to come.

'It's really busy here in the harbour tonight,' Carla said to Simon as they squeezed past yet another group of tourists. 'Do you think it's because we're earlier than usual coming down, or have more people arrived on the island?'

'I'm not sure but it's a fantastic atmosphere. I love the buzz.'

'Yes and also how everyone goes to the effort to get dressed up for an evening out. Now, shall we have a drink first and then a little walk or would you like a walk before the drink?'

'I think a drink first, a large gin and tonic.'

'A gin it is then. We need to find somewhere with a view and ... bingo! Quick, make a run for that table before anyone else gets it,' she said, pointing.

Simon laughed as Carla ran ahead, and it crossed his mind to go in the other direction as a bit of a joke, but no, he needed that gin. Whether that was because he was excited about the next day or he was nervous, he wasn't entirely sure, but he suspected the latter. He really liked Polina.

'You are so funny. If only you could have seen the people's faces as you sprinted along the harbour. It was like you were on fire,' he said as he caught up to Carla.

'Well, if you want something you have to really go for it – no half measures – and if I had only walked to this table someone else would have grabbed it first and then I would have been disappointed. Good evening,' she said, turning to the approaching waitress. 'Could we have two large gin and tonics, please.'

The drinks quickly arrived and they sat taking in the views and escaping into their own thoughts for a while.

'Do you think Angela is having a nice day?' Simon finally asked. 'Something tells me Lambros will be treating her like a queen. It would be nice if she got the confidence to travel back here to the island by herself for little holidays. I'm sure Lambros would love to see her again.'

'It would be so nice. I wish I could travel back with her. I'd love it if this island became a little part of my life for many years to come.'

'Why limit it? It could become a big part of your life if you let it.'

'No, don't go there. Any talk of the future is off

limits tonight. We're simply living for the moment.'

Simon was glad to agree as he wanted to put seeing Polina tomorrow to the back of his mind for now. The drinks were going down a treat and there was plenty to entertain them. There was a juggler performing in front of the bars and restaurant with a little girl holding out a hat for tips, who looked like she could be his young daughter. A few minutes later an elderly couple walked by with a small handcart, the man turning a handle on an old machine and making it play Greek music. A sign on the cart said they were raising money for a children's charity.

'Come on, Simon, drink up. It's time for a walk before dinner, and you never know, we might manage another drink first. I know! We can walk that way and I'll show you where the party was held.'

It was a part of the harbour Simon hadn't been to and as they got to the end of the wall Carla spotted Zeta and waved.

'Hi, Zeta, I just wanted to thank you for a lovely party. I had a really great night.'

'It was good, wasn't it? I'm suffering today though, and I could do without having to work!' She laughed.

'Sorry, this is Simon, a friend I'm on holiday with,' she said, making introductions.

'Hello, you should have come last night! I'm sure you would have enjoyed it.'

Simon smiled and nodded as he took in the restaurant and bar behind Zeta. It looked nice and he was wondering if he should suggest they eat here but thought better of it, as Carla seemed to have her heart set on seeing Sakis.

'Did you want to carry on in this direction or turn around?' he asked a few minutes later, once they'd said goodbye to Zeta and continued on their walk.

'It's still early so why don't we carry on for a little bit? The view is spectacular from here, isn't it? Just rocks, the sea, and a few boats out in the distance.'

She took her phone out of her bag to take some photos and then they carried on for another fifteen minutes or so, until the path turned into a track that neither had the right footwear to be going along.

'Time to turn around, Simon. My stomach is telling me it needs some food.'

'Agreed. Also it's getting on for ten-thirty so the restaurant should be starting to get quieter.'

As they neared Alina's Restaurant Carla spotted Nectarios serving a table outside. He hadn't spotted her, but Sakis had, and he came running out to greet them.

'I'm so sorry for deserting you last night! It was terribly rude of me and I really didn't know what came over me ... well, I suppose I do. Trifon is so handsome, how could I not stand and chat to him?'

'You weren't rude at all. Your lovely friends entertained me and we laughed and danced all night. It was a fabulous party and I've just told Zeta how much I enjoyed it. Do you have a table for two? We're starving!'

'Of course. No Angela tonight?'

'No, she's been out with Lambros all day.'

'Not in his old van, I hope. If so, you may never see her again! I'm surprised it ever gets started.' He laughed as he led them to a table for two. 'Did you spend any time at the party with Nectarios?'

'Yeah, we chatted and had a dance.'

'That explains it then... Excuse me, I just need to see to these customers before they leave.'

As Sakis departed, Alina arrived beside their table ready to take their drink orders.

'I take it the party was a success,' Alina said wryly, once they'd exchanged hellos. 'It's all Sakis has talked about. He's a little bit ... how can I put it? Oh yes, up in the clouds tonight. I get the impression someone paid him quite a bit of attention, which he seemed to enjoy. As for Nectarios, I thought he would be tired and late for work but it's been the complete opposite. I have never known him to be here before me and get so much work done; It's like having a different son working here today! I will have to ask Zeta to have a party every week so he keeps it up.'

Alina went off to get them each a glass of wine and Carla was left feeling a bit confused. Surely one kiss from her couldn't have changed Nectarios's attitude to work altogether? No, that was bonkers!

'I think we're in for an interesting evening,' commented Simon. 'This restaurant is like a soap opera ... and I mean that in a good way! Here's Sakis with the wine.'

'So tell me,' he gushed to Carla, 'what did you think of Trifon?! Isn't he gorgeous? He's invited me to go and stay with him on Corfu.'

'That will be nice for you.'

'Yes, but it won't be until the season is over and the restaurant closes. It's a seven-day-a-week job here until October and I can't leave Alina in a mess as she won't manage with just Nectarios. Still, at least I'll get to see him again while he's here. Trifon is meeting me after work, and we're going to go to one of the late bars for a drink. Did you like the clothes he was wearing? It's all designer, he is so stylish.'

Simon was laughing to himself, wondering if they would ever get to order any food, or if the whole evening would be about Trifon, but he didn't mind really. Sakis was nice and it was good to see him so happy. He also thought that as much as a loud and raucous party wasn't his thing, a small part of him wished he'd been a fly on the wall for a few hours.

As they were waiting for their food Carla looked over to the harbour wall and spotted Trifon. Apparently he was just as eager to see Sakis again!

When Sakis returned with their starter a few minutes later he bid them goodnight.

'Nectarios said I can go early as it's Trifon's last night here on Vekianos. He's really going out of his way to be helpful, which is great, but no doubt before the end of the week he'll want something in return. I'll have to wait and see if this new Nectarios sticks around.'

They waved him off and then got stuck into the starter and topped up their wine glasses. As Carla looked over towards the other tables, she caught Nectarios's eye and he smiled back at her, causing the butterflies in her stomach to take flight.

She couldn't take her eyes off Nectarios. For some reason he looked different tonight. She couldn't really put her finger on it but it was as though he was more caring than usual with the patrons. Or was she just imagining it?

'Are you ok? You look a bit dazed,' Simon observed.

'Yes, I'm fine,' she said quickly. 'This is good. Everything is lovely.'

'Almost perfect, I'd say.'

'Why just almost?' she asked.

'I think to make things perfect you and that young man over there need to talk to each other. I sense something special is brewing between you two.'

Chapter 15

Holiday day 6

As Simon made his first coffee of the day he hoped Angela would be up soon as he wanted to speak with her before he had to leave to meet Polina. He also wanted to hear about her day with Lambros as she had gone to bed before he and Carla had returned last night. If he was honest with himself, he was mostly hoping for some reassurance that he was doing the right thing today by meeting Polina. Thankfully, he was in luck and she walked into the kitchen just then.

'I hope we didn't disturb you when we came in last night,' he said after greeting her. 'We thought you'd still be up.'

'I didn't hear a thing. To be honest, I was so tired I could have slept through anything. Did you have a nice evening out?'

'We did, thanks. How was your day out with Lambros? Did you have fun?'

'We did. We laughed, had some gorgeous food, and best of all we swam in the beautiful sea and chatted. It was very special.'

'I'm so pleased to hear that. Would you like a coffee?'

'Thank you, that would be nice.'

Angela suddenly remembered what Lambros had told her about Polina's mum. As they were alone it was the perfect time to tell Simon.

'There you go,' said Simon as he handed over the drink. 'Did you see a lot of the island?'

Angela talked him through the day, from leaving

the villa to grabbing a drink in the harbour at the end of the day.

'It sounds lovely! So what have you got planned for today?'

'Well, and please don't laugh, but ... I'm going to finish yesterday off.'

'Sorry? I don't understand.'

'We were meant to go for dinner, but we had eaten too much and then we ran out of time so tonight will be part two of our day out.'

'A bonus evening.' Simon smiled.

'Yes, but before that I think I'll stay here by the pool. Have you got any plans?'

'Yes, I'm meeting Polina. But no painting today – just chatting.'

'That will be nice and I'm sure you'll have a good time.'

'I hope so. I haven't met someone so on my wavelength like this before, but all the secrecy with having to keep things from her mum, well ... it feels wrong to me.'

'I actually might be able to shine a little light on the situation. Lambros was asking me yesterday if you and Carla were having a nice holiday and I explained about Polina, and he said he knew her and her mum Calliope. Apparently, Calliope's husband went off with another woman many years ago and she's never really got over it. That's why she's so protective of her daughter, she's trying to stop Polina getting hurt in the same way.'

'That explains a lot. How sad for both of them.'

'Yes, very. I wanted you to know as I know you're quite torn about the situation, but perhaps you should let Polina explain things to you. I'm not saying what Lambros said isn't true, but it's always good to have both sides of a story. Anyway, I'm sure you'll have a lovely day. You and Polina have so much in common with your passion and talent for art.'

'Good morning, you two! Did I hear the word passion? Has that got anything to do with your day out yesterday?' Carla winked at Angela.

'Yes, Lambros and I spent the whole day rolling around naked on the sand,' said Angela, completely deadpan.

There was a beat of silence before all three of them broke down in hysterics.

'Very funny!' Carla managed to wheeze out between giggles.

'On that note, I think I'll go and get ready. And before you ask, Carla, I can guarantee that I will *not* be spending my day rolling around naked,' Simon reassured her.

'All joking aside,' Carla continued once she and Angela were alone, 'did you have a nice day out with Lambros?'

'I did. Part one of the date was lovely and I'm looking forward to part two this evening.'

'Part two?' asked Carla, looking confused.

By the time Angela filled Carla in on everything she had already told Simon, he'd reappeared in a smart pair of shorts and a brightly coloured t-shirt. It was clear he had really put a lot of effort into his appearance.

'How do I look? Is this too dressed up? Should I be wearing something more beachy? More importantly, why am I in such a tizzy about the whole thing?'

'Because you want it to be the perfect day,' said Carla, kindly.

'What you're wearing is perfect so stop worrying and go have fun. Enjoy the day for what it is: two people talking about art and enjoying being with one another.'

'Thank you, Angela. I hope you both have a nice day as well.'

With that Simon was gone.

'I never asked where you went to eat last night,' said Angela.

'We went down to Alina's as I wanted to find out how Sakis got on with the chap from Corfu. We had such a laugh. Now I'm looking forward to another pool day. A week of our holiday has nearly gone which means—'

'Don't say it! I'm not counting down, just taking every day as it comes. I'm going to make some toast, would you like some?'

'I would but we don't have any bread so I'll nip down to the bakery.'

'Are you sure? I don't mind going.'

'Don't be daft, I can be down and back in no time. I'll just go and get changed.'

Carla quickly threw on a loose top and her cutoff jeans, and tied her hair back. Popping on her sunglasses, she was out the door in two minutes flat. As it was still quite early she hoped there wouldn't be a queue at the bakery just yet, and she was in luck as there were just two people in front of her. As she was there it seemed wrong not to buy a few sweet pastries for a mid-morning snack along with the bread, so she added them to the basket. As she exited the bakery she saw Nectarios heading towards her and her stomach did a little flutter.

They greeted one another and he asked about her meal the night before.

'The food was lovely, but I admit I was a bit disappointed with the service.' Nectarios looked taken aback and she rushed to continue before he thought she was serious. 'When Sakis left early, he said you were going to be looking after us, but you didn't come near the table at all.' She smiled shyly.

'I really wanted to come over to you, but I was worried I would make an idiot of myself after the night before. I also didn't want you to think I was giving you the typical waiter's charm.'

'I know you wouldn't have.'

'I don't want to be too forward but ... would you like to have a day out with me? Perhaps go to the beach tomorrow? I don't need to be at the restaurant until five in the evening. But that's only if you want to, no pressure.' He suddenly looked a bit awkward, as if he was regretting his offer.

'I would really like that.'

'Good!' His relief was palpable. 'I could pick you up around nine-thirty, if you're ok getting on the back of my bike. If not, we could catch a bus.'

'No, your bike will be fine.'

'Ok great. I need to get going as we have the restaurant to prepare for the lunch trade, but I'll see you tomorrow.'

'I'm looking forward to it.' She smiled and waved as he headed off, then took a deep breath. Did she mind getting on the back of Nectarios's bike? No, of course not, as it meant she would have to put her arms around him and hold on tight. And what was there not to like about that?

Chapter 16
Holiday day 6

Simon made his way to the bus stop a bit early as he knew where he was heading but wasn't sure of the bus times. He had to admit to himself he was excited and not at all disappointed he wouldn't be getting any painting done that day.

There was a queue at the stop but that wasn't a problem and within minutes the bus arrived. As he was by himself he decided he would make an effort to look out the window for more of the ride as last time he'd missed it all, he and Polina too busy chatting away. He liked how the bus went from being close to the water's edge and then into little villages and back out again. There really was so much more to this island than he, Carla, and Angela had originally thought.

He arrived about an hour early but that wasn't a problem as he wanted to make sure he would be somewhere he could see Polina arriving in her mum's car, but where Calliope wouldn't be able to see him, just in case she recognized him from the bakery the other day.

He found a nice spot where he could see the sea as well as the little road leading to the car park. He was feeling even more nervous now. He'd never really felt such a strong and instantaneous connection with a woman like this before, and the feeling was so new to him. He had thought he'd been in love before, but given the depth of his complicated feelings for Polina he knew now that he hadn't. He'd always thought the concept of love at first sight was a bit ridiculous, but maybe there was something to 'love at first painting'? There was no denying that seeing his own style mirrored in Polina's work has created a connection between them that went far beyond emotions.

But no matter how he felt, he knew that realistically there could be no future with Polina as he only had a week left of his holiday before he would return to England. Even putting aside the issue of Calliope's over-protectiveness, perhaps meeting up today was a stupid thing to be doing.

With one eye on the little road he saw a car pull up and ... yes, it was Polina. She got out of the passenger side and went to the boot of the car. His heart was racing, he was so excited to see her. Once she'd retrieved all of the bags that she'd had with her the other day, she waved to her mum who then turned the car around and drove off.

'Good morning!' he called as he loped towards her. 'Let me help you carry some of that.'

'Thank you. I know it's silly to have brought all this as a sort of cover, but ... well, it just makes life a lot easier. What my mum doesn't know won't hurt her and all that. But enough of my strange life, do you fancy a cold drink in the beach café? To be honest, if we aren't painting I'm not sure what we're going to do for the day.'

'You can paint if you'd like. I'm more than happy to watch, and it would mean you wouldn't be lying to your mum and you'd have evidence of how you'd spent your day.'

'No, it's not that bad that I need to produce evidence when I get home.'

'Coffee it is then.'

Between them they carried the bags and headed across the beach to the café where two cold drinks and two bacon and cheese croissants were swiftly ordered. Taking a seat on the little decking Simon made sure he wasn't looking at Polina but towards the sea. The situation was awkward enough without having to stare into each other's eyes.

The drinks and croissants arrived, and they got stuck right into eating, which relaxed them both considerably.

'Are you still having a nice holiday with your friends? What have you been up to?'

'We're very spoilt having the villa with such a gorgeous pool and a view that's to die for, so we've stayed there most of the time. In the evenings we wander down into the harbour for food and a little walk around.'

'There are some lovely restaurants in the harbour and even if you were here for a month, you could eat somewhere different every night. I expect you've found a favourite though? Most people seem to.'

'Yes, we go to Alina's. The food is really good, Sakis the waiter is very funny, Alina is welcoming, and of course it means Carla can make eyes at Nectarios.'

'Ah, I see.' Polina laughed. 'A lot of girls enjoy going there and it's not just the food that they're attracted to. Nectarios does have a bit of a reputation, but he's young and has a right to enjoy himself.'

'That croissant was great. Would you like another drink or did you want to find somewhere on the beach to sit?'

'I'm fine with just the one drink and I know the perfect place to sit. If we follow the path behind the beach there's a little trail that leads to a rocky bit with a nice view. We'll have something to lean on there and there won't be so many people.'

'Perfect. Here, let me carry all the heavy things.'

'They're not that heavy really. I've scaled everything down and only bring the things I know I will definitely use, so I can always manage it by myself.'

They started walking and chatting and after about fifteen minutes Polina pointed to the little gap, and they made their way down to the beach.

'Is this ok for you? I always think these rocks here are like sitting in a theatre and what a show we have with that stunning view, don't you think?' asked Polina.

'This is perfect. Hey, isn't this where you paint? I recognize that bit of the view in your paintings,' he said, pointing it out.

'It is. Fancy you remembering one of my paintings,' she said, giving him a playful nudge with her shoulder.

'I remember them all because they're so good. How often do you paint?'

'Everything works around the weekly craft fair. It's on a Wednesday so I treat that as my last day of the week. In the evening I look at which paintings have sold to help me decide what to paint next. Say, for example, that a painting of this beach has sold and I don't have a similar one to replace it, I make a plan to come here before the following week's fair. Or if some of the harbour ones sell, I'll spend a few days down there painting.'

'That's really interesting. You're so organised.'

'It works for me.' She shrugged.

'Have you been doing the Wednesday market for very long? It really is lovely with all the different stalls and artists.'

'I've probably been doing it for five or six years now. You're right, there's a really lovely vibe, and I know visitors from other islands come over especially to go to the market. Setting it up and taking it down each week can be a bit of a headache though. It takes over an hour each time to wrap or unwrap all the paintings, and inevitably I'll damage one and it will need touching up after. But I shouldn't be complaining. I know many people would love to be displaying their work in such a beautiful location.'

'What about displaying your work in a shop or gallery?'

'That's my dream. It's actually my goal in life to have my own little gallery, but the reality is that I would have to open seven days a week, which would make it difficult to find time to paint, and the overheads would undoubtedly be high. Years ago I thought I could paint in the winter because the gallery would only be open between April and October, but then, what if I produced the wrong work and I didn't have anything to replace the things that did sell? No, I'll just carry on as I am with the Wednesday market and think of the good times, not the setting up and taking down.'

'It's good to have a positive outlook on these kinds of things.'

'Completely. If I was miserable and fed up with life all the time I really don't think I would be able to paint and create my work.'

'I totally get it. Back in England I have to be in a really good space in my head to paint. If I set time aside and then for some reason I'm not feeling like doing it, but I persist because I had specifically scheduled that time to paint, the work I produce just isn't good, and I feel like I haven't achieved anything. If it was my full-time job I could paint as and when the inspiration strikes me.'

'You must enjoy your decorating work though? I imagine it must be very satisfying for you to see happy homeowners when you've finished.'

'Yes, I do. Some jobs are nicer than others but then the same can be said about painting a picture as you don't get the same buzz from every piece of work.'

'Very true, and it's the same with time. A painting that you think will take just a day to paint could end up being three days, whereas another time something you plan to do over four or five days is done in two.'

Simon nodded and there was a long silence. It was clear they were both struggling to fill the conversation, but the last thing he wanted was to ruin the day by bringing up the subject of her mum. In the end he didn't have to be the one to broach the difficult topic.

'I'd like to talk about the elephant in the room, if that's ok with you,' said Polina, her hesitance clear in her tone.

'Ok,' he said, suddenly a bit nervous.

'First of all, please believe me when I say my keeping our friendship from my mum has nothing whatsoever to do with you ... or with me, come to that. The whole thing goes back many years. When I was five my dad suddenly left us and it turned our world upside down. Up to that point everything had been perfect – or at least what I can remember of it. Of course I was very young, so I probably didn't understand everything that was happening at the time.'

'You really don't need to explain any of this, it's none of my business,' said Simon, giving her an out if she wanted it.

'No, I'd like to explain. I don't want this stupid thing with my mum to spoil our day.'

'Ok, but only if you're sure.'

He was uncomfortable but if it helped her, he would sit there and listen.

'If you chatted to people here on Vekianos who know my and my mum's situation, they'll tell you that my mum is protecting me and controlling me because she doesn't want what happened to her to happen to me. She comes across quite horribly to most people, never letting her guard down, and I've heard what people say. "Poor Polina this" and "poor Polina that". And though that's what we let everyone believe, that's not the truth.'

'What do you mean?' he asked.

'It's true that when my dad left us for another woman my mum went to pieces. Even though I was only five that time is so clear in my head because my mum was a complete mess and the crying went on for months. It got to the point that she could barely function and my grandparents stepped in to do the basic things that she wasn't able to do. She's come a long way since then, but sadly there are still occasionally days like that now. They don't happen very often, but when they do it's heart-breaking.'

'That's terrible. Is there no help she can get?'

'She's had all sorts of meetings and sessions with numerous professional therapists, but it's as if there's a high wall she just can't get over. But none of that explains why today has to be a secret. The truth is that her biggest fear, and the thing she gets the most screwed up about, is the possibility of me leaving her, too. She's terrified.'

'I don't know what to say. That's a lot for you to have to carry on your shoulders.'

'There isn't anything anyone can say. My life has to be committed to her. I know that sounds so overly dramatic but I've spent many years trying to figure a way out and there just isn't one. It's just going to have to be me and her.'

'Do you at least have outlets to relieve some of the pressure? Like, do you have friends you can vent to?'

'Of course, but I always feel my time with them is limited as Mum says that every minute I'm away from her feels like an hour and every hour a day. It's even affected my art. I've been asked to exhibit over in Corfu, but she won't leave the island because that could be where my dad's moved to, and if she doesn't go there's no way I could.'

'What a really sad situation to be in, not just for you but for your mum as well. It's not normal, Polina, and it's not how a life should be lived.'

'Sadly, I can't see it changing anytime soon. If you can think of a way to change it I would be very grateful to hear it.'

There was nothing Simon could say in response. As much as he wanted to help he didn't know how. Sitting there in silence he could see Polina had said all she was going to about the situation.

'I'm really sorry to put a dampener on our day out, but I wanted to be honest and clear. The last thing I needed was someone telling you their version and you getting only a partial truth. My mum isn't controlling, just very fragile, and I don't want to do anything to rock her little boat.'

Simon wanted to point out that not allowing her daughter to live her life the way she wanted to, and demanding Polina be by her side almost twenty-four-seven, was all about control, not fragility, but he wasn't quite sure how to say it without offending Polina.

'What are you thinking? I didn't say all this to upset you, it was just so you'd understand a bit better where I'm coming from.'

'I do understand, and I really can see the difficulty of the situation, but... No, nevermind. Do you fancy getting something to eat or a drink?'

'What were you going to say? Please, I'd like to

hear it.'

Simon took a deep breath. 'I was just wondering what would happen if, for instance, you told your mum about our day out, if you were just honest and said you met an artist that was here on holiday, and you wanted to spend time with him painting and talking art? Then, when his holiday was over, he would leave the island and you would get back to your routine. Surely she would see there was nothing wrong with that?'

Polina looked uncomfortable.

'I understand what you're saying and the only answer I can give you is ... I don't know what would happen. And that scares me, it really does.'

Chapter 17
Holiday day 6

'What another lovely day we've had! I think I'd best start getting ready now though as Lambros said he would be here for around seven-thirty and I don't want to be rushing.'

'Why don't you have your shower and sort out what you're going to wear and then come out and we can have a glass of wine on the patio. Do you know where he's taking you?'

'No, but I have insisted that I'm paying, which he wasn't happy about, but he knows I won't go if he doesn't let me. Right, I'll see you in a while,' she said, heading inside.

As Angela went off Carla checked the time. Perhaps she would put all the lounge chair cushions away and then move back up to the patio to take in the last of the late evening sunshine.

As she closed the door to the pool room she thought about her plans to go out with Nectarios the next day. Was she actually becoming one of those girls who thought they were the only one who truly mattered to him?

Oh, snap out of it, Carla. All you're doing is going to the beach for the day with a nice lad, nothing else.

Opening the wine and taking the bottle and two glasses outside she realised how much she would miss this place; not just the villa but the island as well. This little harbour town was such a happy, comfortable place and to be honest even if she was in a small studio apartment with no view she suspected she would still feel the same. But enough thoughts about going home. They still had another week here, and she was determined to make the most of it.

'I've chosen between two dresses and I'm hoping you'll help me decide which one to wear,' Angela called through the open door.

'Of course! Why don't you model them?'

'Excellent idea.'

While she waited for Angela, Carla called out, 'Can I ask you something? Do you think I'm one of those girls who naively believe everything Nectarios says?'

'Of course not! You and Simon are so similar, both taking things a little too seriously. Remember that you're on holiday and you're meant to be having fun and not thinking too much about every sign and situation.'

'Of course you're right. I need to be more like you.'

'What do you mean?' asked Angela as she stepped out in the first dress.

'Well, you're very laid back about Lambros and the time you're spending together. Alina told Simon and I that she had never seen him like this. She said he had pulled his socks up and was starting to enjoy life, and she thinks that's all down to you. That's a great dress, by the way. Definitely a contender.'

Carla could tell Angela was thinking through what she'd said as she nodded absently and stepped back inside to change.

'I'm sure if you decided to come back for another holiday he would be very happy to see you,' Carla called through the open window. 'You get on well together and there doesn't seem to be any pressure.'

'You've definitely given me something to think about,' said Angela as she stepped out in outfit number two.

The next twenty minutes were spent talking about the pros and cons of each dress. Carla thought they were both nice and encouraged Angela to pick whichever one she felt most comfortable wearing, so Angela opted for the bright yellow, which was so summery and perfect for a night out in Greece.

'Decision made! Now to put on the final touches before I change my mind again.'

Carla sat back in the comfy chair. She was so pleased for Angela and with both of her travel companions out for the evening she was looking forward to a big bowl of pasta, more wine, and perhaps a little music while she enjoyed looking out to sea. Yes, she was really looking forward to some time alone.

'You look fabulous, Angela! Lambros is a very lucky man to have you on his arm.'

'Thank you. And you're sure you don't mind being here by yourself?'

'Not at all. You go and have fun.'

'I will. I think I've just heard a car pull up but it doesn't sound like Lambros's old van.'

Peering over the edge of the patio, Carla said, 'He's just opened the gate and it looks like he's made an effort as well. Go on then, don't keep the young man waiting!'

Angela kissed Carla goodbye and headed down to meet Lambros, who looked very smart in his cream trousers and crisp blue shirt.

'Good evening, Angela, you look lovely.'

'Thank you. You look very dapper as well.'

She was surprised to spot a taxi and shot Lambros a questioning look.

'I thought I'd leave the van at home so you don't have to worry about it breaking down on a dark road later on,' he joked.

He held the door open before going around and

getting in on the other side. The driver said good evening to Angela and they were on their way, heading away from the harbour.

'I thought we would go to a lovely little town not far from here called Keriaphos. It's on a hill with a little beach, and though the town gets very busy during the day with people there to enjoy the sunshine, at night there is a lovely buzz when all the restaurants open. The atmosphere is very special and completely different from being in the harbour.'

Before long they pulled to a stop on the top of a steep hill. After paying and thanking the driver, they got out of the car.

'I thought it would be nice to walk down to the little town, but I promise you we won't walk back up. I've not booked anywhere specific to eat because there are a lot of nice restaurants to choose from and it might be nice to have a walk around first.'

As they slowly walked down the curvy hill Angela could see the sea between little gaps in the houses. They eventually got to the bottom and the road levelled out as shops full of tourist gifts appeared, bracketed by restaurants that were all very quaint and pretty.

'I thought you might like to see the beach first. If we turn down here we can walk along the boardwalk by the beach cafe.'

The little cove was very quaint and quite small compared to the beaches they had seen yesterday, but the view of the boats all lit up on the water in the distance was really nice.

'I expect during the day the beach gets very crowded,' she said.

'Oh yes, a lot of visitors stay here in Keriaphos because it has everything they need for their holidays – the beach as well as shops and restaurants. I have very fond memories of coming here as a child, but in those days it was very quiet, and the only people you saw were locals. Now, are you hungry? Shall we go and find somewhere to eat?'

'Lead the way!'

They headed back to the road and carried on in the opposite direction to which they'd come from. The road got wider in places and there were little lanes and alleyways off of it, just begging to be explored. This really was a very pretty town.

'What do you fancy eating?' asked Lambros.

'I would like a surprise meal, please. You didn't disappoint me with the food or the lovely places we went to yesterday so I know you won't tonight either.'

'Oh dear, no pressure then.'

'None whatsoever! Go with what you would do if you were here by yourself. Come on, where would you eat?'

He smiled. 'There's a place up a little lane that all the locals go to. It's sort of shoved in between a couple of buildings and they only serve old fashioned Greek dishes. It's all very rustic and by that I don't mean a tasteful, traditional looking Greek tavern, I mean *rustic*.'

The way he emphasised the word 'rustic' made her grin.

'I can't wait to see it. You've painted quite the perfect picture!'

'It's good we're going in the evening as it will be dark and you won't be able to see the full horrors of the place. But jokes aside, it serves some of the best food on the island. I should also warn you that I'll probably know nearly everyone there as it's inevitable that I either went to school with them or worked with them, so there will be a lot of chat. And of course the fact that I'm bringing you with me will really get the tongues wagging.'

'I do love a bit of village gossip, and for it to be about me? Even better.'

'Put it this way, before we've even eaten a bite of food Alina will have received a phone call saying I'm here with a woman. But saying that, I think it will do my ego good as it's not happened for many years.'

'I'm glad to be able to help.'

He pointed out which way they had to go, and they giggled all the way up the street before turning up another lane. It was very uneven and the further they got the more Angela could hear laughter and music.

'Are you ready for a shock?' asked Lambros.

He hadn't been embellishing; their destination wasn't a restaurant so much as a selection of tables and chairs in the middle of a lane. It was very busy and the chatting was so loud, but the biggest impression Angela had was the aromas. The smell was to die for! As they got nearer some people called out to Lambros while others waved. It sort of reminded her of a film, and also gave her the oddest feeling of having stepped back in time. One thing was for sure, this wasn't like anywhere she had ever been to eat before.

Lambros pointed to a table near one of the buildings and he stood back to let her go first through the crowd, more people greeting them with friendly smiles and waves as they passed.

'A glass of wine, Angela?' he asked once they were seated.

'Yes, please, white.'

Lambros nodded and then turned and told the next table their order, who then told the one next to them, and on and on until finally a bell rang.

'Order placed,' said Lambros, proudly. 'I bet you have never seen that happen before! Don't worry,' he added, 'the wine will be brought by someone, not passed from table to table. Look, it's on the way already. Here comes the lovely Maria, she is the owner's daughter.'

Lambros introduced Maria to Angela and then he chatted away to the young girl in Greek. It looked like he was asking about the food as he gestured to several of the tables around them. Angela was fascinated by the place and felt so relaxed.

'That's a very big smile on your face,' said Angela once Maria had drifted away to help another table.

'Because I can't believe I have brought you here. Wait until Alina finds out, she will be horrified.'

'I think it's nice. The wine is good and I suspect the food will be as well. What do you recommend?'

'I asked Maria what the specialty for the day was and I'm glad to say it's one of my favourites – beef stifado. The way they make it here is just like how my mum and grandmother used to make it.'

'Perfect. I'll have the same.'

'How about a starter as well?'

'That would be nice. Surprise me.'

'You're putting me under so much pressure!' said Lambros, pretending to sweat.

Then, once again, he turned to the next table and the same thing happened, with the order relayed back to the kitchen. The only word she recognized was 'feta', which made her happy as it was her favourite and given Lambros knew she loved it, it appeared he was out to please her.

The wine was going down a treat and she was feeling so happy. This was a part of Greek life she never knew still existed and it was wonderful to spend an evening somewhere that hadn't changed for decades. It harkened back to simpler times and was such a lovely feeling.

'All these people here and I can't see one person looking at their phone,' she observed. 'They're all talking away to the person they're with and to the customers on either side of them. It's so refreshing to see. Thank you for bringing me here, it's something I will remember for a long time to come.'

He smiled, looking like the cat that got the cream, and so he should. He had made their couple of days out very special. With that the starters arrived and of course it was her favourite – feta cheese in filo pastry covered with honey and sesame seeds.

'If you don't like this I can order something else for you,' said Lambros, sounding a bit nervous.

'The only thing you'll be ordering is a second one of these – it's my favourite! It's one of the things I'll miss most when I go back to England.'

'If that's the case, then you will have to keep coming back to Vekianos.'

'You could be right there. I think I've found a gem of a place ... and the people aren't bad either,' she added cheekily.

Another huge smile spread across Lambros's face as he topped up the wine and ordered another bottle. They settled into a comfortable silence as they ate, the relaxed nature of the moment confirming for Angela that she would definitely be back very soon.

The main course arrived and was just as delectable as the starter. The meat was so succulent, and the rich sauce was full of flavour. This could easily become her favourite meal.

'That was very special indeed,' said Lambros as he finished. 'Just like my mama used to make. I'm not sure if you have room for dessert, but if so I'd suggest we go elsewhere. There isn't a lot of choice when it comes to desserts here, but we could walk down and have an ice cream from one of the little ice cream parlours by the seafront.'

'I'd love an ice cream, but I am absolutely full to

the brim. I could probably manage a coffee though.'

'We have several places to choose from down by the sea. I will just get the bill.'

'You can get the bill, but I am paying, and if you won't let me there will be no stopping for a coffee. I will not hesitate to get a taxi right back to the villa,' said Angela, determined to pay after all of Lambros's generosity the day before.

'I'm not happy about this but I'm also not ready to go home yet, so I guess I have no choice but to give in. You can pay on this one occasion,' he said, begrudgingly.

Half an hour later they had strolled down to the main street, walking along until they came to a few restaurants that were still serving drinks.

'It's a shame none of them have a sea view,' Angela observed.

'I might have a solution to that.'

They approached one of the restaurants and Lambros was greeted by someone he knew – she got the impression he was the owner – and they hugged each other and had a conversation that Angela couldn't decipher. With that the chap turned and spoke to one of the waiters while Lambros turned back to Angela.

'Coffee is ordered. If you would like to follow me this way?' Lambros said, pointing.

They headed back down onto the boardwalk and went to the very end. Next thing Angela noticed was a waiter was following them with two chairs. She smiled, feeling very spoilt. She could not get over what a romantic gesture it was. If being at the restaurant they had just eaten in felt like being in a film, this was the equivalent of the end of a really special movie. As they sat down another waiter arrived with a tray of coffee. Looking out to sea as she sipped the delicious blend, she didn't know what to say apart from thank you.

'It's funny, isn't it?' she said at last. 'We came out tonight because we ran out of time to fit everything in yesterday, and the same has happened tonight as we couldn't manage a desert, not even an ice cream. Perhaps we need to have another evening out just for dessert?'

'Are you saying we should have another date before you go back to England?' Lambros asked, hopefully.

'Only if you can fit me into your busy schedule,' she said with a wink.

With that Lambros's smile lit up the beach. They were both definitely on the same page.

Chapter 18
Holiday day 7

Angela thought she was the first one up but walking past Simon's bedroom door she could see it was open and the curtains were pulled back. Walking into the kitchen/lounge area she noticed the doors to the patio were closed and touching the kettle, it was cold. She was confused. She knew she was the last one in last night as both Carla and Simon's bedroom doors had been closed, so the only conclusion she could come to was that he must have gone out very early. Making herself a coffee and heading out onto the patio she thought about last night with Lambros. It really had been the perfect night, and she knew it was one she would look back on as one of her favourite parts of the holiday.

As she sat looking out at the boats in the far distance, she thought back to the day she'd left London to travel back to Norfolk. She had felt so numb and empty on that train. Her brother had died, and it felt as though all she had to look forward to in life was getting old and lonely in Saltmarsh Quay. Coming here to Vekianos had made her realise that wasn't the only option for her. Yes, the death of her brother was devastating in so many ways, but her life wasn't over and she didn't need to just count the hours in her little cottage. There was so much more just waiting to be discovered, and all she had to do was what she'd done coming on this holiday – take a leap of faith.

Just as the revelation hit her the gate opened, and Simon strolled through it with a bag from the bakery. Oh how she wished that the bakery was back in Saltmarsh Quay so she could enjoy it all the time.

'You're up and out early!' she called down to him and he smiled, indicating that he'd be right up.

Digging into the pastries a moment later, Angela asked Simon how his day with Polina had gone.

'It's a bit of a long story. How was your evening out with Lambros?'

'Another long story. Looks like we have quite a bit to catch up on today.'

As Simon put the kettle on Carla appeared all bubbly and excited.

He wasn't really in the mood for it today but then he remembered she was off out with Nectarios today, and he knew he could cope with her enthusiasm for the next hour or so. But he did take his time making the coffees...

'Here we go, ladies.'

'Thanks! I was just telling Angela that I fancy Nectarios, and he is rather keen on me, but in seven days I will be getting on a plane never to return so I'm just going to enjoy it for what it is.'

'I do think that's the right attitude, but wouldn't you like to come back to Vekianos at some point?' asked Angela.

'Yes, but I'm not sure when the opportunity will arise. Once I've started on my career path back in England it will be full-on and you know what these holiday situations are like, once back in the real world everything that happened in the two weeks away is forgotten. I should add that I haven't a clue what that career path will be yet, but I'm putting that right out of my mind until I'm back in Norfolk.'

Simon sat holding his coffee and thinking he wished that could be the case for him as well, but somehow he already knew that getting Polina out of his head would be very difficult. Looking over at

Angela he saw she looked equally deep in thought. Hopefully her thoughts were happier than his own.

'Thank you for the coffee and pastries. I need to go and get myself ready for a day on the beach now though.'

As Carla scooted off to her room Simon said he would go down to the pool room and get the mattresses and lounge chair cushions out.

'I was thinking I might also get all the pool toys out – the beach balls and the pool volleyball net.'

'Oh yes please. A real activity day could be just what we both need, don't you think?'

The two of them couldn't stop laughing at Angela's jokey suggestion and as Simon walked down to the pool, he hoped the rest of the day would also be full of laughter. It would be just the thing to take his mind off of Polina.

'Nectarios should be here any minute. Do you think I look ok?' asked Carla a few minutes later.

'You look lovely as always, and just on cue as I can see your date has just come through the gate. Have a wonderful time,' said Angela.

'Thank you. I should be back by four at the latest as Nectarios has to start work at five o'clock.'

Angela could see Nectarios had a big smile on his face as Carla turned and walked towards him. They really looked like the perfect couple.

The pool felt lovely and Simon was pleased he was starting the day off with a swim. It was something he'd really miss once back at home, but then he suspected that everything about this island would take a long time to get out of his head. This villa, for a start. He would likely never have the opportunity to stay somewhere like this again as it was way out of his price range. But like it or not, this time next week the cases would be packed and the three of them would be getting the boat back over to

Corfu, ready to fly home.

'I think I'll leave my swim for an hour or two and wait until it gets really hot so I can get in to cool down.'

'You can dive into your book instead of the water,' he joked.

'I don't think I'm in the mood to read yet. I'd rather hear all about your day out with Polina.'

Simon was more than ready to tell her but where to start because it was a day of two halves really: the nice part of laughing and chatting with Polina, and the second half, which was the serious side, where she'd revealed the world that she was trapped in.

For the next three quarters of an hour, he recounted his day with Polina, starting at the beginning as that felt easiest.

'Oh Simon, that poor girl! What a very sad life she is living – not that she *is* living, more like merely existing. After she said she was scared of what might happen if her mum found out, what happened then?'

'That was the end of the conversation and her mum wasn't mentioned for the rest of the day, though as I'm sure you can imagine, the tone of the day really changed.'

'It was good you said what you did though, and Polina did ask what your thoughts on everything were.'

'I suppose. We went for lunch after that and things lightened up a bit as we walked to the other part of the beach, which was completely different – no rocks, just sand – and very busy. We found a nice little spot though and settled down and talked about how we started off on our painting journeys, recounting all the mistakes we had made over the years to finally reach what we liked – our signature work that we both do now – which was very interesting. It was good to hear that someone else had faced the same pitfalls and it wasn't just me who struggled.'

'So the day finished well? That's good.'

'I wouldn't go that far, as I stayed on the beach away from the car park so her mum couldn't see she was with someone, and then waited ten minutes before walking to the bus stop, so that did spoil the day in some ways. But just being with Polina was nice.'

'Try to focus on only the good parts if you can. Do you think you'll have another day out?'

Angela could see she had asked the wrong question as Simon turned away and focused on the pool. Oh dear, she knew the answer that was undoubtedly coming.

'No, that was it. The day out was Polina's idea, and it was just to tell me the situation with her mum.'

'But that isn't right! Surely you can see one another again.'

'I get the impression she doesn't think it's necessary as we both left knowing where we stood. It's all very sad but I'm ready to leave it behind me. Can I get you a drink? I'm thirsty all of a sudden.'

'Yes, thanks, but I can go and get something.'

'No you're fine, I need to go to the bathroom anyway.'

Angela felt so sorry for Simon. The situation really was sad and silly. It was clear that Polina must care or think something of Simon as she wanted him to understand her hesitation in spending time with him had nothing to do with her not liking him or him doing anything wrong. Oh how she would love to meet this Calliope woman and see for herself which of the two stories was the right one. Was she a fragile woman scared to lose her daughter, or was she a controlling monster who insisted on everything being her way? There had to be a lot more to this situation than the two black and white versions Angela had heard.

Simon returned with two cups of tea and he immediately jumped into questioning her about her evening with Lambros. It was clear he didn't want to continue their discussion about Polina, which was fine with Angela. It would do her no good to push Simon.

'Where did Lambros wine and dine you? Some gorgeous flash restaurant, I expect, where all the glamorous people on the island go.'

Angela burst out laughing and she couldn't stop. The rustic restaurant they had eaten in must be the least glamorous place on Vekianos! Not that she was complaining as it was fabulous and just right for her. She wouldn't have wanted to go anywhere else.

'What's so funny?' asked Simon.

'You! You're so far off the mark.'

Angela told him all about the beautiful little town of Keriaphos and the steep hill going down to the lovely little beach. She worried she wasn't doing the restaurant justice with her description as it had to be seen to be believed. She was a little hesitant to tell him about the end of the evening with the coffee on the beach, but she knew she had to. Simon had been honest with her and he deserved that same honesty in return.

'Of course it wasn't the evening I had expected, but then I suppose I didn't know where we were going so any place would have been a nice surprise.'

'How romantic of Lambros. I would never have thought he had it in him to think of that.'

'It was a really lovely end to a special evening. Whoever thought I would be having so much fun here on Vekianos?'

'When we first talked and planned this holiday it

was all about the villa, the pool, and enjoying the chance to rest and recharge our batteries – a sort of breathing space for a couple of weeks – and look at the three of us now. I never would have thought we would get to talk to people here apart from restaurant staff, and after just a week we know what's going on in so many of the island's residents' lives, and they know about ours. Do you find that all very strange?'

'Completely bonkers, but saying that, I do feel as though I belong here, as though I was meant to be here on the island. Imagine we had chosen somewhere else to go? The holiday would have been so different.'

'I hope you don't mind me saying this, but in a way, for me, that would have been nice as it would mean I'd never met Polina and I wouldn't have this strange situation where she's screwing up my head.'

'I understand. The holiday has impacted each of us in ways we haven't expected. For me, being here is a lot more for me than a holiday. I really can't explain what I'm trying to say, it's hard to put into words...'

'Go on, give it a go,' Simon encouraged her.

'You see, I thought that once I got back to Saltmarsh Quay that would be it, my adventures would be over. I'm in my seventies so life would inevitably start to slow down, my existence settling into something very mundane and boring. But coming here and having time to think and do things that are out of the ordinary for me has made me realise my life doesn't need to be like that. I'm not ready to sit in my armchair every day of the week with my book or the television, and though the time will come – I'm not daft enough to think it won't – I want to be able to look back and say I've had some fun in my seventies, and not just napped my time away.'

'That's a really good attitude to have. I'm looking forward to hearing all your stories of your adventures.'

'I'm not sure they will all be "adventures", probably just little things like going off to the theatre in Norwich and staying overnight, or having a coach trip to Devon and Cornwall, seeing places I've never seen before and making the most of every moment. This holiday has taught me that my life is for living, and I'll always be grateful to you and Carla for coming along and helping me realise that.'

'I don't think Carla would mind me speaking for her and saying that it's our absolute pleasure. I'm curious though, and please don't think you need to answer as it is likely none of my business, but does Lambros feature in your adventure plans?'

'To be honest, I'm not sure. I really like him and enjoy his company very much, and we both seem to be in similar situations – both lonely and in need of regular interaction with people rather than being by ourselves. You know what? Now you've asked the question I think yes, I do want him to be in my life.' Her voice got more confident with every word. 'Yes, I think coming here to Vekianos a few times a year and spending time with him would make me very happy indeed. Hopefully he feels the same.'

Chapter 19
Holiday day 7

As Carla walked down to the gate to meet Nectarios, she was feeling good, happy and very comfortable with the clothes she had chosen. As she got closer to him, she could see the smile on his face. He was obviously pleased to see her as well. Switching her phone off and putting it in her beach bag she was looking forward to a day out with no disturbances.

'Good morning! You look nice.'

'So do you. I'm a little nervous about getting on the bike. I can't remember when I was last on the back of one; it was probably many years ago I think.'

'You'll be fine. It's not like the roads are busy or we're going that far, just a few kilometres around the coast road. Now, if you give me your bag, I'll swap it for a crash helmet.'

They walked over to the bike and Nectarios opened the box at the back of the bike and took out the helmet and then put her bag into the space, snapping the lid closed.

'Hopefully that shouldn't be too big for you. Just pull the strap underneath your chin like...' He paused to help align the helmet and secure it snugly. 'That's it, perfect. I'll get on first and start the engine and then you swing one of your legs over and just hold me tight around the waist. We'll be at the beach in no time.'

Carla did as instructed, knowing that holding him around the waist was not an issue for her. If she was honest, it was the bit she was looking forward to the most! They headed up onto the main coastal road, Nectarios going slower than perhaps he normally would have, and after about twenty minutes he slowed right down and turned down a little track.

'Can you hear me under the helmet?' he asked over his shoulder. She gave him a quick thumbs up. 'Good. This lane is a little bumpy so hold on tighter.'

She happily obliged and it wasn't long before she spotted some cars and bikes parked at the side of the lane. Nectarios stopped behind another bike and she got off and waited for him to put the kick stand down and lock the bike. She struggled with undoing the helmet strap, so Nectarios did it for her, and she relished the opportunity for them to look into each other's eyes. She felt herself blushing, but also started wondering how many times he had played this exact scene out with other women. Then she felt bad. If she was going to think like that all day then she shouldn't have agreed to come with him. She shook off her concerns and vowed to live in the moment for the rest of their time together.

'We can head off down to the beach from here. It's only about a two-minute walk.'

Carla went to take her bag off him, but he insisted on carrying it. As they stepped onto the beach the first thing that hit her was the fantastic view of the beautiful clear blue sea. It was an amazing sight and she almost couldn't take it all in.

'This is so gorgeous. You are so lucky to have this on your doorstep!'

'I am, and I definitely don't take it for granted. Which bit of the beach would you like to head towards, left or right?'

'I don't mind. Why don't you choose where you'd normally go when you come here. I'm happy anywhere.'

'If we walk over there,' he said, pointing, 'we can

avoid ending up in the middle of all the families with the children playing.'

She agreed that was fine and followed him as he led them down to the edge of the water. They took their shoes off and walked along the waterline for a bit before he pointed to a spot away from other people, not that there were many on the beach. He put the bags down and then opened his up and took out his towel.

Carla found she was suddenly a little nervous about revealing her bikini underneath her dress. She made a point of looking away from him before she did it, and then took a deep breath before turning back to look at him. When she did her heart made a little jump. Nectarios had taken his shorts off to reveal a pair of bright red swimming trunks, but the big shock was the perfect six pack that had been revealed by him taking his shirt off. She tried not to stare but it was almost impossible. It was clear that Nectarios and the gym were no strangers.

'Shall we have a swim first, Carla, to cool down?'

'Great idea.'

She could certainly use the cool down but she wasn't so sure her temperature wouldn't skyrocket again once Nectarios came out of the sea all wet. No, she would be far from cool – if anything, she would be positively hot!

Once in the water she felt a lot more in control and relaxed.

'A little different from your villa's pool, isn't it?' he asked.

'It certainly is. Not that the pool isn't lovely, of course, but this is very special. Thank you so much for bringing me here. Are there many beaches like this on the island?'

'Yes, and there are a few that you can only get to by boat.'

'That sounds so romantic.'

'I know what you mean by that, but I assure you I've never done that with a girl, just a few times with groups of friends when we were teenagers.'

'I didn't mean to suggest—' she rushed out.

'I know. I just didn't want you to think... Sorry, I'm being silly and likely digging a hole for myself. Are you ready to get out?'

'Yes, but I'm sure it won't be long before I get back in. It's so lovely.'

Carla followed him out of the water, quickly checking her bikini was looking ok and hadn't slipped, revealing more than she meant it to.

Once back on the beach she was determined not to look at him while he dried himself off. But she caught him looking at her while she was rummaging in her bag for her hairbrush and smiled to herself. She liked the appreciative way his gaze floated over her. Two minutes later their towels were on the ground, and they were laid out, ready to enjoy the sunshine. She closed her eyes and all she could hear was the sound of the gentle waves. She felt so content.

'This really is what holidays are all about, isn't it?' she said, her eyes still closed.

'I thought you would like it here and I'm glad I was right,' answered Nectarios. 'I should tell my grandfather to bring Angela here. My mum and I can't get over the change in him since he met Angela. All the new clothes and actually taking a bit of pride in his appearance. I hope he hasn't been a pain, inviting her out multiple times.'

'Not at all. She's loved spending time with him and they seem to have hit it off, which is so lovely. With Lambros's help Angela has really fallen in love with this island and even better I think she'll now have the confidence to travel back here by herself.

That is something I wouldn't have been saying even just a couple of weeks ago.'

'I think my grandfather would like that. I just hope she feels the same way about him as he does about her. It never crossed my mind that after my grandmother died that he might fall in love with someone else, but I think he really has fallen head over heels.'

'I know Angela enjoys being with him, but as for falling in love... I'm not entirely sure that's how she sees it.'

'Well, as long as they're honest with one another I think they'll be ok. And what about you? Would you consider coming back?'

'Oh yes, definitely, but I can't see it happening for a few years as I need to get stuck into my career and throw everything at it. Holidays will be the last thing on my mind.'

He didn't answer her, and she got the impression she had disappointed him. They laid there in silence for quite a while after that and Carla wasn't sure if he hadn't fallen asleep, but she was getting thirsty and needed to get her water bottle out of her bag. The bag was near his head and the last thing she wanted to do was disturb him so she waited another fifteen minutes, but by then she really needed that drink.

When she opened her eyes and turned her gaze towards him she found she was wrong. He wasn't asleep but instead leaning back on his elbows looking at her. Had he been like that for all that time? As their eyes met he smiled and there was something different about that smile to the one he wore when he was working in the restaurant. No, this was not a happy 'I'm here to entertain you and make sure you're enjoying your evening' smile, this was a relaxed and content smile that showed the real Nectarios.

'I just need my water out of the bag,' she said, pointing.

'Don't get up, I can pass it to you. I was thinking about going back in the water to cool down as I'm quite hot. Join me?'

'Yes, that would be nice.'

After a big drink of her water, she got to their feet and walked side by side with Nectarios down to the sea.

'Shall we run in?' he suggested.

Carla didn't answer, just grinned and then sprinted into the sea. She could tell he was taken unaware but it was silly of her to think she would be in first as he quickly overtook her, and she was covered in his splashes before she was even in the water.

Both swam out a little way and ended up next to each other.

'I suppose I was a bit daft to think I could beat you,' she said, sheepishly. 'For a start, you're a lot fitter than me, and for another, you've spent countless hours of your life diving in the sea.'

'It did cross my mind to let you win but then you would have realised I had only been pretending, and that's not how I want you to see me. I want you to see the real Nectarios, not the charming, flirtatious one that performs seven nights a week in the restaurant.'

She believed him and his confession made her want to swim right up to him and wrap her arms around him, to feel him holding her tight, and to kiss him and not let go.

Instead, she turned and swam the opposite way.

She needed time to calm down and get rid of all those passionate thoughts in her head. Was she really considering making love with Nectarios?

'Are you ready to get out? Do you fancy a little

walk along the edge of the sea to the end of the beach? It will help us to dry off but more importantly, it will help with the tan,' he suggested.

'Anything that helps with my tan is good for me.'

As they made their way out of the water Carla stepped on a stone and started to lose her balance. She made an involuntary squeaking noise and before she knew it Nectarios had turned and grabbed her to stop her falling. This was the first time they had touched so intimately and her whole body tingled with excitement. She managed to get her balance and smiled at him as they carried on walking out of the sea. He was still holding her hand and she momentarily wondered if she should try and let go, but would he think she was pulling away from him?

'Which way are we walking, left or right?'

'To the right. You see that big rock in the distance? There's a little path that goes behind it and out the other side to a lovely viewpoint looking back towards the harbour.'

They were still holding hands as they walked, and Carla quickly shook off any hesitations she had been feeling. This was a magical day and she was so happy. Why shouldn't she embrace this growing connection she felt to Nectarios? There was no use stopping now she was falling for him, and though this day out on the beach with him was meant purely for them to have some fun, that touch and the looks they were sharing had turned into something completely different. Something more.

'Are you ok?' Nectarios asked as they picked their way across the rocks to the pathway to the viewpoint.

'I'm fine with the walking, and like you said, we're getting an all over tan. Well ... apart from my hand,' she joked, looking down at their joined hands.

'I can let go if you like, but something tells me

you don't want me to. Or is that me being a little presumptuous?'

'I am more than willing to not get that hand tanned.'

They shared a secret smile, the look saying so much more than words, and kept walking, eventually reaching the rock. From back where their towels were Carla had thought the rock was blocking any way through, but that was just a trick of the eye and now, up close, she could see the path behind it. They walked the few metres through to the other side, a beautiful view of the harbour in the distance opening up before them.

As she stood looking at the sights Carla realised they had the lookout entirely to themselves. They were the only two people here.

'Perhaps we should have had something on our feet,' said Nectarios, sounding a bit nervous. 'Are you sure this is ok?'

'Totally fine. Look, it's not so rocky over there. We just need to climb over a little bit.'

'You didn't tell me you were an adventure girl.'

'There is a lot about me you don't know. And one of those things is that I like to be kissed, but not just by anyone. They have to be very special, and of course it helps if they are gorgeous and Greek...' She arched an eyebrow suggestively.

'Well, you're on the right holiday then as this island is full of gorgeous Greek men. You'll have to keep your eyes peeled when you're out and about.'

'Shut up and just kiss me,' she said, pulling him close.

Chapter 20
Holiday day 7

The journey back to the villa was quick and as Nectarios stopped and turned the engine off Carla wished she didn't have to let go of his waist. She reluctantly climbed off the back of the bike and waited for him to put the kick stand down before getting off himself.

'Thank you for a lovely day. I've really enjoyed seeing a little more of this beautiful island and the beach was very tranquil and special.'

'I'm glad you've had a nice time because I have as well, especially the end of the afternoon. That was ... unforgettable. Not that the rest wasn't lovely as well,' he rushed to add.

'I know what you mean. Look, you need to go or you'll be late for work and the last thing we both need is to be in Sakis's bad books.'

'Sakis won't mind if I'm a little late.'

'In that case, perhaps you should kiss me again.'

She didn't need to ask twice. Nectarios smiled at her before placing his hands either side of her face and leaning in close. The minute their lips touched she was transported back to the lookout, instantly reliving the magical day they had just had together.

They pulled apart a few moments later and she waved goodbye as he got back on his bike.

As Carla closed the villa gate behind her she heard Nectarios drive off. She paused to take a breath and process everything that had just happened before walking over to the pool to see Angela and Simon. Because what had happened was pool. Before she got down to them, she told herself she wouldn't be going into all the details of her day on the beach. No, before either of her friends found out about the kissing, she wanted to get it all straight in her own head.

'Here we go! Have you both had a nice day? Have I missed anything?' she asked, trying to divert her friends' focus.

'Yes, it's been lovely. Very quiet, hasn't it, Simon?' said Angela.

'Is that because I've not been here?' Carla joked.

'Of course not. What I meant was that I've been stuck in my book and Simon's been reading on his phone, but now you are back we can let the party begin.'

'I don't think I'm ready to party. No, a quiet, relaxed evening in for me, please. I'm quite tired after all the swimming and a nice walk along the beach. It's been a great day.'

'It's a shame Nectarios had to go to work. You could have continued on and made an evening of it.'

'That would have been nice, but because it's such a short tourism season he has to work seven nights a week, just like everyone else here who works in the restaurants. Still, it was nice to have the day together on the beach. Speaking of food: do either of you have a date tonight? If not, do you want to go out or stay here?' asked Carla.

'You make it sound as though I'm out dating all the time. I'm not like Angela, she's the one who's been out the most!' Simon laughed.

'You know the problem? You youngsters just can't keep up the pace! But no, I'm not out with Lambros tonight and I was thinking we should start to use up some of the frozen things we bought on our first day. There are pizzas and potato wedges in the freezer, which might be quite nice.'

that she had spent the last three hours of her day o kissing and cuddling Nectarios, and she was just ; happy. She really couldn't remember ever feeling th way she did right now. The way he held her an made her feel so special, the gentleness, and as fo the kisses ... there had been so many and they were all so beautiful.

'Carla, we're over here,' called Simon.

'Sorry, I was miles away,' she said, walking over to join them and hoping her steamy memories weren't written all over her face.

'I was just saying your timing is perfect. It's wine o'clock time.'

'Great! I'll just go take my bag in and change. Shall I bring the wine back down with me?'

'Yes please.'

As she closed her bedroom door behind her, she knew she had a problem, a big one.

She had fallen hook line and sinker for every one of Nectarios's charms and there was nothing she could – or even wanted to – do about it. But she only had one more week here on Vekianos and then she would be back in Norfolk looking for a job. Looking in the mirror she could see a different Carla looking back at her. The Carla that morning had been in control, off to have a nice day out and that was all. But now the face looking back at her was a confused mess, someone who wasn't really sure who she was or what to do about how she was feeling.

She changed from her bikini into shorts and a baggy t-shirt, quickly washed her face, and tied her hair back. She was as ready as she was ever going to be for the questions from Angela and Simon. Picking up her sunglasses and placing them on her head, she went back out to the kitchen. Taking a bottle of whit wine out of the fridge she uncorked it, then picke up three wine glasses and headed down towards th

'Sounds ideal. Carla?' asked Simon.

'A night in with wine, food, and that gorgeous view? Sounds perfect and I'm more than happy to cook it all. Just tell me when you're both ready.'

'I think I'm ok for a while. Angela and I didn't have our lunch until three o'clock,' offered Simon.

'That's fine. It means we can enjoy the last of the sunshine and work our way through a couple bottles of wine.'

'And you can tell us all about your day out with Nectarios!' Angela said to Carla.

'There isn't a lot to tell.' She shrugged. 'We laid in the sun, had a few swims, took a nice walk along the beach ... and that's about it really.'

Neither of them answered and she hoped it was because they believed her, not because she wasn't convincing enough. Nectarios made her feel so special, and she wanted to believe all his talk about her being different than all the other girls, but to what end? She was on holiday and that was it. There could be nothing more because sooner or later she *would* go home.

Two hours later the three of them all went off to their rooms to get cleaned up for dinner. Carla was first back and got the pizza and wedges out of the freezer. She started the oven, put some music on, and poured another glass of wine. She was feeling a little more relaxed now, so the wine had obviously kicked in.

Angela joined her next and Carla topped her wine up before putting the wedges on a tray and then into the oven. They took a lot longer than the pizzas so needed to go in first.

'Are you ok, Angela?' asked Carla, seeing a conflicted look on her friend's face.

'Yes, fine. I've just had a text from Lambros asking me out again tomorrow.'

'Oh that's nice! During the day or the evening?'

'Both. He's actually asked if I would like to go over on the boat to Corfu and stay overnight, coming back the following day.'

'Um ... wow. And what do you think, do you want to go?'

'I don't think so. A meal out or a day on the beach is one thing, but going away for the night is a completely different thing. To start with, I'm seventy; the last thing I need or want is a night of romance and passion.'

'But you don't know that's what he has in mind... Actually it could be,' said Carla with a shrug. Who was she to know what was going through Lambros's mind?

'What do you mean?'

'When I was with Nectarios today, he mentioned that he and his mum have never seen Lambros like this before. Apparently, he's a completely different man since he met you. They reckon he is very taken with you so perhaps love and passion *is* what he has in mind.'

'Well it's certainly not what's on my mind! Ok, I enjoy his company, and I would be lying if I said he hasn't opened my mind up to enjoying my life a lot more than I have been in the last few years, but spending time with someone you really like is one thing ... sleeping with them is another. No, I'm going to text back and say I'm busy or something.'

'Try not to worry too much. Perhaps it would be best if you just forget about it for now? The food won't be too long so you could head outside and sit on the patio with your glass of wine.'

Angela nodded and near-marched out the door. Carla could see she didn't have her phone with her, which was a good thing, as it meant there would be no quick reply back to Lambros. Better for Angela to think through what she wanted to say.

Talking about phones, she realised hers was still turned off in her bag and she would need to put it on in case her mum called. Before she could do so, Simon appeared. Carla decided it was best if she left it to Angela to tell him about the text she'd received from Lambros, if she wanted to.

'Can I help with anything?' asked Simon.

'No, you're good, thanks. Why not top up your wine and join Angela outside? The food won't be long.'

'It's nice being waited on, don't you think, Angela?' he asked as he settled in one of the chairs at the outdoor table. 'I could get used to it!'

'I suspect it all evens out as you've been going to the bakery every day, and more importantly, lugging all the bottles of water back here.'

'Too true.'

'I was going to ask, will you go to the craft fair tomorrow, or do you feel you don't want to?'

'It's not tomorrow but the next day – Wednesday – and to be honest I'm not sure if I want to. Yes, it would be nice to see, but I think it'll be awkward if Polina's mum sees me chatting to her. No, I'm not going. I've made my mind up. I need to put her out of my head. I have come here for a holiday, not to get involved in a complicated relationship.'

Angela smiled.

'If it makes you feel any better, you're not the only one to get all confused and mixed up with relationship things. I've had a text from Lambros inviting me for an overnight stay in Corfu.'

'Oh! That's slightly different than just going down into the harbour for a meal or spending a day out on the beach,' he hedged.

'Yes, exactly.'

'Dinner is served! Freshly made pizzas – well, as

fresh as a pizza can be when it's out of a box – and I think I've gone over the top with the spices on the potato wedges, so consider yourselves warned. Dive in, I won't be a minute, I just need to go and get my phone as it's still in my beach bag.'

Angela started to cut up the pizzas and when Carla came back they all got stuck in.

'I think it's a lot warmer tonight. There isn't a breeze. It's actually something that surprised me on the beach today – it was so calm and still.'

'That must have been nice for you and Nectarios. Are you sure everything went ok? I asked because you've not said a lot about it,' asked Angela.

'I did, but in one way I wish I hadn't gone. I mean, I am glad I went, but I think Nectarios is, shall we say, a bit like his grandfather in that he's taking our time together very seriously.'

'Oh dear. That's not what you want, is it?'

'Actually, I think it is what I want, but I know I need to snap out of those kinds of thoughts. We're on holiday and the last thing I need is to go home all screwed up and pining for a gorgeous Greek hundreds of miles away.'

'I think your phone's just beeped, Angela,' Simon interrupted.

'No, it's not mine, it must be yours, Carla.'

She looked at it to find it was a text from Nectarios. Should she open it now or wait until they had finished eating? No, now. Best to get it over with.

When she was silent for a long moment, Simon gently asked if everything was ok.

'Yes, thank you. Apparently today on the beach was one of the happiest days of Nectarios's life. Not exactly something I needed to hear.'

'The three of us have got ourselves into quite the muddles, haven't we. Whoever would have thought when we sat down in my cottage planning this holiday we would all end up in the middle of confusing relationships,' observed Angela.

'You're so right, and we're only at the halfway mark, with seven more days to go. What on earth will happen next?' Simon pondered.

'I don't know, but one thing is for sure – I don't need all these complications at my age!'

'You don't need it, and I certainly don't either. How about you, Carla?' he asked.

'No, thank you, my plan is to top up my tan, enjoy the pool, and certainly no more kissing.'

'Kissing?' Simon and Angela said in unison.

'Sorry, didn't I mention what a lovely kisser Nectarios is?'

'You certainly didn't.' Angela grinned.

'Oh, sorry. Yes, he's got such beautiful lips on a gorgeous face, and that face comes with a perfectly formed body...'

'Somehow I think next week won't be as straightforward and as easy as you're hoping for,' said Simon.

'You could be right. So how am I going to make it less complicated without escaping this island?'

'You've nailed it in one, Carla. We should escape! Why don't we take a boat trip tomorrow to another island, somewhere where no one knows us, so we can switch off from everything. No Lambros, no Nectarios, and no Polina.'

'That sounds perfect, Simon, it's a date. This one without strings attached! What do you say, Angela?' asked Carla.

'I say let's take a trip to somewhere new before any of us gets another text!'

Chapter 21
Holiday day 8

The three of them were all up early and they had their breakfast on the terrace before going in and getting ready for their day out. After lots of looking on the internet last night they had settled for a boat trip over to the mainland and the little town of Parga. They'd pre-booked their tickets online and needed to be down in the harbour for nine-fifteen. The crossing would only take about an hour, so they'd have most of the day to explore.

'I'm really looking forward to this,' said Angela as they prepared to depart. 'The boat is completely different to the one that brought us over from Corfu.'

'Apparently the shopping is to die for, with lots of clothes and handbag shops.' Carla nearly squealed with excitement.

'Are we ready?' asked Simon.

'Yes, let the adventure begin!' Angela cheered.

'When has shopping for handbags ever been called an adventure?'

'I'm telling you, Simon, you've never really lived if you've not been handbag hunting. Don't you agree, Carla?'

'Completely! But if you don't want to join us on our massive expedition to find the perfect bag, you can just sit and relax in the gorgeous sunshine.'

It didn't take long to walk down to the harbour and find the boat. There were several people on board already and the three friends found seats on the side nearer to the back. The seats all faced out to sea, perfectly displaying the view. It was another beautiful day with not a cloud in the sky.

'We managed to get down here without being spotted,' Carla observed as they waited for the boat to depart. 'I did get a text from Nectarios this morning, just telling us all to have a nice day.'

'No text for me, but then I wasn't expecting one from Lambros after I replied and said I didn't think going away together was a good idea for either of us. But enough of that. Today we are leaving it all on Vekianos. Let the fun begin!'

The boat was quite full by the time they set off. There were three crew members – an older man who was obviously the captain, and then a younger girl and boy who did all the things with the ropes and bits and pieces. Carla didn't really understand what they were doing but they certainly seemed to be efficient and good at it. Once they had left the harbour the captain came over the loudspeaker and welcomed everyone on board before explaining how long the journey would take, and saying he would point things out – sights and places of interest – along the way.

'...So just sit back and enjoy the journey, and if you have any questions, please ask away.'

The three of them sat in silence just taking everything in. The graceful arcs of the sea's waves around the boat as it cut through the water and the little breeze that sprinkled them with a hint of sea salt. Even though there were lots of people on the boat, it was so quiet and very tranquil, everyone appreciating the journey instead of talking through it.

Before long the boat was turning and they passed a very small island, which the captain explained you could only get to with a small boat as there were a lot of rocks in the surrounding waters. In the far distance the island of Paxos was just visible and the captain informed them that they were about halfway to their destination.

'Have you both got enough suntan lotion on? I think with the breeze it's very deceiving how hot the sun is,' Angela asked as she rummaged in her bag.

Simon replied that he did and was covered in it.

'How about you, Carla, do you need some?' She offered the tube, which she'd found at the bottom of the bag.

'Sorry, what did you say? I was miles away.'

'Suntan lotion ... have you got some on?'

'Yes, I'm smothered in it today. I thought with the breeze it would be a little dangerous not to put it on.'

'Good. I'm glad to hear we're all prepared. Would either of you like a drink? I've brought plenty of water.'

'Angela, take a breath. You don't have to be mum to Simon and I today. You're meant to be relaxing just as much as we are,' admonished Carla.

'I'm sorry, I don't mean to nag. I don't want to come across as old and bossy.'

'You could never come across like that. Actually, I was thinking only yesterday about how your age doesn't come into it.'

'What do you mean?'

'It really never crosses my mind that you're a lot older than Simon and I. We all just get on so well.' Carla shrugged.

'We do, don't we. Before we came here on holiday I was very aware I'm more than twice your ages, but once arriving at the villa it's not even entered my head. We just gel so well.'

With that the captain came back on the loudspeaker and said you could just about see Parga in the distance. 'To the left is the beautiful Valtos beach, and to the right is the harbour, where we'll be dropping you off. The harbour at night, with all the twinkling lights, is an experience not to be missed. We won't be much longer and we hope you enjoy your day in Parga. Remember to set your alarms for the return sailing back to Vekianos. We will be leaving at five-thirty and, unfortunately, if you miss the boat you'll have to find a bed in the town for the night.'

As the boat got closer Simon spotted the ruined castle on the top of the hill that separated the town from Valtos beach. He hadn't realised how much bigger Parga was compared to the little island of Vekianos, and he was looking forward to seeing the sights.

As the captain manoeuvred the boat in beside another one, everyone got their things together, ready to get off as soon as they were given the ok to rise from their seats.

'It looks exciting and so much busier than Vekianos. What would you two like to do first?' asked Simon.

'Let's have a coffee before we walk around,' suggested Angela.

'Fine by me. Carla? Do you have time before the hunt for the perfect handbag begins?' joked Simon.

'Yes please. I'll need as much caffeine as I can get! Here we go, it's time to dismount. Is that what you say when getting off a boat?' she asked as they all made their way along the aisle of the boat.

'I always thought dismount was when you get off a horse. I think the word you're looking for is "disembark",' offered Angela.

Five minutes later they were on dry land, though all three said it felt a little odd after the swaying of the boat, and they stumbled a bit, setting off a laughing fit that saw them all the way down the stone jetty. A big anchor had been cemented into the ground at the jetty's end, and to the right of them was a long row of restaurants that looked just like what they needed.

'Lead the way, Carla. If you can, try to pick one that has an empty table on the front row, so no one is blocking the view.'

'This looks nice,' said Carla, leading them towards one of the restaurants. 'It looks like they have waitresses, not waiters, so there will be no temptation for us here today, Angela,' she joked.

That sat down and ordered three coffees and three vanilla pastries, then settled in to watch people heading to and fro, many looking as though they were off for a day on the beach.

'I read there's a little sea taxi that goes from here to Valtos beach several times an hour, so that people don't have to traipse up that steep hill and down the other side.'

'No sea taxi for me and Angela, thanks,' said Carla. 'The hill is full of gorgeous little shops and we don't want to miss any of them.'

After their coffees were finished they walked around by the sea wall and then past the small town beach before turning around. It was time to head up the hill and discover all the pretty little shops.

'While you two hunt down the perfect handbag, I'm going to go off to the gallery I read about online, which I think is behind here, just up past a school,' he said, pointing down the street. 'I just need to check the exact address on my phone. Shall we meet up somewhere for some lunch later? How about at the top of the hill by the castle around two-thirty to three o'clock? That will give us plenty of time to eat and be back down to catch the boat back.'

'Sounds good to me! Just text me when you get near the castle,' said Carla.

'Enjoy your walk and mooch around the gallery,

Simon.'

'I will, and you both remember not too many purchases as we only have so much baggage allowance on the plane back to England.' He shot them both a cheeky grin before heading on his way.

Walking back past the restaurant they'd had coffee in, Angela and Carla started up the lane leading up the hill. It was very pretty and thankfully in the shade of the buildings, which would come in handy as the day was already warming up.

'You just watch, Angela, I bet we'll spend the next three hours going in and out of all the shops and then will end up not buying anything.'

'As long as we have had a really nice time I don't mind. And it will take our minds off of Lambros and Nectarios, which won't be a bad thing.'

'Can I tell you something? I don't think I do want to take my mind off of Nectarios,' Carla admitted.

'And why should you? Your face lights up when you see him and it's the same for him. You're both young with no commitments so there's nothing to stop you from living life to the fullest. I say, what will be will be. Now, I spot a shop with handbags in the window!'

Simon looked at the map on his phone, grateful he now understood where he was and where he had to head to. These streets were a lot quieter than down by the harbour wall, but he could imagine at night everywhere would be bustling. As he crossed a little road he saw what he was looking for – there was the gallery on the corner. Putting his phone back in his bag he could see through the open door that there was no one else inside apart from a lady behind a desk.

'Hi, is it ok to take a look around?' he asked.

'Yes of course. Were you looking for anything in

particular?'

'No, I'm just here on holiday and I was interested to see some of the local art. I'm an artist myself,' he said, liking the way it sounded out loud.

'That's nice to hear. Please take your time and don't hesitate to ask me anything. Hopefully I'll be able to answer any questions you might have.'

Simon didn't know where to start as there was so much to look at. It was an eclectic display of work, with everything from classic oil paintings right through to his style of abstract work, and everything in-between. After a few minutes he came across a group of paintings – all of olive trees – that were very modern and almost photographic, they had so much detail. The way the artist had used the light was stunning and he instantly loved them. He just wished he had the talent to paint something like that. It was a few minutes before he moved on to other works, taking in many paintings of Parga – the harbour, the castle, and of course every shape and style of boats you could think of. In the middle of the gallery was a display of pottery, a few different collections from different artists, some of which were quite plain and rustic, and others that were bright and bold with oranges, reds, yellows, greens, and the blue that was so synonymous with the Mediterranean.

Moving back to view the art on the walls, he noticed a piece that was very similar to Polina's work, but nowhere near as good, and he was shocked to note the price – it was so expensive! Of course the gallery had to put a mark-up on the price to ensure that both they and the artist got paid, but the number on this particular piece was very over the top in Simon's opinion. As he got to the last wall of art, he decided to return to the olive tree paintings that had really taken his eye.

'Do you like them?' the woman asked as she came to stand next to Simon. 'They're by one of our most popular artists, who lives here in Parga. People keep asking me what it is about them that draws the eye and all I can think is they are just so simple, very cleanly painted but still so detailed.'

'Yes, they are sharp and so clear, and the way the artist gets the light on the subject is so special. I do really like them but you have a lot of art that is just as lovely.'

'Thank you, that's very kind of you to say. I try to vary the work I display so that there's something for all tastes. What do you specialise in?'

'Nothing as good as anything you have here. My style is quite abstract and living in England we don't have the beautiful summer skies and light as you have here. For most of the year we can only dream of painting outdoors.'

'Are you staying here in Parga? Perhaps you can do some work while you're here.'

'No, I'm only here for the day with some friends. They're off looking at a different type of art, in the form of handbags.'

'Serious art then.'

'Apparently so, and even though it can be very expensive they were bursting with excitement. We're staying over on Vekianos, which is lovely.'

'You must have been to the Wednesday craft market then? We have a few artists on display here who also sell their pieces at the market.'

'Yes, I really enjoyed it last week. I'm not sure yet if I'll have time to go again tomorrow.'

'Every so often I like to take the day off and go over on the boat as I love it. There is a girl who has displayed there for many years that is so talented. We would love to display her work here because we know it would sell so well, but sadly, she apparently only sells her art from the market.'

'It sounds like you're talking about Polina.'

'Yes, do you know her? She is so talented and just like the olive tree paintings her work really stands out.'

'It does and I can see what you mean about her being a great fit for this gallery. Her work would fit in here really well.'

'Please tell her that when you see her. Perhaps you could persuade her where I've failed in the past.'

'I think there will be a barrier to cross first: her mother.'

'Yes, I've long suspected that is the reason she won't let us have any of her paintings. I have met her mother and she has instructed me in no uncertain terms to not approach her daughter ever again. Excuse me, that's my phone ringing. Feel free to carry on looking around.'

'Thank you, but I need to be heading off to meet my friends. It's been lovely meeting you.'

With that he said goodbye and left, and then walked back down to the harbour wall. Checking the time he saw that he still had over an hour before he had to meet Angela and Carla up at the castle, so he took a few minutes to sit on the wall, trying to take in the conversation he had just had. The only conclusion he came to was that the more he heard about Polina, the sadder her story and life appeared. The whole point in coming to Parga today was to get away from the romantic complications all three of them were facing, so he really didn't need this following him around. He sighed and grabbed his phone out of his pocket, texting Carla to say he was on his way.

'Angela, that was Simon. He'll be here shortly so did you want to head towards the castle? I think there should be somewhere to sit overlooking the harbour.'

'Yes, that's fine by me. Simon is going to be so shocked when we tell him that after all that talk of handbags, we've not bought a single thing between us. That's if you don't count the two large glasses of wine, of course.'

'Perhaps we should trick him by saying we bought so much that we're having to get everything shipped directly back to England.'

'Can you imagine the look on his face?' Angela laughed. 'Here we are. This last bit seemed even steeper, but we've made it and if we give ourselves plenty of time for going down after lunch it will be fine.'

'There's a wall there, the perfect spot to catch our breaths and we'll be able to see him when he gets to the top. I'm ready for some food, aren't you?'

'Yes. I fancy garlic bread and moussaka, but should I have something lighter now and then a bigger meal tonight instead?'

'You should have what you like. We're on holiday and what better time to throw caution to the wind? Here he comes.' She pointed. 'He certainly has done the hill a lot faster than us, but I suppose he didn't stop and go into twenty little shops along the way.'

'I'm shocked you managed the hill, Angela, it's so steep!' Simon said, pausing to catch his breath. 'Have you both had a nice time? And more importantly, did you find the perfect bag?'

'We did ... but we didn't buy it.'

'Why not?'

'Because we figured out that we could probably have another holiday for the price it was. No, that's unfair of me. We did see lots of lovely bags and clothes that weren't too expensive, but we just thought, do we really need them? And of course the answer was no. But we did buy something really nice: two glasses of wine. And now I'm ready for another.'

'Good because I could do with a glass as well. I checked the map and there's a little road just that way with restaurants that look down onto Valtos beach. Would you like to go and see if any take your fancy?' asked Simon.

'Perfect! You're like our own personal tour guide. Please lead the way.'

They took their time wandering along and they all agreed that the first restaurant they came across had a nice view so they would go in. As it was late afternoon everywhere was very quiet, most people still on the beaches, and they were seated in no time at a table on the terrace. To their right they could see the beach, to their left was a view of the back of the castle, and out in front the sea stretched to the horizon, with cabin cruisers and yachts moored just off the beach.

'This view was well worth the hike up the hill. Just to look out from here is such a treat,' said Angela, Carla and Simon nodding their agreement.

All three ordered moussaka with garlic bread and they opted to share a carafe of white wine. The view was magnificent, and they all said how magical it must be of an evening with all the boats out at sea lit up.

'Here it comes, the food is on its way. I am so hungry.'

'I've never seen you like this, Angela, it must be all the sea air on the boat and of course the walk up the hill must have given you an appetite as well,' said Simon.

'I just know I'm going to really enjoy this. By the way, I hope one of you is keeping an eye on the time as the last thing we need is to miss the boat. Could you imagine the three of us having to top and tail in a hotel bed?'

'I will definitely make sure we're on that boat as neither you nor Simon would be able to put up with my snoring.' Carla laughed.

'Tell us how you got on at the gallery,' Angela encouraged Simon. 'Was it as interesting as you'd hoped?'

'It was a lovely place and the lady who works there was nice and very chatty. The artwork was really good and there were so many styles, all displayed in clever little collections that were brilliantly done. There was this set of paintings of olive trees by an artist who lives and works here on Parga, which doesn't sound that exciting, but they were honestly exquisite. If I could produce work of that calibre I would be over the moon.'

'I'm so pleased you had a nice time and got the chance to see something different to what you've been looking at on Vekianos.'

'You'll be interested to hear that when I said where we were staying and mentioned the Wednesday craft fair, Polina's name came up. The lady who owns the gallery said she's been trying for many years to get Polina to display with them as the paintings Polina creates would just walk off the walls because they're so good. She's apparently approached her a number of times but Polina's mum has now put a stop to it.'

'That's so odd. In one way she is encouraging her daughter's art by allowing her to display at the Wednesday craft fair, but then to turn away such a great opportunity for Polina to sell her work further afield? That's so sad,' said Angela, shaking her head.

'That's what I said, it's so sad that a talent like that is being wasted.'

'Do you think Polina knows how well she could do if her work was displayed here in Parga? Surely it would open doors to opportunities on Corfu and Paxos as well, as they're also just an hour away from Vekianos,' suggested Carla.

'I really don't know.'

'Perhaps tomorrow you should wander down to the craft fair and tell her. She's told you she's ambitious and wants to make a name and a big career with her art, so I think you wouldn't be a friend if you didn't tell her,' said Angela, gently.

Chapter 22
Holiday day 9

The first person up the next morning was Carla, which was odd as she was normally the last one out of bed. The only reason she could think of was that they had all gone to bed before ten o'clock, exhausted after their day over on Parga, and she usually stayed up much later than the other two.

After their lovely meal yesterday they had walked back down the hill to catch the boat, and the early evening journey back to Vekianos was just as nice as the morning one. Taking her coffee out onto the terrace she could see they were in for another lovely day. After the excitement of their day out, she was looking forward to a lazy day by the pool.

'Good morning, Carla.'

'Hi, Simon. You look as shocked as me to see I'm up already. I think it's because I had an early night.'

'I can't believe how tired I was.'

'It was a long day and so much walking but what a lovely time we had. Parga was such a nice town but the best part of the day for me was just the three of us all being together on our adventure.'

'I have to agree. Can I get you another coffee?'

'No, I'm fine at the moment, thank you.'

Simon made his coffee and headed back out to join her.

'I'm going to miss this view when I get back to England. I know we live in one of the most beautiful parts of the UK, and I'm lucky that there hasn't been a day since I moved back from university that I haven't seen the sea, but it's not quite the same is it?'

'I get what you mean. I drive on the coast road all the time getting glimpses of it, but we don't get constant sunshine like this in Saltmarsh Quay. But no, we shouldn't moan. I have a very good life so there's really no reason to complain.'

'Yes, but it's not exactly the life you want, is it? Decorating pays the bills, but if you could earn a living with your art that would really be the perfect life for you. I wonder, do you think you could make a living as an artist if you lived here in Greece?'

'I don't really know. People do, I suppose, but it all comes down to outgoing costs. You have to be living somewhere with cheap rent that also has room to paint, and it's such a short tourist season here. The whole thing would be very stressful, I think, and those thoughts aren't good for creativity. It sounds glamorous and exciting in theory, but in reality, it would likely be very scary.'

'True, but it's still a lovely dream to have and to work towards, don't you think?'

'Perhaps the dream bit is right. I'm realistic enough to see that it will probably never happen for me. No, after this holiday I will get back to my old life and be happy with it. I have nothing to complain about.'

'I suspect it will be the same for Angela. She'll be like you and just slip back into the old routine. And as for me? I haven't a clue what to do next. Now my mum's back to work I haven't got her jobs to use as an excuse anymore. When I land in England it will be with a big thud that says "Carla, get yourself sorted. Your schooling days are over and it's time to become a responsible adult".'

'I really think you're looking at it in the wrong way. You should be excited that there's nothing to tie you down – no responsibilities, your life just a blank piece of paper. You can go and do anything you like.'

'Yes, but the problem is that I don't know what I'd like to do. I haven't a single clue or idea. Apart from staying here in this villa fifty-two weeks of the year, of course,' she joked. 'Now *that* would be perfect. Day trips to the beach and over to other islands, lounging by the pool in the sunshine, enjoying nice food... I could really cope with that.'

'But you left something out: Nectarios.'

'Oh yes, he would be the cherry on the cake for sure.'

'The thing is, it could become a reality and not just a dream. Ok, you might have to forfeit this villa and pool for something a little simpler, but there's really nothing stopping you living and working here on Vekianos and being with the chap who is just as obsessed with you as you are with him.'

'I know that but I don't know if I'm brave enough to do it.'

Walking back inside to refill their mugs, Carla thought about what Simon had said. He was right, she could stay here with Nectarios and live a happy life, but it wasn't as easy as that. This was real life, not a fairytale.

'Good morning!' said Angela, walking into the kitchen.

'You have perfect timing as I'm just putting the kettle on. How are you feeling today? Are your legs and feet hurting after all that hill climbing yesterday?'

'Believe it or not, I'm bouncing. Well, perhaps not *bouncing*, but I've had a restful sleep and I'm feeling fully recovered from that hill and the boat trip. I'm ready to take on another fun packed fulfilling day ... after I've had a couple of coffees to kick start it.'

'Go take a seat outside with Simon and I'll bring your kick start coffee out for you.'

'How are you feeling?' asked Simon as Angela stepped outside.

'Fine, thank you. All ready to get going again.'

'Coffee is served!'

'Thank you, Carla, that's kind of you.'

'Yes, thanks. Now, plans for today? I presume a lazy one by the pool with a few swims and quite a lot of napping?' Simon suggested.

'Actually, I thought this morning I might come with you to the craft fair,' Angela responded.

'But I'm not going.'

'After yesterday, with what you learnt in the gallery, don't you think you have a duty to tell Polina what the lady said? Sorry, duty isn't the right word. I just think that if you were in her shoes, wouldn't you want someone to tell you if you had a chance to sell your work to a wider audience? I also suspect Polina would really like to see you again.'

'I think Angela's right. You don't want to leave here with any regrets, Simon. I hope you two won't mind if I stay here in the sunshine.'

'Not at all. I don't think we'll be there for very long as the market's only on in the mornings,' Angela replied.

Simon smiled at his friends' encouragement, but he wondered if he would be doing the right thing, or if it would just cause more problems for Polina.

'Before you both go, would you like some breakfast? I can do some toast or there's also cereal, fruit, and yogurt.'

'I think just another coffee for now, and then I'll have a pastry down in the harbour. How about you, Simon?'

'No, nothing for me, thanks. I'm going to go and grab a quick shower before we head out.'

'I'm not sure he wants to be going down to the market, let alone seeing Polina. Are you sure it's a good idea?' Carla whispered to Angela once Simon was back inside the villa.

'No, I'm not sure, and to be honest it probably will cause more problems than it solves, but at least he won't be going back to the UK thinking he should have done something and having regrets for many years to come. Also, if I'm honest, I'm very intrigued by Calliope. I've heard two very different stories about her, and I'd like to find out which one is the truth. Is she a fragile woman who is dependent on her daughter, or is she a very controlling mother who is holding Polina back from achieving her dreams?'

'If anyone is going to find out, it will be you.' Carla smiled with affection at her friend.

An hour later Simon and Angela headed off down to the Wednesday market. Apart from exchanging a few words to point things out along the way, they were both very quiet. Simon was nervous. He didn't really know what to say when he saw Polina, and he was glad Angela was with him as she always seemed to know the right thing to say and do, and she would be very sensitive to the situation. He so appreciated her encouragement.

Once down in the harbour he knew they had to decide whether to turn left or right. The craft fair was to the right, just a few hundred yards along the sea wall, but it was still early and the traders would be still setting up. The last thing he wanted was to disturb Polina while she was getting everything together, especially given how stressful she'd told him that process was.

'I'm sure there's a lovely little restaurant near where the fair is taking place so why don't we have some breakfast?' suggested Angela. Simon had been right, she knew exactly how best to approach this.

He nodded and as they walked along they

spotted Nectarios coming towards them.

'Why are you both up and out so early? Another boat trip? Carla texted me yesterday and said you were going to Parga.'

'No, today we've come to look at the craft market,' Angela answered.

'Did you have a nice day yesterday?'

'We did. The hill was a bit of a struggle at times and we were really tired last night, but after a good night's sleep we're relaxed and ready to take on another day. Sadly, I can't say Carla is the same. She's having a quiet day by the pool by herself. I don't think we'll be back at the villa until at least two o'clock, so hopefully Carla won't be too bored.'

'Oh, well, have a nice time. Goodbye.' With that, Nectarios went.

'I know what you're doing,' Simon said with a smile.

'Whatever do you mean?' asked Angela, looking the picture of innocence. 'I was just letting Nectarios know Carla was up at the villa all alone. If he took that as some sort of hint that she might like some company, what can I do about it? Now, here we are, this place will be the perfect spot to watch everything that's going on, and we can also see the pier with all the traders so we'll know when is best to head over.'

Simon could tell Angela was on a mission today, not just to sort out his life, but Carla's as well. Coffee and omelettes were ordered and while they settled back and waited for the food, they quietly took in everything that was going on around them. Crafters were arriving with boxes of their wares and helping one another set up. There seemed a real community spirit between them. But there was no sign of Polina in her normal spot, which was still empty. Perhaps today she wasn't coming? In a way that would be a relief because he wouldn't have to chat with her, so he could stop worrying about what to say ... or not say.

'Here comes the food, Angela. Look how good these omelettes look.'

'Yes, I'm rather pleased I suggested them. Can you see your friend yet?'

'No, she's not here. Perhaps she's taking the day off?'

'Not to worry. No matter what happens, it's not been a wasted journey because this food is gorgeous, and we can still have a little walk around to look at the other stalls.'

'That would be nice. Anyway, we can't go back to the villa too early.'

'Why not?'

'Because you've told Nectarios we're staying down here for a while, and we can't go and disturb him and Carla.'

Angela looked thoughtful for a moment. 'Do you think he'll go up and see her? I hope so.'

'Of course he will. You almost told him he *had* to go! Oh, I think Polina will be here today after all. I've just spotted her wheeling some boxes up to her table and she has someone helping her. It looks like Calliope.'

'Can you point them out to me?'

'Just over there,' said Simon, angling his chair so he could point Angela in the right direction. 'It looks like they're going back to get more stock.'

'I have to say that her mum's not at all like I'd imagined.'

Simon didn't know what to say so didn't answer, and they finished off their breakfast. By that point the harbour was getting very busy with visitors.

'I think it looks like Polina is all set up and her mum has gone, maybe to park the car or perhaps she's left altogether and won't be back until it's time to pack everything up.'

'Right then, why don't you go and have a word with Polina, and I'll putter around and look at the stalls here against the wall. I'm sure we'll be able to spot each other in the crowd when you're done.'

'Do you really think I'm doing the right thing by mentioning the gallery over in Parga? Or should I just say hello and leave it at that?'

'I think you need to do what you think is right. The last thing I would want is for you to be left feeling upset or unsettled with anything you've said. Just remember that you aren't out to upset her, only to help her.'

'Ok, wish me luck.'

Simon's stomach was in his throat as he got nearer to Polina's table. He could see her sat on a chair behind it looking at her phone. This was it, there was no going back.

'Hi, Polina. It's another gorgeous, sunny day with no wind. Perfect for the craft fair.'

'Hello, yes, it's lovely. How are you?' she asked, looking a bit flustered.

'Fine, thank you. I've popped down with Angela; she's just over there, looking at the stalls by the sea wall.'

'That's nice. I better warn you that my mum will be here any moment. I have to nip off for an hour and she's going to mind the stand while I'm gone.'

'I'd best go then. I'm sorry to have disturbed you.'

'There's no need to be sorry. Look, we can chat? I have to go to the dentist – of course it has to be on a day when the fair is on – but we could talk on the walk over? You see the little alleyway over there? I'll be cutting through there in about ten minutes.'

'Ok, I'll wait for you.'

He walked off and as he got to the end of the

pier, he noticed Calliope heading his way and ducked his head, even though he doubted she would recognize him from the bakery. Walking through to the ally he waited by a clothes shop where Polina wouldn't miss him.

A few minutes later he spotted her, and they waved to each other.

'The dentist is just up the end of this street but I'm in no hurry as I'm actually quite early. Are you still having a nice holiday with your friends?'

'Yes, thanks. We caught the boat over to Parga yesterday. It was lovely but that hill up to the castle is so steep. I still can't believe that Angela made it to the top and back again. Do you go to Parga very often as it's only an hour away?'

'To be honest, I haven't been since I was at school years ago. My mum doesn't like me leaving the island because she gets very nervous and upset, and of course I would never be able to get her on a boat. From what I remember Parga is very nice. The town is a lot bigger than here, with a lot more shops and restaurants.'

'Yes, we all felt so relaxed on the boat and we had a nice meal at the top of the hill, overlooking Valtos beach.'

This was the moment to mention the gallery, it was the perfect opportunity.

'I suspect you would love it over there. While Carla and Angela went to hunt down the perfect handbag, I found this beautiful gallery full of work by local artists. There was this wonderful set of paintings of olive trees that were so striking. If only I could produce work like that. The owner was lovely and she talked me through some of the pieces on display. It was the highlight of my day.'

'I think I know the gallery. The owner sometimes comes to the market to try and get the artists to display their work with her. She once asked me, but my mum took over the conversation while I served a customer.'

'How exciting. Are you going to do it? You would do so well.'

'No, I'm not. The place might look inviting, but she isn't a nice woman.'

'Really? She seemed lovely to me.'

'I can imagine, but she takes a huge commission on every painting.'

'Oh, but if she's like that then why are there so many artists displaying their work in her gallery?'

'I don't know. It's just what my mum told me. I haven't had any dealings with her since that time when she introduced herself, but my mum has a few times.'

'So you haven't actually talked to her directly about her commission structure?'

'No, but my mum has told me it's really bad. Apparently, she takes eighty percent and all I would get is twenty, which wouldn't even cover my material costs, let alone all the hours of work I put into it. Here we are, this is the dentist. I'd best go in, I don't want to be late.'

'Ok. It was nice seeing you again. Perhaps before I leave to go back to England, we could meet up here in the harbour and grab a drink?'

'I'd like that, but I'll need to be careful.'

'I know.'

'Thank you for being so understanding. It's been really nice to see you, Simon.'

As he walked away he was so confused. If the gallery owner was taking an eighty percent commission there was no way she would have any artists agreeing to their work being displayed in her gallery. Polina had either misunderstood her mum and got the eighty and twenty percent the wrong way around, or perhaps this was something to do with her mum not wanting her to expand her horizons. One thing was for sure, something wasn't quite right.

Angela had noticed an older woman take over when Polina left her stand, and thought that it had to be Calliope. Could this be an opportunity to be a little nosey on behalf of Simon? Yes, of course it was.

'Hello! What gorgeous paintings. You're so talented.'

'I can't take the credit as it's my daughter who paints. It's her little hobby.'

'The standard of this work is far more than a hobby. These paintings would sell well all over the world. What a talent and an eye for detail. You must be such a proud mother.'

'No, it's just a hobby. She doesn't want to be a full-time artist as she is happy just to sell a few paintings here in the market.'

'So she has another career? I understand now. Well, if she was my daughter, I would be telling her to give up her career and take her work all over the Greek islands. She would be hugely successful. Does she ever hold exhibitions of her work?'

'Did you not hear me? She doesn't want to be an artist. This is just something she does to pass the time. Now, would you please excuse me? Unless you want to purchase a painting, I must ask you to move out of the way.'

'I'm sorry,' said Angela, taken aback at the woman's rude tone. 'I didn't mean to upset you. I was just saying what a brilliant artist your daughter is, that's all.'

'Well, I don't need or want to hear any more of your opinions.'

Chapter 23
Holiday day 9

Carla had settled herself down on the sun lounger after a short swim. She was surprised to discover she was actually looking forward to being by herself for a while. She felt relaxed and happy, and she was determined that any thoughts about her future were not going to upset her today. There would be plenty of time for that once she was back in the UK. She also thought about what her mum had said before she left for this holiday, how she had told Carla to have a nice time and not to worry because there was no rush for her to start her career because she could still live at home for as long as she wanted.

Perhaps that was the problem. Was she relying on her mum too much? There was no denying that if she had been a nagging mum, Carla might have got into action trying to find a job a lot sooner. No, this was day nine of the holiday and as they had four full days left after today she was going to switch off completely.

Then she laughed to herself. If she wasn't going to think about getting a job, there was only one other thing on her mind – Nectarios, and especially their day on the beach together. Hopefully there would be at least one more of them before the holiday was over, and of course she wanted him to kiss her again.

She looked at her phone but there were no new messages. She was surprised there hadn't yet been a text from him today.

Lying back on the sun lounger she heard the gate open. She was shocked that Angela and Simon were back so early; she wasn't expecting them for at least a few more hours.

'Hi, Carla.'

'Nectarios!' she exclaimed, pleased to see him. 'I thought you were Angela and Simon returning.'

'I bumped into them in town and they said you were up here all alone so I thought I would come up and say hello. Maybe even keep you company?'

Carla smiled. 'I'd love that. Would you like a cold drink?'

'Yes, please. How was your day was over in Parga? Did you have a nice time?'

'We had a lovely time. You're not working today?'

'No, I'm not in until this evening. Sakis and my mum are covering the day shift today.'

'How is Sakis? I keep meaning to message him.'

'He's fine. Still in love and counting down the weeks until he can go over and see Trifon on Corfu.'

Carla went in and fetched the drinks. It had really made her day, Nectarios popping in.

'Here you go. Help yourself to some biscuits as well.'

'Was it a spur of a moment thing to go over to Parga? My granddad reckoned it was something to do with him upsetting Angela.'

'Oh no, he hasn't upset her. We all just needed a day of escape. I have to admit though, I couldn't get you out of my head,' she admitted, shyly. 'I didn't intend to tell you that, but I've said it now, so there's no going back.'

'I don't know what to say. Actually, I do because I feel the same about you. It's not like me at all. I'm usually just good old Nectarios who flirts with all the girls that come to Vekianos on holiday. I'm not saying I'm a joke, but I do have a reputation, which I used to be proud of but not any longer. Now, I'm starting to feel ashamed of it.'

Carla didn't know what to say, but she was glad they were both being honest about how they felt. Then she realised that despite not knowing what to say, she did know what to do, so she leaned across the table and kissed him. And it was just as special as it had been when they were on the beach the other day.

'I haven't been able to stop thinking about kissing you. I just don't want you to think I'm taking advantage of you.'

'You aren't. If anything, it's the other way around!'

As she leaned over for another kiss, she heard voices approaching the villa. It appeared that Simon and Angela were back from the harbour. She quickly moved away from Nectarios.

She wasn't sure if her friends' return was bad timing or good timing because goodness knows where the kissing could have ended up.

'Hi, you two. We have a visitor.'

'Hello again, Nectarios,' said Angela, looking very pleased to see him at the villa.

'I actually need to be off as I have some things to do before my shift later on.'

Carla found herself blurting, 'Nectarios just popped in to see if we were going down to the restaurant tonight.'

Why had she come out with that? She couldn't say.

'I hadn't thought about where we would go.'

'I don't mind if we do,' offered Simon. 'Can you squeeze us in around nine-fifteen?' he asked Nectarios.

'Consider yourselves all booked. See you all tonight.'

With that he was gone and Angela's smile grew.

He couldn't get out through the gate quick enough!

'How was the craft fair? Did you see Polina, Simon?'

'Yes, I did, and even better Angela got talking to her mum Calliope. We'll tell you all about it but first I need to change. I can't wait to get into the pool.'

'I'm not going for a swim, but I'll change as well. The temperature has certainly shot up since we left earlier.'

As they went off to their rooms Carla had time to reflect on what had just happened with Nectarios. It had been so good that they had been honest with each other, but what would happen now? She made her way back down to the pool and pulled two other sun loungers into the sun for Angela and Simon.

'Was it nice seeing Nectarios?' asked Angela once she was settled in her chair.

'It was more than nice. I've concluded that he's a nice lad and I really like him. He's been honest that all this business about him flirting is true – not that he could deny it given we've seen it with our own eyes! – and I like that he isn't making excuses.'

'That's great. I think I might have upset Polina's mum down at the craft fair but one thing is for sure, she isn't fragile, she's just controlling. It's so silly. All her daughter wants to do is paint and sell her work and she's stopping her from doing that because ... well, I don't really know what's going on in her head. Here comes Simon.'

'I was right, Angela! I've just called the lady who owns the gallery in Parga and rightly or wrongly I told her I had spoken to Polina and asked her why she didn't want her paintings sold in the gallery. I told the woman what Polina said about the commission, and I was right – she has the numbers wrong. The gallery takes twenty percent, not the eighty Calliope told her, and with what Calliope said to you all I can think is that she doesn't want her daughter to be an artist or live her dream. All this business about her being fragile is rubbish. Where I was sad about the whole situation before, now I'm angry. To think of the hold she has over Polina, who has such a talent...'

'What are you going to do about it?' Angela asked.

'I don't know yet, but I do know I have to do something. For now, I need to get in the pool and cool off – literally and figuratively. By the way, Carla, I think we've both failed.'

'In what way?'

'Our day trip to Parga was meant to get Polina and Nectarios out of our heads but here we are, drawn back to them like magnets. That just leaves Lambros. What do we think his next move will be?' Simon asked Angela.

'Only time will tell. At least we can laugh about it all and not take any of it too seriously because in four days' time we will be heading back to our old lives. Within a few weeks Lambros, Nectarios, and Polina will be all forgotten.'

They all nodded but none of them was entirely sure if that was true...

Chapter 24
Holiday day 10

Carla looked at the time on her phone. It was nine forty-five, which meant she had fifteen minutes to get down to the harbour to meet Sakis. She was really looking forward to her morning out with him. One thing was for sure, it would be a lot of fun. He had made them all laugh at dinner last night, providing the perfect antidote to Simon's long face, his mind on what to do about telling Polina about her mum lying to her, and to Angela's silence because Lambros was hovering around and she feared he might ask again if she wanted to go away for the night.

The only good thing about the evening, apart from Sakis making them all laugh, was the attention Carla had gotten from Nectarios, which she'd enjoyed very much.

She was now on a mission to make sure these last four days of the holiday were packed full of fun.

'Good morning, Carla, I love the outfit,' Sakis greeted her warmly as she met up with him.

'Thanks! I knew I had to put a bit of effort in even though we're only going to the beach. You're also looking fab, not a crease or a hair out of place.'

'By "crease" I hope you mean the clothes and not my face!'

'No, the face... Sorry I couldn't resist. You left it wide open for me.' Carla laughed.

'Very funny, but I will say it takes me longer to get ready for a casual beach day than it does for an evening out.'

'I'm so looking forward to our day out.'

'So am I. Now, if we're quick, we could get the ten-fifteen bus.'

'Lead the way.'

As they got to the bus stop there was quite a long queue and Carla hoped they would manage to get on even if they had to stand. Thankfully, they were in luck, and even better they managed to nab seats.

'Do you go to the beach a lot?' asked Carla.

'Yes, but normally only at the beginning and the end of the season because at the height it's very busy and also far too hot. Come July and August I keep out of the sun during the day. It's bad enough working in that heat and even late into the evening the temperature never seems to drop.'

'So which beach are we off to?'

'It's not just a beach, Keriaphos is a little town. It's small but quite sweet and I think you'll like it. It's also quite a good place to pose. Why are you laughing?' he asked, pretending to look affronted. 'I haven't gone to all this trouble to not be looked at.'

'Ok, not a problem, I can pose as well as the next person.'

'Yes, darling, but not like me. To be honest, it's one of the only things I'm qualified in. I'm useless at everything else.'

'Rubbish! You are brilliant at your job and you bring an entertainment value few people could match. I'm sure people go to Alina's restaurant to see you as much as they do to eat the food.'

'Of course they do. Every night is Show Time! But saying that, there are some people – mainly young women – that go for another reason. And I can't blame them, Lambros is very handsome. I'm only joking! Obviously I mean Nectarios, but more about him later. We're nearly there and our stop is the next one so make sure you've got your bag, and more importantly, make sure you give a good performance when we leave the bus.'

'You are so funny, Sakis. I think it would be better if I leave the performing to you though.'

As they walked down the bus and got off Carla couldn't help but laugh because Sakis really did make sure everyone was looking at him, swishing his hair and extending his neck to be seen above the other passengers. This was clearly a way of life for him, and she loved seeing it.

'As you can see, we have the steep hill to go down first. By the way, have you brought water with you? The last thing you need is to get dehydrated.'

'Yes, two bottles, plus I stopped at the bakery and got us a couple of pastries.'

'That's very kind of you. We can save them for later though as our first stop is a little café at the bottom of the hill. If we're lucky there will be a table free outside, and people will be able to see us as they head to the beach. Plus, I can use the bathroom mirror to check myself out. God only knows what the wind is doing to my hair.'

Carla was nearly in hysterics. 'What are you like, Sakis?'

'Very high maintenance are the words you're looking for, Carla.'

'And there is nothing wrong with that.'

They took their time walking down, Sakis pointing out different things and telling Carla all about the little town, saying what a lovely atmosphere there was here in the evenings as it was a lot smaller than in the main harbour of Vekianos.

'Oh, looks like we're in luck. There's the little café I mentioned, and there's a spare table on the terrace. You take a seat and I'll be right back. I just need to go and check myself in the mirror.'

'What did you want to drink?'

'A double espresso, please. I won't be a minute.'

'I'll believe that when I see it! I expect it will be lunchtime before you get back out here.'

'Very cutting, my darling, but also funny. I see I have competition when it comes to one-liners today.'

Carla ordered the coffees and sat back to take in the view. It was a busy little town with lots of people all going in one direction. She assumed that it must be towards the beach. A quick look at her phone revealed there was a new text from Nectarios.

Have a good time with Sakis. I don't expect you'll stop laughing all day, and please don't believe any of the things he says about me as they aren't true. Also, I wish it was me there with you today xx

'I'm back and in record time for me. What have I missed?' asked Sakis.

'Nothing much, just a text from Nectarios telling us to have a nice day.'

'I expect he also said he wished it was him here with you instead of me.'

'Spot on. Have you worked together very long? You seem like a good team.'

'Oh yes, many years. It works well now but it wasn't always like this, and there are still times when I could scream at him, but he knows how far he can push me before I throw a tantrum.'

'You? A tantrum? I can't imagine you throwing your toys out the pram,' said Carla, sarcastically.

'My darling, you should see me. It's not just the toys, I end up throwing the pram as well!'

'But something tells me you still get your way every time.'

'I do now, but it wasn't always like that. I think it comes with age and earning respect.'

They sat having their coffee and people watching, Carla happily taking everything in. After twenty minutes Sakis paid for the drinks, and they headed off to the beach.

'It's been a while since I've been on this beach. We need to turn here and then walk down the little boardwalk onto the sand. Hopefully we can find a little spot away from other people.'

A few minutes later they had found a spot near the rocks where no one would be able to set up behind them. Once there they got their towels out, and after covering themselves in sun cream, they made themselves comfortable, settling down for a day of sunshine and chat.

'So how many days have you got left of your holiday?'

'Four full days, counting today, and then we have a few hours on the day we leave. The holiday seems to have gone so fast. It really feels like we arrived just a couple of days ago.'

'It's so funny because to me it feels like you've been coming to the restaurant for weeks. I'm going to miss the three of you when you've left and of course I won't be the only one. I have to say, and I'm being totally honest with you, Carla, I've *never* seen Nectarios like this with anyone else before. He really has fallen for you.'

'Give him a few days after I've gone and I'm sure he'll be back to his old self, you wait and see.'

'I don't think so. I think he's grown up a bit since meeting you, and he's realised his playing around days are over and he wants more out of life than all those one night – or should I say one week? – stands. I know how he feels. I've had my share of romances with holidaymakers but since meeting Trifon I've realised I want a different type of life, something a bit more fulfilling. And it's not just me that's noticed how he's changed – the chefs and Alina have as well. I know his mum is holding her breath that he stays the course with this new attitude. It's not just about the romance side of things, he seems to be taking on more responsibly at the restaurant as well. He's actually interested in it now, not like before when he was late in and always wanting to leave early.'

'When that happened I imagine a lot of the work must have fallen on your shoulders. That doesn't seem fair.'

'It used to annoy me and we would end up rowing about it all the time. The worst thing for me was that Lambros always took his grandson's side. If I heard it once, I heard it a hundred times: "Nectarios is young. He only wants to have fun so why shouldn't he?" Of course Alina looked at it completely differently, but she was always overruled by Lambros. The arguments I used to have with both Nectarios and Lambros were happening more and more frequently until one day Alina sat me down. She knew things were unfair and she also knew I was a hard worker, and she made me an offer. She said that if Nectarios left, say, for example, two hours early, she would pay me his wage for those two hours in addition to my usual wage. Ok, I'm not daft, I'm sure she didn't take the two hours pay off of Nectarios's pay because at the end of the day he's her son, but it did mean I've been able to earn a lot of extra cash. There were even some weeks when he didn't disappear early and I found I was wishing he would so I could get the extra payout.'

'But you both seem to get on ok together now.'

'Yeah, but it's taken many years of working together to gel like we do. If, say, I get a table who I know are going to be good tippers, he will let me spend a bit of extra time with them by stepping in to help with my other tables, and vice versa. At the end of the day we both want the same thing: to earn enough money to get us through the winter months.'

'That's good you have that sort of relationship.'

'It helps that he finally acknowledged that many customers come specifically to see me camp it up and be silly and funny. He realised we could work together, rather than against one another.'

'You do it very well. Surely there are some nights though when you just can't be bothered. Do you still have to go through the motions?'

'Oh of course. But I don't mind really. At the end of the day Alina pays me to do my job and that bit of camp is all part of it. I can tell you there aren't a lot of waiting staff on Vekianos that earn the money I do, and I am very grateful for my job.'

'I have to say you earn every penny. You work so hard! So, what's in the future for Sakis? Where does Trifon fit into the plans? Or perhaps I should asking where you fit into Trifon's life?'

'That is the million-dollar question, and the answer is quite simple: I don't know. It's all a bit scary at the moment.'

'Scary? I'm not sure I know what you mean.'

'Well, Trifon has asked me to go and live with him on Corfu. He's even said I wouldn't need to work if I didn't want to and from where I'm standing, heading into the busiest and hottest months of the year, that sounds like an exciting and welcome prospect.'

'I sense a "but" coming.'

'Oh yes, a big one. First of all, I couldn't expect anyone to keep me; I need to work and earn my wage. And secondly, you know as well as I do that I only met him at the party last week. I couldn't give everything up – leave behind my whole life here – and move in with someone I barely know only to have it all go wrong. A holiday romance isn't a real romance, and it's certainly not enough to base life decisions on.'

'I understand that but you obviously want to spend time together so aren't you tempted to just go over to Corfu for a holiday and see how you get on living together? You never know, there could even be a job on the island that you love. I suppose what I'm saying is, you wouldn't want to miss out on what could be a life-changing situation for you because of "what if's".'

'Oh, completely. It's definitely my plan to go over and see him, but the first opportunity for that to happen will be in October when the restaurant closes for the winter, and by then you never know what will have happened. I might have lost my opportunity to someone else. Ugh! This is too depressing. Let's change the subject. Why don't you tell me about your life in England?'

'There's nothing to tell really, as it's all very boring and not a patch on yours here in beautiful Greece.'

'Don't be silly! I know you live near Angela and Simon, and you've just finished university, but what else can you tell me?'

'Well, I actually left university a while back but then my mum had a fall and broke her leg quite badly and I took over all her little jobs, doing everything from dog walking to cleaning people's houses, and my least favourite activity: ironing. But now she's back to work I need to get a job ... well, actually a career.'

'A career? That sounds very high flying. So what will you be careering at?'

'I don't have a clue. Once I get back I need to sort my life out.'

'I see. Well, the important thing is you've had a lovely holiday before the real world beckons.

'I think it's time for a swim, don't you?' She was very ready to talk about something – anything – else.

Sakis gave Carla a look that said he knew exactly what she was doing, but he stood and they headed down the beach and into the beautiful clear blue sea. To her surprise, Sakis dunked his head under the water, and before she could say anything he started to splash her. He was dreadful, acting just like a child.

'You didn't think that was going to happen did you?' he asked.

'Not at all, but no doubt there's a reason behind it.'

'Are you saying it wasn't a spur of the moment thing?' Sakis put a hand to his chest, an expression of mock outrage on his face that quickly dissolved into a grin. 'Well, you would be right. I actually think I look quite good getting out the sea with my hair wet and flicked back.'

This had her in fits of laughter and she lost her balance and ended up with her head underwater.

Back in the sun on their towels a while later, having sashayed their way across the sand, they were still laughing and of course taking the mickey out of each other.

'Pastry time! I have two vanilla ones and two spinach. Which would you like, Sakis?'

'Could I have the savoury one first? In this country we always have the sweet one last.'

'Of course. You're very witty, Sakis,' she said, thinking about how good he'd been with the quick retorts all morning.

'You always have to be one step ahead, darling. I learnt that the hard way when I was bullied at school for being different. Oh, I hated those days and that place. I was horrible at sport, just ok at art, and didn't have a head for history. No, it wasn't until I got old enough to work during the season that I realised people laughed at what I said when I was serving them. That's when I came into my own, realising it could be my strength, and all these hundreds of years later I'm still doing it.'

'And may you continue doing it for many more hundreds of years to come.' Carla mimed raising a toast and Sakis playfully pretended to tap her invisible glass with his own.

'That's another thing to consider. If I did go and live with Trifon on Corfu, would I miss bringing fun and entertainment to the holiday makers?'

'The only way you'll find out is to go and stay with him for a few weeks. Surely Alina must know someone who can stand in for you and do your job?'

'No, that's the problem. Everyone who can work is already working. There's no such thing as people waiting and looking for work around here as the island is always short of workers as it is.'

'So it has to be October then, but maybe that's a good thing as it will mean you can stay longer than a couple of weeks with Trifon. Do you think you can wait that long for the months to tick over?'

'I don't know. Like I already said, if I wait too long I might lose my chance through no fault of my own. But I've just had a thought. Answer me this question, Carla, when you get back to England, what will you miss the most about the holiday? Will it be the island itself, the villa, the food, or perhaps something else?'

'I'll miss everything,' she said, shrugging her shoulders.

'No, come on, if you only can say one thing, what would it be?'

'You know exactly what I'm going to say – Nectarios, of course.'

'But you don't need to miss him.'

'You've lost me now. What do you mean?'

'It's very simple. Why not stay here on Vekianos

and do my job for a couple of weeks? That way I'll be able to go over to Corfu and see Trifon, and you'll have Nectarios's lips to kiss twenty-four-seven. You did say you haven't got a job to go home to, so everyone will be happy. Come on, Carla, just think how much kissing you can do in a couple of weeks!'

There was no denying that Sakis made a very good point...

Chapter 25

Holiday day 10

'I'm off to meet Polina for a little bit. Is there anything I can get you while I'm down in the town?' Simon asked Angela.

'No, I think we're ok for every essential. Before you go though, and please don't think I'm trying to interfere, but ... I want you to be careful. I know you're angry at how Calliope seems to be controlling Polina but at the end of the day, we're strangers to her compared to her mum. You need to approach this gently, not going in all guns blazing.'

'I know, and to be honest, Angela, I don't really know or understand why I'm getting involved with all of this. It's none of my business and I don't have anything to gain from it but ... I want to help Polina. I really care about her.'

'I know you do. All I'm saying is please be careful.'

'I will. I might take a walk afterwards so I could be a while.'

'Take all the time you need. I'll be perfectly fine here, and Carla will be back later on this afternoon as Sakis has to start work at five.'

'Ok, see you later.'

Polina wanted to meet away from the harbour and shops so he needed to walk along the road behind the promenade. He found the road and turned left, eventually coming to a shaded little square where local people sat and chatted. From there he had to go up a side street that led to an old church, and that was where Polina would be. A check of the time reassured him he was doing ok and wouldn't be late.

Strangely, he wasn't nervous. If anything, he felt very comfortable as he turned a corner and spotted the church. There was no sign of Polina just yet so he walked over to the building and sat in the shade. A few minutes passed and then he jumped as someone touched him on the shoulder.

'Oh dear, I'm sorry, I didn't mean to startle you,' said Polina.

'That's fine. Thank you for agreeing to meet me. I hope it's not caused you too much trouble with your mum.'

'No, it's fine, she knows I'm out doing a few errands. I'm just sorry we can't spend the whole day together. I would have enjoyed that.'

'So would I. Now the thing is, and I don't want to cause a problem or upset you by telling you this, but I found something out by complete accident and given what we talked about last time I saw you, I thought I'd best tell you even though it might be upsetting.'

'Simon please slow down. I'm very confused and I think you are as well. Let me get this right, you've found out something I might want to know, but which could be upsetting?'

'Yes, that's right. You see, I talked to the woman at the gallery in Parga again, and I asked her about her commission structure. Polina, she doesn't take eighty percent. The artist is the one who gets the eighty, and she gets only twenty, and most of the artists put their prices up so that they don't lose out at all.'

'No, I'm sure you have it wrong, Simon.'

'I'm sorry but I don't. The owner told me herself. I also know for a fact that it's exactly what she told your mum.'

There was a long silence and Simon could see Polina was trying to process what he'd just said.

'I'm really sorry for upsetting you, but you are *such* a talented artist and you deserve to have your work shown across Greece and beyond. I hoped to help by telling you.'

'But ... but... Why would my mum lie to me?'

'That's something you'll need to ask her. I can promise you this though, the gallery would love to sell your work. They think you could do really well.'

'Look, I need to go, I have jobs to get done and... Yes, I need to be off right away.' Polina looked flustered and Simon felt helpless, wanting to make things better for her but not knowing how.

'Will I see you before I leave to go back to England?' he asked hopefully.

'No, I don't think so. Goodbye.'

With that abrupt farewell she was gone and suddenly it was like a huge boulder had fallen on Simon. He had made a huge mistake by telling her.

He sat there for a while thinking about how he might be able to put things right, but he kept coming to the same conclusion: he couldn't. Because what he'd said could not be unsaid. The damage was done.

Angela had made herself a sandwich for her lunch and was sat at the table on the terrace when she saw Lambros at the gate. As he closed it behind him, he paused, as though thinking what to do next. She wasn't sure if he had spotted her on the terrace so she took a deep breath, stood up, and waved. He waved back and started to walk towards her.

'Hi, Lambros, this is a nice surprise.'

'Just thought I'd stop by and say hello, if you aren't too busy?'

'Busy? I'm on holiday! I have all the time in the world. Why don't you take a seat while I fetch us a drink.'

Taking a bottle of water and the two glasses out onto the terrace she caught her reflection in the glass door. She looked so serious and she told herself to cheer up. This was just a friend popping in for a chat, nothing more.

'Here we go.'

'Angela, I think I need to apologise to you,' he announced abruptly. 'You see, I've been very stupid – well, my daughter has used stronger words than that – and it wasn't until last night in the restaurant that I realised something was wrong. I'm worried I said something that might have sounded as if I said something else. And now I'm getting tongue-tied and making everything worse.'

'Why not take a big swig of water to clear your throat and then tell me what the problem is ... or was.'

'I'm just an old fool really.'

'I will be the judge of that,' she said primly. 'Now, come on, explain.'

'Ok, here goes. You know how I invited you to go away for a night?'

She nodded.

'I couldn't understand why you turned me down, and I have to admit I was upset because we had been getting on so well with each other up until that point. Then, last night in the restaurant, you weren't your normal self and you hardly said two words.'

'I'm sorry if I came across rudely.'

'Please don't be sorry. It's not your fault. Alina noticed you seemed off and I explained about having invited you to come away with me for a few days, and you turning me down. She just stood there staring at me blankly, then she slapped me on the arm and told me how stupid I had been. Of course, me being an old fool, I hadn't given what I said to you any thought. You see, when I asked you out I didn't mean it to come across as if I expected that we would have the same bedroom – not at all! – and Alina said that was the reason you said no and why you were very cool with me. Angela, I haven't been intimate in that way with a woman for decades and I really don't think I would even know what to do anymore. Please stop laughing at this old fool. I have made myself look so stupid, haven't I?'

At this point Angela couldn't stop giggling and eventually Lambros gave an embarrassed smile.

'I admit, I did think you wanted to whisk me away for a night of passion and I wasn't ready for that. That's why I said no.'

'I did deserve that slap, didn't I? I really don't know what to say apart from I'm so sorry. I am definitely no Romeo!'

'But I bet you were in your day.'

'You're being too kind about all of this.'

'Honestly, now that I know the truth, it's all very funny. I was just shocked at the time as it's only my first visit to the island. Who knows, maybe it would be different if it had been my second or third.' She smiled cheekily and took a sip of her water, leaving poor Lambros speechless.

Chapter 26
Holiday day 10

Walking back into the villa after her day out with Sakis, Carla's head was ready to burst. One minute she was thinking about how silly the idea of her staying here and working while Sakis went to Corfu for a few weeks was, and then the next her head was saying it's only two weeks, why not go for it? But then the doubt crept in. Could she actually do the job? No, it was nonsense to even consider it.

Walking back into the villa and putting her bag down, she went to the fridge to get some water. Hearing a noise coming from the other room she called out, 'I'm back!'

'Give me just a minute, Carla, I've just got out of the shower,' Angela replied.

'Ok, shall I pour you a glass of something?'

'No, thank you. I think I've had too many today already. I'll explain in just a moment.'

Simon came through the door just then.

'Good day?' asked Carla.

'Don't ask. Sorry, I didn't mean to sound so snappy. I told Polina about the commission thing and, well ... I shouldn't have. Now she's upset and so that's it for us. I messed up. How was your day? Hopefully a heck of a lot better than mine.'

'As you can imagine, it was a laugh a minute with Sakis, but also very interesting because-'

'You're both back!' exclaimed Angela, looking delighted to see them. 'Let's sit outside.'

Angela headed out onto the terrace with a bottle of water, but Carla poured herself and Simon each a glass of wine as it sounded like they both needed it. Sitting in the sunshine they heard the whole story about Lambros and the mistaken night of passion, which had the three of them giggling from beginning to end.

'You are so wicked teasing him, Angela, but you have to admire him for coming up here and explaining. We have to go down there and eat tonight now, don't you think?' asked Simon.

'You and Angela go. I'm not that hungry so I'll just snack up here,' said Carla, hoping there would be no follow-up questions, but of course there were.

'Excuse me? You? *Not* hungry? Those are words we've never heard!' said Simon.

'Ok, the truth is I'm starving but can we go somewhere else to eat?'

'Why? What has Sakis said to upset you?' asked Angela, concerned.

'Nothing. It's fine. I'm fine,' Carla answered dismissively.

'Look, after spending the past week and a half with you two, I can read you like a book. You both need to get out tonight, and we need to go and see Lambros as no doubt he'll still be feeling embarrassed. So, come on, you two. Go off and shower then get the glad rags on. We're on holiday and tonight we're going to have some fun.'

Two hours later they were sat having a drink in the harbour before heading over to Alina's for something to eat. Both Simon and Carla had relaxed thanks to a few glasses of wine, and they were still laughing about Lambros and Angela's mix-up. It was turning out to be the start of a nice evening.

'So, Angela,' began Carla. 'Now that the sharing the bedroom thing has been sorted, the question is: are you now going to have a night away with

Lambros?'

'We actually talked about that and because we have only a few days left here we've decided not to, but I'm sure I'll be back soon and then we can see how we feel.'

'So you're definitely coming back to Vekianos then?'

'Oh yes, why wouldn't I? I've found a place I love, and I feel comfortable, relaxed, and very safe here. And if I'm coming by myself those are the things that are very important to me. Ok, I won't be staying where we are now at the villa – that experience is a one-off – but as long as I have a nice, clean, modern studio with some outside space, whether it's a terrace or a balcony, I'll be very happy. There are gorgeous restaurants, fabulous shops, beautiful beaches, and lots of friendly faces. Who wouldn't want to return as often as possible?'

'I get that because after the thing with Polina today I had a lovely long walk and literally every few metres I found I was saying to myself I could easily sit myself down here and paint. I would move here at a drop of a hat if I could earn a living from my paintings. Oh yes, it would be goodbye decorating, hello Vekianos!'

As they sat in silence for a moment, different thoughts going around in their heads, the one thing they all had in common was their love for this beautiful Greek island that was new to all of them, but which they already felt so connected to in such a short space of time.

'Time for food. Are you two ready?' asked Angela.

They paid for the wines and then strolled back across the harbour to Alina's Restaurant, which was still surprisingly busy. Sakis spotted them and came out, showering them with lots of hugs and kisses. He pointed out a table that would be leaving in about fifteen minutes if they wanted to wait.

'Thank you, Sakis, we'll just be over there by the sea wall. There's no hurry.'

They crossed over the little pathway to lean up against the wall and while Simon and Angela looked out at the boats, Carla looked back into the restaurant. There were Nectarios rushing around, Alina taking an order, and of course Sakis laughing and joking in his own special way. It was a happy place, but could she see herself working there for a couple of weeks? The answer to that was ... yes. It would be hard work but also so enjoyable, and what was two weeks out of her life? Time with Nectarios after work would also be very nice...

But there was one downside to it all, and it would be a huge problem: she already knew that after two weeks she wouldn't want to leave and go back to England.

'You ok?' asked Angela. 'You looked like you were miles away.'

'I was. No Lambros tonight by the looks of it,' she said, not ready to talk through what she was thinking just yet. 'Your afternoon at the villa must have worn him out.'

'Perhaps so. That or he's avoiding me. You know, I've never stood here looking in before. It's very different than being sat in there, don't you think? It makes a lovely picture with people sat at the tables and all the bright colours of their clothes. It looks like a really joyful scene.'

'I agree. I'm actually kind of glad we didn't just go in and sit down right away. It's been nice to stand here and look over for a few minutes. A nice holiday memory to take back with me.'

Carla spotted Nectarios walking towards them just then.

'Your table is ready. I'm sorry to disappoint you, but you're on my side of the restaurant tonight, not Sakis's, so it might not be as much fun.'

'That's not a problem at all. And who knows? It might still be fun. We'll have to wait and see how you entertain us,' joked Angela.

They followed him over to a table for four and he pulled the chair out for Angela to sit. Angela was in control tonight and firing on all cylinders, the complete opposite to the night before, when she'd looked so uncomfortable.

'Good evening and welcome,' said Alina. She handed them each a menu and placed a carafe of wine on the table. 'Sakis tells me you had a nice day on the beach, Carla. I expect you're exhausted though as it certainly wouldn't have been relaxing. A few years ago I spent the day with him and oh my goodness! I never knew there was a special way to walk down to the sea, and then there's the walk back with all that flicking of the hair.' Alina shook her head while the others laughed at Sakis's antics.

'Did I hear my name?' asked Sakis, sidling over to their table.

'Yes, I was telling them about the day we went to the beach and you had me walking like a fashion model across the sand. I was exhausted by the end of the day.'

'Yes, but you had fun, didn't you?'

'I did, Sakis, it was a lovely day. I'll leave you with the menus for now,' she said, addressing the table. 'Just shout over when you're ready to order.'

'Is your dad not here tonight?' asked Angela.

'No, he called me to say he was tired as he had a few drinks this afternoon, so he was having an early night.'

'I'm afraid that's my fault as we had a few glasses more than we probably should have. But at least we cleared up our misunderstanding.'

'What is he like?! Did he tell you I hit him? I can't believe how naive he was.'

'It's all ok now, and very funny really. I'm glad we both know where we stand.'

Alina left them to look at the menus but Carla wasn't really concentrating. She couldn't take her eyes off Nectarios, and she could see that he was looking at her, too.

'Just three more days and three more nights left of the holiday. All of a sudden the days are flying by,' said Angela.

'I was thinking that earlier, and there's still so much to get sorted before we leave. But saying that, you've sorted your little problem, Angela, and hopefully you and Lambros will be able to have another day out before we go. I think I need to text Polina and see where I stand. I might do that in the morning. Whoever would have thought my holiday would become so complicated? I was most looking forward to painting while I was here and it's the one thing I haven't really done.'

'You'll have to come back again sometime. Perhaps in the next couple of days we should enquire about accommodation here in the harbour,' mused Angela.

'No, I don't think I'll be back. I've had a lovely time with you two but with all this hassle with Polina I somehow don't think I'll be welcome. So that just leaves you to sort your situation, Carla.'

'You've lost me completely, Simon. My situation?'

Carla immediately wished she had just smiled and laughed Simon's comment off. She already knew exactly what he was going to say.

'You and Nectarios, of course. The tension between you both has been building more and more every time we come here to eat. You can't take your eyes off of him and he's the same. You must have noticed how many times he's walked into tables and chairs while we've been sat here tonight. He only has eyes for one thing, and that's you.'

'Is it that obvious?'

'Yes. Simon's right. Now, time to order. What are we all having? Would you like to share a tzatziki to start with? I'm having the swordfish for my main.'

Thankfully, Angela's query changed the subject completely. The food was ordered and arrived, and as per usual it was beautiful. They chatted away as they ate, and Sakis kept popping over to them with his little one-liners, which had them almost constantly in fits of laughter. Any tension that was there when they'd first sat down was now well and truly gone.

'Has everything been ok for you?'

'Oh yes, thank you, Alina. As always, the food has been top-notch and of course Sakis's entertainment has had us in stitches. Gosh, we're the only table left,' said Angela, looking around them. 'This is becoming a habit. You'll likely be glad to see the back of us when we leave in a few days' time.'

'Excuse me, I need the bathroom.'

With that Carla got up and headed inside and Alina sat on the empty seat.

'To be honest, I'm dreading the three of you leaving. I know my dad will be going around with a sad face and as for my son... What can I say? Both Sakis and I are desperately hoping we don't get the old Nectarios back.'

Nectarios grabbed Carla on her way back to the table, saying, 'We've nearly finished here so I was wondering, would you like to go for a drink? A few of the bars stay open late and it's always a nice atmosphere. I'm sure you would enjoy it.'

'I'd love to have a drink with you, but perhaps not in a bar. How about in your apartment? I think I would enjoy that a lot more.'

Chapter 27
Holiday day 11

Nectarios smiled at her. 'Good morning, would you like a coffee?'

'What time is it?' Carla asked groggily.

'Eight forty-five. It's still early so you can go back to sleep if you'd like.'

'Have you been awake long?'

'Just a little while.'

'Ok, I'll get up too. And yes, coffee would be nice.'

As Nectarios walked out of the room Carla realised this wasn't a dream. She really had woken up in Nectarios's bed! Her first thought was that she wished she could look in a mirror as she must look a mess. Nectarios returned with the coffees before she could move though, so there wasn't anything she could do about it for now.

'Thank you. Do you need to be getting ready to go to the restaurant? I can make a move and go,' she offered, feeling a bit uncertain about what she should or shouldn't do now that they were face to face in the bright morning light.

'No, I'm good. I have the morning off so we can spend it together. That's only if you want to of course,' he rushed to add.

Maybe he was feeling the same nerves she was? The thought was reassuring.

Carla smiled and sipped her coffee. She wasn't quite sure what she was feeling, but right now it felt a lot like happiness. And as she looked over to Nectarios, she could tell he felt the same.

'If you like, we could go to the beach or take a walk. Or would you like to go out for some breakfast?'

'I'm more than happy to stay here. But if it's ok with you, could I have a quick shower?'

'Yes, of course. While you're doing that I could go to the bakery and fetch us something nice.'

'Thanks.'

They sat in the bed quietly sipping away at their coffee for a moment and Carla wondered how Nectarios was feeling. She had invited herself into his apartment and she couldn't actually remember if he had said yes. What she could remember was whispering to Angela that she wouldn't be back to the villa last night. And then she remembered Angela's smile and her quick, 'Have fun.'

'What are you laughing at?'

'Nothing really, just something Angela said to me about having fun.'

'And did you?'

'Oh yes.'

'Me too. I'm glad you invited yourself back here.'

'That was probably very rude of me. Sorry.'

'It wasn't rude at all. It was actually a blessing because I was too scared to ask you myself. Now, you have your shower. There are plenty of clean towels in the cupboard there,' he said, pointing into the hall, 'and feel free to use any of the toiletries you see.'

She sat and watched as he put on a t-shirt and flip-flops, then waved him off. The bakery wasn't very far away so she needed to rush in and out of the shower before he got back. Once in the bathroom a look in the mirror revealed that she looked a mess and very tired, but that wasn't too surprising as they'd probably only had about four hours of sleep.

The shower was powerful, the water was hot, and she could have quite happily stood under it for hours, but there was no time for that now. She was just drying herself when she heard the apartment door open. Quickly wrapping one towel around her and a smaller one around her hair she took a final glance in the mirror. She looked a bit more awake now and felt tons better. Nectarios had left her some clean clothes on the edge of the bed, and she slipped on one of his t-shirts, wearing it like a dress.

'That is a lovely shower,' she told him as she walked into the kitchen. 'And you have a really nice apartment. Have you been living here long?'

'About three years. My granddad owned it and he thought it would be good for me to have my own place because it would have been a lot for my mum and I to work and live together. And he was right. Take a seat on the balcony and I'll bring the food out.'

Carla made her way out onto the little balcony, which had just enough room for two chairs and a small table between them. The apartment was two floors up, above a clothes shop, and there was a nice view of a street, which was increasingly busy as the harbour came to life.

'There you go. I brought a selection of pastries so dive in. The coffee won't be a minute.'

Carla waited for Nectarios to come back before helping herself to the treats.

'The coffee here is so good, it's really rich and fresh tasting, and there's just something about having it here in the sunshine on the island.'

'There's nothing quite like a coffee, especially first thing in the morning. It sets me up for the day, and if I'm on an early shift at the restaurant I have a cup on the go all morning long.'

'I'm the exact same. The pastries are really good today. I dread to think how many Simon, Angela, and I have had since we arrived. Probably too many, but we're on holiday, so...' She shrugged.

'The bakery has been in the same family for many generations. I can remember going there when I was very young, so it holds lots of great memories for me.'

There was a silence and for the first time that morning Carla didn't know what to say.

Nectarios laughed. 'Look at us, sat here talking about coffee and the bakery. Why does it suddenly feel so awkward?'

'I know what you mean. Perhaps I should get dressed and—'

'*Or*, perhaps we should go back to bed? There was definitely no awkwardness there.'

Carla smiled as a wave of memories from the night before washed over her. 'I'd like that.'

As they both stood up someone shouted up from the pavement and Carla recognized the voice – it was Sakis. Should she head back inside and pretend she hadn't heard him? Looking at Nectarios they both froze before breaking out in laughter. There was no denying they'd been caught out!

'Can you hear me?' shouted Sakis.

Carla was pretty sure the whole island could hear him.

'I was just saying that shirt really suits you, Carla, the perfect thing to wear when you've just got out of bed. Hope you too have a lovely morning,' said Sakis, making the words sound as suggestive as possible. He waved and strutted away, clearly pleased with himself.

'We deserved that, didn't we?' She laughed.

'Probably. We should count ourselves lucky for getting off so lightly considering I've said a lot worse to him over the years. Now, are you sure about this?'

'I'm very sure. That coffee we couldn't stop talking about has given me a real buzz of energy...'

*

'Right, I've done it, Angela, I have texted Polina and apologised. I also said that if she wanted to meet up, I'm here for three more days.'

'I'm glad. There's no more you can do as it's out of your hands, so try to forget about it for now. Have you anything nice planned for today?'

'Nothing apart from a swim and time spent around the pool.'

'Why don't we go out? Not to the harbour but somewhere else. How about the little town where Lambros and I went to have dinner? Keriaphos. We could get a taxi over and have some lunch and a little sit on the beach. It will do us both a world of good.'

Half an hour later they were ready and stepping into the taxi.

Like all the people who lived and worked on the island, the driver was lovely and very chatty, explaining that the little town was at the bottom of a very steep hill and asking where they would like to be dropped off.

'Definitely at the bottom, in the town,' Simon quickly replied.

'Oh yes, I'm not dressed for hills today,' agreed Angela.

The driver said that was fine and in no time he had pulled into a little parking space. Simon paid and thanked him, and they headed off towards the beach.

'I think we need to turn here, Angela, as the people heading this way are carrying beach things. Oh yes, here we are. I can't see any sunbeds so we might have to sit on the sand.'

'I worry that once I get down, I'll never get back up! I think we might need to look for a rock or something to sit on.'

Simon carried Angela's bag for her as they

walked across the sand towards a rock they could put their towels down on. It looked like it should be ok for a short sit down.

'This is lovely!' enthused Angela after they'd been sitting and enjoying the sunshine for a while. 'I can now see why Carla enjoyed it so much when she came with Sakis. Look at the sea, it's so clear. This island never fails to surprise and delight me and I've still only really seen a very small part of it.'

'Yes, we made a really good choice with Vekianos, and none of it would have happened without your generosity—'

'I'm going to stop you right there, Simon,' interrupted Angela. 'You and Carla have both said thank you more than enough, and as I've told you many times, it's my pleasure. I would have happily paid double or even treble for this as I've gotten so much more out of this visit than just my fabulous tan because it's taught me that every day we get should be cherished and lived to the fullest. Now, my behind is starting to hurt on this rock. Shall we head off and see what else this gorgeous little town has to offer us?'

Once off the beach and shaking the sand off their feet Simon was feeling a little shaky.

'Could we go and have a cold drink somewhere? Not alcohol, just water or lemonade. I feel like I need to sit down in the shade and collect myself.'

'Of course. That restaurant over there has big umbrellas we could shade under.'

'Perfect.'

Angela could see Simon looked a bit off and worried he was feeling ill. Had they had too much sun? Whatever it was, she would wait as long as it took until he felt better before they continued their exploration of the little town.

'I need to thank you again,' he said once they

were settled and he'd had some water.

'I'm not sure what you're thanking me for as you've bought the drinks,' she joked.

'I want to thank you for what you said back there on the beach about how every day we're alive is a gift and not one minute should be wasted.'

'It's true. I only wish I had learned that years ago.'

'It's made me realise that I'm wasting my life dreaming of being an artist. The only way it's ever going to happen is if I do something about it. I need to put all the reasons I've used in the past to not do it out of my head for good, and I need to say goodbye to the decorating and just paint. And do you know, I'm going to start tomorrow. Yes, tomorrow there is going to be a whole new world starting for me.'

Chapter 28
Holiday day 12

It was only six forty-five in the morning, but Simon was up and dressed, and he'd already had two coffees. He was ready and eager to get going. With only two days left of the holiday there was no time to waste, so today he was off to do what he should have been doing from the day they arrived: painting. He was still shocked and slightly numb from his day out with Angela. He had so much to thank her for because if it wasn't for their chat on the beach, he wouldn't be heading out now to produce some art. Of course, he was nervous. Though he knew where he was going, and he knew exactly what he was going to paint as he had been looking at the scene for nearly two weeks, the question was: could he transfer it to the canvas and do it justice?

Closing the villa gate behind him he started out on the ten-minute walk down to the harbour. There was one point in the middle of the night where he thought he could start painting, the image he wanted to capture was that clear in his head, but no, he needed to be there with it right in front of him to get it just right. As he was walking down the little street, he thought back to last night's dinner in the villa. Angela was quite quiet as she was tired – it had been a long day and they had done a lot of walking – and Carla was in a very mellow mood, not just happy but truly content. He suspected it was because she was in love.

As for him ... well, he probably bored them to tears with all his art talk, but he couldn't help it, he had never been this excited in his life. There would be no more ifs, ands, or buts. No, this was it. He was ready to follow his dreams and become a true artist.

He had realised that if he didn't believe in himself, no one else would.

Carla had asked what his parents would say when he got back to Norfolk and told them he was giving up the painting and decorating to concentrate on this art, and though he knew they would support him no matter what, in truth it didn't matter what they said or thought. This was what he wanted to do for the rest of his life. Painting was his passion, and no one was ever going to stand in his way.

He was nearly at the spot where he planned to paint, right at the very end of the harbour wall where the promenade changed into a rough path, and though he didn't have an easel, he was determined to make it work. Thankfully, the boat he wanted to paint was still moored exactly where it had been the whole holiday.

He found a rock to sit on, which wasn't exactly comfortable or perfect, but he wouldn't let that little obstacle stand in his way, and getting everything out of his bag that he needed, he was soon ready to get going. But just as he was ready to put paint to canvas, big, dark doubt clouds rolled in. Who did he think he was, building himself up to be this great artist with so much potential?

Standing up and walking a few steps nearer to the boat he did his best to ignore the naysaying thoughts and snap out of the doubt. If he didn't at least try he knew he would regret it for the rest of his life. Sat back on the rock once more, he placed his bag in front of him and used it to balance the canvas against, muttering to himself 'please work, please work...'. It did, just, but he needed a counterbalance in front of the canvas to stop it from rocking as he painted. Looking around he spotted a stone that looked heavy enough to do the job. Once that was sorted, it was now time to face the blank white canvas. This was it.

The paintings of the olive trees he'd seen in the gallery in Parga were his inspiration for how he wanted to approach the light within the piece, and he hoped to achieve with the boats what the other artist had achieved with the trees. To begin, his focus would be the boat and the light, nothing else.

Three hours later his back was hurting and when he tried to stand up it was so uncomfortable. He walked around a little bit to try and loosen up his tensed muscles, and then he stood looking at the boat from different angles. Walking back to the rock he looked at what he had painted on the canvas, seeing it as a whole for the first time, as he had been focused on it in pieces as he painted.

He was a bit disappointed with the actual boat, which he felt still needed so much more work, but he at least had captured the dimensions and character of it the way he'd hoped to. And he was pleased overall with what he'd accomplished so far, and knew the rest he could achieve back at the villa later.

Sitting back down he felt himself welling up and then the tears started. It was a feeling of relief that he could do it, but more than that, joy that he was now living his dream, a dream that he'd had since he was about thirteen years old. Taking his water bottle out of his bag he took a long sip and then breathed the hugest sigh of relief.

Packing up all his tools a while later, he left the harbour and started to make his way back up to the villa. He couldn't believe he had been painting for so long, and he was thrilled that he had started two pieces of work he was already so proud of. Whether he would be saying that later when he tried to focus on making the two boats stand out might be a completely different story, however...

With all the time and concentration he had put into the paintings he should be tired, but he was the opposite. Apart from needing to get some food, he was ready to drive straight back into working on the paintings.

Looking at his phone he saw he had missed a text from Carla to say she and Angela were off to do some shopping, and that they might eat early before heading back to the villa. It was just what Simon wanted to hear as it meant he could quickly make something to eat before getting stuck into painting with no one to disturb him.

Waiting for his pasta to cook back at the villa, he placed the two paintings next to each other. They still needed a lot of work, but they looked like a pair and that meant they could be part of a collection. As he stood there, he realised that if it wasn't for the paintings of the olive trees he might never have created this type of art. Once again he was so glad he'd wandered into that gallery on Parga.

Chapter 29
Holiday day 12

Angela was sat quietly reading her book on the terrace and for once she wasn't waiting for the others to get up. No, Simon had gone out early to paint and Carla had spent a second night at Nectarios's after meeting him when he finished in the restaurant the night before.

Angela couldn't get over the difference in Simon. One minute he was upset with the whole Polina situation and had no interest whatsoever in getting his paints out, and the next he had changed the course of his whole life and was almost running out the door to go and paint. Oh how she wished she'd had his confidence thirty years ago.

When Mark ended their relationship she should have pulled herself up and took on the world, but no, she just plodded on as she was. What a waste of years.

Well, no more. Angela was determined to enjoy every moment she had left.

As for Carla, the big question was how this latest development in her relationship with Nectarios would affect her next step. Would she go home and find a career, or would the gorgeous Greek tempt her to turn her holiday into a permanent relocation? One thing was for sure, the last two days of their holiday would be anything but boring! Going back in to make another coffee, she wondered if she would have a visit from Lambros today. It would be nice to see him and perhaps she should just check her appearance in the mirror as a precaution. Was she dressed acceptably to welcome a visitor? The thought made her laugh. She sounded like a teenager, and not a seventy-year-old woman!

This time she took her coffee down to the pool. There were only two swimming days left and she was going to make the most of them, wanting to embrace the things she wouldn't be able to do when she got home. Thinking of home, she realised that one thing she needed to do in the next couple of days was to buy a gift to take back to Carla's mum, Jan, as a 'thank you' for taking care of Molly. Ok, she was paying her to do so, but it would still be nice to do something extra. Jan deserved it.

When her drink was finished she decided to do a few lengths of the pool – both for happiness and for her health, which had flourished being here on the island and being so active. Yes, she had put on a bit of weight over the holiday – mostly down to the wine and the nibbles and snacks in between meals, and of course the treats from the bakery hadn't helped either – but vacations were meant for indulging in all that the destination had to offer, and so Angela didn't regret a single moment.

An hour later she had dried off after a lovely swim in the morning sunshine, and she settled into a lounge chair in the shade, already assuming that she would probably nod off at some point before repeating the whole cycle.

Carla came through the gate just then and the two women greeted each other warmly.

'I wasn't expecting you so early.'

'It's Nectarios's day to work the lunch shift,' explained Carla.

As Carla walked up to the villa Angela could see how happy she looked. And as much as she wanted to ask her lots of questions, she also knew it was really none of her business.

'No Simon? Oh, of course. He's gone out painting hasn't he. I do hope it's a success.'

'Me too. I suspect it will all be well as he seems very determined. I'm glad he's put that business with Polina behind him. In a way I wish he had never met her as I think it's sort of spoiled some of his holiday.'

'Yes, but he's also had some great moments, and he's said over and over how much he's enjoying the time the three of us have spent together. We've all laughed so much and I like how we tease each other. There's definitely been no pussy footing around each other!'

'I have to agree. Hopefully we can continue with our close friendship once we're all back in Saltmarsh Quay.'

'I'm sure we will. I have to admit that I'm not sure if I'm ready to go back to Norfolk just yet.'

Seeing how close Nectarios and Carla had grown in recent days, Angela had been expecting this. Carla was a young adult and she needed to do what she thought was best for herself. Whether she and Nectarios would have a future together was something only time would tell, but it was something they would figure out together. She knew Carla wasn't quite ready to discuss it yet though, so she changed the subject.

'I thought I might wander down to the shops at some point today as I want to get your mum something nice for looking after Molly.'

'You don't need to do that, Angela. You're paying her and that's enough. She really won't be expecting a gift, and if anything, it's me that should be buying her something ... and it hadn't even crossed my mind. How bad is that? I'll go with you. What sort of time were you thinking?'

'I thought late afternoon so we could grab

something to eat after and then be back here before it gets too late. I'll need the rest as it's our last day tomorrow and I expect it will be a late night.'

'Sounds perfect, and it gives us a few hours here in the gorgeous sunshine before we need to get ready.'

'Yes. I was planning to take a little nap.'

'You sleep away, Angela, and I'll lay here pondering my future.'

Carla lapsed into silence as she contemplated all the thoughts swirling in her head. Last night with Nectarios was even more special than the night before, and she loved the fact that she could just say whatever was in her head without second guessing. She was one hundred percent herself when she was with him, and she really believed he was the same.

But the future was something neither had talked about. There were a couple of times where she'd thought she should mention what Sakis had said about her stepping in to cover for him so he could go over to Corfu and spend time with Trifon, but just as she was about to, Nectarios started to talk about something else. And the more she thought about it, the more unsure she was. Sakis would only be away for two weeks so what would she do afterward? Alina wouldn't need another member of staff.

Come on, Carla, your head is in the clouds. This isn't a prince and princess fairytale, it's real life – your life – and that is back in England ... not necessarily in Norfolk, but certainly not here on a Greek island.

'You look lovely, Angela, I haven't seen that dress before.'

'Thank you. I went through all of my clothes to see what I haven't worn yet and there were about three tops and two dresses, so I picked one of the two for tomorrow night and that just left this one.'

'I wish I was as organised as you. I dread to think how much I've not worn. But saying that, I think this is the first time this top has had an outing,' she said, looking down at herself. 'Are we ready? I've texted Simon to tell him what we're up to, but he's not messaged back yet.'

'I'm ready. Perhaps we could go a different way when we get down among the little shops? I feel we always cut through the same little streets and there are so many more to explore.'

'Of course!'

They took their time wandering down as it was still very hot. It wasn't really the best time to be out and about but it did mean the streets were a bit quieter, most of the tourists either on the beaches or staying inside.

After perusing the gift shops and then the exquisite lace shops they agreed it was time for a sit down and a drink.

'I'm not sure I'm ready for any wine yet, Carla, just some water for me I think.'

'I'm craving the same. Why don't you sit here on this bench in the shade while I fetch us a couple of bottles? I'll only be a couple of minutes.'

'Oh thank you,' said Angela, relieved to have a chance to take the weight off her feet for a while.

Sitting down, Angela realised this was the little courtyard square where she'd first met Lambros and was rude about his house, but this time she was looking in a different direction.

'There we go. I went right to the back of the fridge to get the coldest bottles I could.'

'Thank you. I was just remembering this is where I was rude to Lambros about his scruffy house. That seems ages ago now but it was actually less than two weeks ago.'

'Which house is his?'

'It's behind us. If you turn around you won't need me to point it out as it's very obvious.'

Carla turned around so she could see all the houses behind them but was she missing something? There wasn't a scruffy façade in sight, though one did have scaffolding up on the front of it.

'You'll probably think I'm daft, but I can't see a scruffy house.'

'Just a minute while I get up and point it out...' Angela turned and froze, a look of shock on her face. 'Oh my goodness, you're right! His is the one with the scaffolding. It looks like it's being painted.'

'Didn't he tell you he wasn't going to do anything with it?'

'No, he said that the more his family and friends nagged him about it, the more he was going to stick his heels in the ground and refuse to do anything about it.'

'Well, something has evidently happened to change his mind. I know you might not want to hear it ... but I think it's you. Nectarios told me Lambros had been out and bought new clothes to impress you, and it looks like he's now doing the same with his home.'

Angela didn't know what to say, but she instinctively knew there was some truth in what Carla had said. Here she was thinking Carla and Simon were having a strange last few days of their holiday, and now it looked like hers might be quite unexpected as well!

Chapter 30
Holiday day 12

'Just a few more yards, Angela, and we'll be at the gate.'

'I really should have listened to you, Carla, when you suggested we get a taxi. I suppose all the walking around from one shop to another has added up, but I've had a lovely time and it's been fun and different. The meal was also nice, though it felt strange eating that early compared with most other nights we've been here.'

'The light is on. Simon must be back.' Carla checked the time on her phone. 'Believe it or not, it's not as early as I thought. Nearly a quarter to nine.'

'Really? Some nights we've been going out at this time.'

As they walked up the path they could see Simon with his canvas on the kitchen worktop. Carla smiled. He really looked like an artist and that made her so happy. At last he was doing what he'd come on holiday to do, and even more importantly, he was doing something he really loved.

'Hi, you two, have you had a nice day?' he asked.

'We have, haven't we, Carla? Now, you carry on. We don't want to disturb you and anyway, I need to go and change and get my comfortable slippers on.'

'You aren't disturbing me at all. I'm just fiddling, putting a bit of paint here and a bit there, not knowing when to stop and say enough is enough.'

'That is so good!' Carla exclaimed as she looked over his shoulder. 'Look, Angela, it's that boat from the harbour. You must be so pleased with yourself,

Simon, it's fabulous.'

'It really is,' agreed Angela. 'I suppose we don't need to ask if you've had a nice day.'

'I have had the perfect day and I really am so happy with the result, mainly because I didn't know if I was capable of this. The inspiration I got from the olive tree paintings over on Parga has helped so much. It was all about the simplicity and the light, nothing else, so that's all I focused on when I was out today, and the work I've done in the last three or four hours has pulled everything together. That's it! No more painting talk. I bored you both yesterday and I'm not doing it again. Once you've changed we can talk clothes and handbags.'

'Oh no, no clothes talk, just scaffolding talk ... isn't that right, Angela? Open the wine, Simon, and we'll tell you everything.'

They both went off to change and Simon took one last look at his two paintings. He knew he could improve both, but he'd achieved what he'd wanted to in such a short time and that was a promising start. Putting all his art things away, he knew everything depended on tomorrow. He likely wouldn't sleep well but in just one day he had come so far, and he was looking forward to carrying his plan forward.

Wine poured, and crisps and nibbles put in bowls, Simon was ready to hear what sounded like a very strange story. As he sat at the table waiting for the others he glanced at his phone and then he realised something – he hadn't thought of Polina all day. But was that a good thing or a bad thing? He didn't know. What he *did* know was that he missed her, but how could he when they'd spent so little time together? Was it the art talk that had created this connection between them? Or was it perhaps a desire to protect her from her mother? Whatever it was, there was no denying that he really liked her.

'So, are you ready to explain what you meant?' he asked Carla. 'What have you and Angela been up to?'

'I should wait until Angela comes out.'

'I'm here! You tell the story though, Carla.'

'Ok, now, Simon, you know how when Angela first met Lambros she was not so nice about his house? Well, it's being painted! We spotted the scaffolding covering the façade and given that we're both nosey, we walked up near the house to take a closer look—'

'I want to add at this point that it wasn't my idea to do that,' Angela interjected.

'It doesn't matter whose idea it was,' said Carla, brushing past the interruption. 'When we got sort of close to the house we could see the whole place is being gutted. What do you say to that?'

'I would say Lambros is having his house refurbished.'

'Yes, that's obvious, but the big question is why?'

'Because he wants to, I presume.' Simon shrugged.

'But don't you think it's suspicious timing, him deciding to finally do something about his house right before Angela leaves? Especially as he knows she wants to come back to Vekianos.'

'You could be right, but then you could also be wrong. There's only one way to find out, and that's for Angela to ask him, and she only has one day to do it. Now, talking about one day ... I know we originally said we would spend tomorrow here by the pool, but I need to nip out for a few hours as I want to take my two paintings over to Parga to that gallery.'

'That's fabulous, but please don't feel you need to rush back. I will be perfectly happy here by myself.'

'You won't be by yourself, Angela, I'll be here.'

'I thought as tomorrow is Nectarios's morning off you would spend it with him? Anyway, it would be good for me to have some time to myself as I need to get my packing done. I don't want to leave it until the day we leave. Speaking of Nectarios, what time are you meeting him tonight?'

'He said he hoped to finish by eleven-thirty, but if he's any earlier he'll text.'

'Great! So we're all sorted for tomorrow. You will spend the morning with Nectarios until he has to go to work, Simon will take a nice boat trip to Parga and back, and I'll pack. Who knows, maybe I'll have a visit from Lambros telling me his news about his house and inviting me back to stay when it's finished.'

'You are being very presumptuous, Angela.'

'I am, and if that's not the case I have to admit I'll be very disappointed. Now, I think we could have another glass of wine, don't you both?'

For the next hour they drank wine and reminisced about their two weeks on the island – all the lovely days spent at the villa, all the gorgeous food they had eaten, and all the little dramas and misunderstandings they had been involved with.

It was just gone ten o'clock when Angela and Simon both said they were ready for their beds. They were both very tired and Simon wanted to be up early to catch the first boat over to Parga.

'I might go and change and head down to the harbour to have a little mooch around while I wait for Nectarios, perhaps sit and have a drink. Are you sure it's ok for me to not come back until the afternoon tomorrow?' asked Carla.

'Yes of course, and then in the evening I presume we'll eat down in Alina's Restaurant as it's our last night? Is that ok for you, Simon?'

'Perfect, thank you. For now, I'm off to my bed. Have a lovely evening, Carla.'

'Thank you and good luck at the gallery tomorrow! I can't wait to hear all about it.'

Twenty minutes later Carla was heading down to the harbour. The little town seemed quieter tonight. Her first stop was the restaurant to let Nectarios know she was down in the harbour and as she got closer, she noticed there weren't that many occupied tables left. She could see Sakis waving to her so she walked over to him.

'Carla, you have perfect timing! I was just going to stop for a ten-minute break so we can sit and have a drink and a chat. We've been quiet tonight as there doesn't seem to be as many visitors walking around. By the way, I'm doing you a favour. Once my break is over, I've said I can finish off here and Nectarios can leave early. Now, take a seat and I'll fetch us a couple of glasses of wine.'

'Thank you, that's very kind.'

With that Nectarios came over and gave her a kiss.

'Has Sakis told you he's letting me leave early? I just need to get all this cleared away while he takes his break. It won't take long.'

'Stop chatting and get some work done!' Sakis ordered as he returned with the drinks.

All three laughed and off Nectarios went to clear the empty tables.

'Thank you again, Sakis.'

'Not a problem at all. I'm actually glad you popped down early because I wanted to ask you something. You know how we talked well about me going over to see Trifon on Corfu and I sort of suggested you could step in and do my job for a couple of weeks?'

Carla nodded.

'Well, since that conversation things have obviously changed. You and Nectarios are a lot closer and I know the last thing he wants is for you to go back to England. I still haven't mentioned my idea to anyone apart from you, and I realise time is running out, so I was wondering how you're feeling about the idea? I know you're more than capable of doing the job and that you would have the full support of Nectarios and Alina.'

'I don't know... Don't you think it all sounds a bit fairytale-like? Girl comes on holiday, falls in love with the gorgeous waiter, and they end up working together.'

'Yes, and then they live happily ever after.'

'Exactly. That's a fairytale and not real life.'

'Well, Carla, I have to say that if you don't have faith or believe in happy endings then you might as well head back to England and forget the whole holiday romance ever happened.'

'That told me, didn't it? I'm sorry, Sakis, but the whole thing just seems a little too perfect.'

'And what's wrong with perfect? It's what we all strive for, isn't it? We all want a happy ending but to get to that point we have to take chances along the way. Sometimes they pay off and other times they don't work out, but you don't know which way it will go unless you try. We're talking about a two-week commitment that would see you working here and also getting to know Nectarios a little better. The ball, as they say, is in your court. I'd be happy to mention it to Alina tonight and see what she says.'

'What do you think she might say?'

'Oh, I know exactly what she'll say because she is loving the new Nectarios. He's thrown himself into the restaurant these last couple of weeks and has worked harder than ever before. His whole attitude is different and that is down to you, Carla.'

As she sat there she wondered if she was brave enough to take the risk and give it a go. She wouldn't know if it would work out unless she tried. And if it did? Could this be her fairytale happy ending?

Chapter 31
Holiday day 13

Carla couldn't sleep. Even though it had been another late night her head was all over the place. She didn't know if Sakis had said anything to Alina or not, but she suspected that if he had, he would have texted her. As she climbed out of bed and closed the bedroom door behind her, she hoped she hadn't disturbed Nectarios. Heading into the kitchen she really wanted a coffee but putting the kettle on would make too much noise, so she settled for a cold glass of juice. Gently opening the balcony door and then sitting down she could see the little town was still asleep, just one or two people in the street below.

Instead of coming right back here last night, she and Nectarios had gone for a drink with a few of his friends, who were very nice, and she'd liked them very much. But the best part of the evening was the fact that even though there were eight of them sat around a table, laughing, joking, and chatting, Nectarios hadn't been able to take his eyes off of her. And every time their eyes met, he had a smile on his face that made her feel special and very happy.

She realised Nectarios was the icing on her cake but there was a lot more to that cake – the beautiful island of Vekianos, the people... It was everything here, really. But could she make a life here? For a start, her mum would be back in England. Could she really move to a different country without her? Surely they would miss each other too much. But thinking that, she had lived away from home at uni and had been contemplating moving away from Norfolk to start her career anyway. She nearly jumped out of her seat as the door behind her opened, startling her out of her thoughts.

'You're up early, and you've not made yourself a coffee.'

'I didn't want to disturb you.'

'Who says I didn't want to be disturbed?' Nectarios winked. 'I'll go and get the coffees. Did you want it out here or back in the bedroom?'

'Do you mind if we sit here to drink it?'

'Of course not.'

While he made the drinks Carla nipped to the bathroom. Looking in the mirror she wasn't really bothered with how messy her hair was, or the fact that last night's make-up was smudged. Those things just didn't really seem important to her at the moment.

'Thank you, that smells lovely,' she said, accepting the mug once she was back outside.

'You're welcome. Did you enjoy meeting my friends last night? You weren't disappointed we didn't come right back here, are you?'

'Not at all. It was really nice and such a laugh. They were a lot of fun.'

'Yes, even though they were teasing me and telling you far too many stories about me.'

'I liked that. It was honestly a lovely evening... I think that's your phone beeping.'

'It likely won't be anything important. What would you like to do today? How about while you think about it I nip and get us some pastries? I think that's *your* phone beeping now.'

Carla had a look at her phone, and found a text from Sakis to say he had spoken to Alina, and she'd told him she'd have to think about it and talk it over with Nectarios. As she finished reading the text she looked up to find Nectarios was looking at his phone.

'It's my mum. She wants to know if I can pop into the restaurant for five minutes as she needs to ask me something.'

'I think I know what it's all about, and I'm not sure if you'll be happy.'

'What do you mean?'

'Sakis wants to go to Corfu to visit Trifon but obviously it's the busiest time of the year for the restaurant, so he's had this brain wave ... that I could do his job while he's away.'

'What a fabulous idea! We'd have a great time working together. How exciting.' Nectarios smile stretched wide.

'Yes, it will be fun, but do you think I'm capable of doing the job? Sakis works very hard and I just worry I could never be as good as him.'

'You aren't him and you don't need to be him. You'll be bringing yourself to the job, just like he brings Sakis, and the customers will love you.'

'You think so?'

'I do, and I am so happy because it will give me two weeks to convince you to stay on Vekianos permanently. On that note, I'll go and grab our breakfast and then pop in to see my mum and I might even wind Sakis up and tell him you won't do it so he can't take time off.'

As Nectarios went out the apartment door singing away, Carla sat on the side of the bed lost in her thoughts. It was good that Nectarios was so happy but would they work as well together as he thought?

She was starting to panic. What had she got herself into? It was one thing staying overnight with Nectarios, but working with him day in and day out for two weeks was another matter entirely. She had to get out of the apartment and go back to the villa.

She needed time to think. Getting out her phone she texted Nectarios.

sorry, can't stay for breakfast. Angela has an emergency at the villa. see you in the restaurant tonight, Carla xx

Chapter 32
Holiday day 13

Simon was in the harbour way before he needed to be as the boat over to Parga wouldn't leave for another hour. He sat on a seat near where the boat was, drinking a takeaway coffee from the bakery. No pastries today as he couldn't face any food; his stomach was turning with nerves and his head was full of questions and doubts. Was he believing his own hype? Did he think his work was better than it actually was? Most important of all, was he kidding himself that he could make a living selling his paintings?

He couldn't sit still and so he walked a little way down by the sea wall. He needed to give himself a good talking to, and he needed to calm down. It was what it was. Within a few hours he would be at the gallery and hearing the opinion of the owner.

He checked the time on his phone – why wasn't it moving? – then looked up and recognised the person walking towards him.

Polina.

Would she speak to him? This was so awkward.

'You're up and about early,' she said once they'd exchanged shy greetings.

'I'm catching the first boat over to Parga.'

'That will be nice. You must be heading home soon now.'

'Yes, it's the last day. We leave tomorrow right around lunchtime.'

'Have you been able to do much more painting?'

'Not much, just that day with you and yesterday.

I found a spot down at the end of the sea wall overlooking a couple of boats. I really enjoyed myself. How is your painting going? I expect you're busy keeping up with everything and making sure you have enough work to display at the weekly market?'

'Yes, it's getting to be the busiest time of the year now.'

'I think they're starting to board the boat so I need to get going. It's been really nice seeing you though. I've missed spending time with you.'

'Me too,' she said softly. 'Simon, you were right about the commission. I called the gallery and the lady explained, and I confronted my mum. She isn't really talking to me at the moment and it's all a bit of a mess.'

'I am so sorry I said anything in the first place.'

'No, I'm so glad you did, I really am. Look, you'd best get on board before the boat goes without you. Have a nice day over in Parga and if you ever come back to Vekianos we should meet up again.'

As Simon boarded the boat he was filled with regret. He would sooner have spent the day with Polina now that the air between them had been cleared. It was such a relief she wasn't upset with him. If only this had happened at the start of the holiday and not the end. Things could be so different.

The journey flashed by and Simon couldn't remember any of it. One moment he was looking at Vekianos disappearing, and the next, there was Parga in front of him. Another few minutes and he would be getting off. Then it would be the moment of truth. What would the gallery owner think of his work?

Before he made his way to the gallery he needed

to compose himself and concentrate. Any thoughts about Polina had to go from his head. Stopping to get a coffee in one of the seafront restaurants and thinking through what he wanted to say, it crossed his mind that he needed to be business-like and go in there without any emotion. This could be a new start for him, a future he had only ever dreamed of, and he wasn't about to waste this chance.

Taking a deep breath he walked to the gallery. This was it.

'Hello again!' the woman greeted him warmly. 'Welcome back to Parga. I'm so sorry, I don't think we shared names when you came in last time. I'm Lydia.'

'Simon.'

'It's nice to see you again, Simon. I also think I need to thank you because I had a call from Polina, and she mentioned that you had explained to her about the commission confusion. I don't really know what's going on with her and her mum – and to be honest I don't want to get involved with any of it – but I'm still very interested in her artwork and she's promised to consider my offer.'

'That's great news. I'm sorry to take up your time but I would greatly value your opinion on something before I head home, if you're not busy? The thing is, I've painted a couple of pictures... They're very different from what I normally paint but I wanted to try something out of my comfort zone, and though they aren't necessarily my best work, and perhaps I should have spent a little more time on each of them, I—'

Lydia kindly interrupted him. 'Simon, please slow down and take a minute to breathe. I'll fetch you some water and then you can show me your paintings.'

She went into a separate room at the back of the

gallery and she seemed to have been gone for ages. Simon realised she was probably taking her time so he could calm down and pull himself together. He moved over to the counter and took the paintings out of his bag. As he carefully unwrapped them, he kept telling himself to slow down and keep calm, that Lydia was a lovely lady and she didn't bite. With that she walked back into the gallery carrying a bottle of water.

'There you go. Now, why don't you sit there and we'll take a look at your work together.'

As he sipped the water he watched Lydia study each painting. It seemed to take forever and all the time he was berating himself. Who did he think he was pretending to be an artist? What an arrogant thing he had done coming over to Parga and into this beautiful gallery with all this wonderful art on the walls. He should apologise for wasting Lydia's time and leave.

Before he could say anything she took the paintings over to a shelf to the side of the counter. She moved the three paintings that were there out the way, stood his on the shelf, and then moved back and looked at them together for a while before going back and removing one. Again she stood back, studying the piece in silence. He desperately wanted to know what was going on in her head.

'Simon, I don't know where to start. I can tell you got your inspiration from the olive tree paintings that are on display here in the gallery. Similar to them, you've uniquely captured the light and the simplicity of the subject.'

All that sounded ok to him, but she hadn't said if she liked them, or if they were any good, or if they might be something she would be prepared to put for sale in the gallery.

'I really like them, and for so many reasons,' she

said at last, and Simon let out a breath he hadn't realised he was holding. 'I think they look good individually but also I could see them as a collection, perhaps three of them altogether.'

'Thank you, that's really very kind of you.'

'I'm just being honest. I promise I would have said if I didn't like them. You have a special talent and there's something very unique about your style that makes it stand out. You should be very proud of what you've created.'

'Thank you.'

He felt so relieved. Her words had been everything he had dreamed of hearing – more, if he was honest! – and apart from thanking Lydia he really didn't know what else to say.

'T-Thank you,' he stammered.

'You don't have to keep thanking me.' She laughed. 'They're lovely and I'm so happy you brought them over to Parga to show me.'

'Thank you— Sorry, I've said it again, but I really do appreciate everything you've said and your taking the time to look at them means so much to me. It's given me the reassurance that I've made the right choice to give up my job and make art my career. If I don't try now, I know I never will.'

'I'm glad I've been able to help in a small way.'

'No, a huge way! I just need to figure out how I go about it now – the practical bits. It's one thing saying I'm giving up my job to become a full-time artist, and quite another to work out how to go about it. And I need to do that before any paint goes on a canvas.'

'You have exciting times ahead! Please do keep in contact once you're back in the UK. I'd love to see more of your work. I can't wait to see the images you create.'

Simon suddenly felt a little wobbly on his feet

and looked for somewhere to sit down. It was the same feeling he'd had when he was in Keriaphos with Angela.

'Are you ok?'

'I'm not sure. Do you mind if I just sit here for a moment? I've just realised that I won't be able to create what I want to create back in England. I would need to be living and painting here in Greece to finish this series and pursue the other ideas I have. I can't believe I've just said that out loud,' he said, the admission startling even him.

Lydia remained silent and for a moment he feared that her praise had merely been to make him feel good on the last day of his holiday. Perhaps his work wasn't as good as she had told him? There was only one way to find out if she had meant what she'd said.

Taking a deep breath, he asked, 'Lydia, would you be willing to put those two paintings for sale here in the gallery? I guess what I'm asking is, is there any chance that this gallery could play a part in my new adventure, and a potential new life in Greece?'

Chapter 33
Holiday day 13

Stood waiting for the kettle to boil Angela realised she needed a plan of action for the day. Looking in the fridge there were things in there for her lunch, so she didn't need to go down to the shops, so she decided she would split the day up between swimming, lying in the sun, and of course packing, a job she wasn't looking forward to. Coffee made, she opened the patio doors, deciding she would sit on the terrace in the morning sunshine and then have a little breakfast before a few hours down by the pool. Before lunch she would get her suitcase sorted, ready for Carla and Simon's return and their last hurrah of the holiday.

It was just gone nine o'clock when she moved to make some toast and jam, and as she stood up she heard a vehicle pull up outside. Surely it wasn't Lambros this early in the morning? When the gate opened she was surprised to see it was Alina. How odd.

'This is a nice surprise,' she called to her guest. 'I was just going to have a snack. Please join me. I have some gorgeous homemade biscuits from the shop in the harbour and they need eating before we go tomorrow.'

'Thank you but I can't stay too long as I need to be at the restaurant for ten o'clock or I'll get a telling off from Sakis. You know, sometimes I do think I work for him rather than the other way around. I mean that in a good way of course. He's a superstar and I know the amount of business we have some days is all down to him and the entertainment he provides.'

Angela went inside to grab the biscuits and they settled at the table on the terrace. It seemed Alina was a bit nervous and Angela wanted her to feel comfortable.

'We're looking forward to having our last night in the restaurant. It will be the perfect end to what has been a very lovely holiday. All three of us have well and truly fallen in love with Vekianos. It is a very special island with such fantastic people.'

'That's actually why I've come to see you. It's about love, actually,' Alina began.

This shocked Angela. Was Alina suggesting that Lambros was in love with her? Angela was now the one getting very uncomfortable, whereas Alina seemed more relaxed now she had started.

'You see, Angela, my son has fallen in love with Carla—'

'This is about Nectarios and Carla? Sorry, I shouldn't have interrupted. Please carry on.' Angela breathed deeply, trying to calm her racing heart.

'Yes, Nectarios is head over heels in love with Carla. I've never seen him like this before and I cannot believe the change in him over the last couple of weeks. The only way I can sum it up is to say that he has grown up. Now, to the point of my visit. I want to know, do you think Carla feels the same?'

'I think ... well, actually, I *know* she feels the same. But I also know that she is an intelligent young woman who knows these sorts of things can happen on holiday, especially on a romantic Greek island. I believe part of her wants to stay and see where things go, but I know she will leave tomorrow to talk everything over with her mum – they are very close – and though I know what I would do if I was in her shoes, that's me not her.'

'Sakis seems to think that if I ask Carla to stand

in for him and do his job while he takes some time off, it will convince her to stay. The work doesn't concern me because I know Nectarios will be there to help her, but after those few weeks are up, what happens then? Will she be up and off, leaving my son broken-hearted? That's what worries me.'

'That's something neither you nor I can predict, and at this moment I doubt even Carla would know if you asked her. Sadly, that's life – nothing is straightforward and there are surprises around every corner.'

'Speaking of surprises, Angela, I have something to thank you for. After all these years of me and friends keeping on at him, my father is finally renovating his house.'

'Yes, I noticed when I was down in the harbour yesterday. I looked up and saw the scaffolding on the house. It will look nice all painted in a fresh colour.'

'It's the inside that really interests me. There will be a whole new kitchen and new bathrooms as he's having the third bedroom converted into a guest suite with its own bathroom so that any guests staying with him won't have to share. Right, I need to get going before Sakis gives me the sack. Thank you for the coffee. I look forward to seeing you down at the restaurant tonight.'

As Alina said goodbye and walked down the path Angela could feel her heart racing, and she knew why. Lambros was spending all this money on his house to impress her? She had told him that she would be coming back to Vekianos but staying at the villa was a one-off and she would have to look for a studio next time. It seemed he was planning ahead. But what if he went to all this expense and then she did come and stay for a holiday but they didn't get on? He would have wasted all his savings for nothing.

Chapter 34
Holiday day 13

As Carla walked through the villa gate, she could see Angela down by the pool. Even just seeing Angela's face helped her to calm down.

'I didn't expect you to be here so early. Is everything ok?' Angela's concern was evident.

'Not really, if I'm honest.'

'Is it to do with working in the restaurant? I've had Alina here this morning. She's worried about what might happen after the two weeks are up and Sakis has returned. She suspects that if you leave, Nectarios will be devastated.'

'I'm worried, too, and I feel like I'm starting to suffocate. Whoever would have thought this holiday would turn out like this? I really don't know what to do.'

'Welcome to the club, my darling. While she was here, Alina happened to mention that her dad is converting a spare bedroom into a guest suite so I think that means that if I do come back he'll be expecting me to stay with him. And if I decide not to revisit Vekianos, he'll have gone to all that expense for nothing. Oh, my dear, what a pickle we are both in...' Angela started to laugh.

'Why are you laughing?' asked Carla, confusion written on her face.

'Because I don't know what to do. Normally I would say let's just open a bottle of wine and everything will be ok, but it's too early to do that, even for us.'

'Two weeks ago we were packing to come here

with no idea what was in store for us, and now look at us. We would never have believed any of this could happen.'

'I know, but we both need to stop worrying and enjoy our last day on this gorgeous island. And the best way to start that is with a cup of tea.'

Simon was back down in Parga harbour, and he was in luck, as there was a boat heading back to Vekianos in twenty minutes, meaning he would be back at the villa by mid-afternoon. His body was still racing with excitement and he still couldn't believe Lydia had agreed to take on his art – both of the paintings he'd brought with him as well as the future paintings he had planned in the series. His dream had come true, and now it was time for the practical part – he needed to find somewhere to live on Vekianos. But even before that, he had to go back to Norfolk and sort his life out there. The first step would be telling his parents and then ... well, he didn't really know, but he was sure he could figure it out.

Once on the boat he started thinking about his finances. He had savings, and he could sell his van, and as he was currently living with his parents, he didn't have to worry about selling or renting out a home. Plus, his room would still be there for him to return to, which was a comforting safety net. But should he be thinking like that? No, he needed to be more positive. He *would* succeed, so there was no point in planning to fail.

Back at the villa Angela and Carla had managed to switch off from thoughts of Lambros and Nectarios and had cheered each other up with all sorts of chat. As lunchtime approached they went through the fridge to see what they had left to use up and get rid of.

'Cheese, ham, and bread it is then, Angela, and given that we have some wine to use up – and it's nearly two o'clock – perhaps a cheeky glass wouldn't go amiss? Oh, and there are also still some crisps.'

'That sounds good to me. I'll get the cutlery and lay the table.'

Carla took everything they had and placed it all in the middle of the table so they could help themselves. As she went back to grab the wine out of the fridge she heard the gate open and turning around she spotted Simon.

'Angela, we're going to need another place setting. Simon's back.'

'How lovely. We can have our final lunch here at the villa all together. You have perfect timing, Simon. You can tell us all about how you got on over in Parga while we eat.'

'That looks great. I'll just go and get changed.'

Simon was soon back out on the terrace and Carla had poured the wine.

'Now tell us, how did it go? I get the impression your visit to the gallery was a success?' said Angela, eagerly.

'Yes, it was. Lydia – the gallery owner – said she would love to display and hopefully sell my work. She even kept the two pieces of art I took over to show her today. She said there was no point waiting to put them on display. We also talked about the style of my paintings and the direction I should go with them. It was all very exciting.'

'So what happens next?' asked Carla.

'Well, I'll head back to Norfolk tomorrow to sort things there, and then I'll be heading back here to Vekianos to get settled. In the meantime, I need to find somewhere to rent. Of course, I'm not daft, I know it won't be in the harbour or one of the other tourist spots as that will be too expensive for my budget. No, it will probably be somewhere remote, but as long as I have the essentials – kitchen, bathroom, and a bed – and of course a place to paint, I'll be happy. I think I'll need to get a scooter as well, to help with getting around to places to paint.'

'If you live here on Vekianos, will you have a stand at the Wednesday craft market?'

'I think it would make sense, Angela, although I would sooner be in a shop or even a gallery here because I'm not sure how I would transport everything on market day. So, that's my news. What have you two been up to? Any visits from Lambros?'

'No, but I did have a visit from Alina.'

'I presume she's worried about her dad and making sure you don't take him back to England in your suitcase,' joked Simon.

'That's funny, but no, she came to ask Angela what my intentions were with Nectarios. Thankfully, for the last three or four hours we've managed to avoid any mention of Lambros or Nectarios, haven't we, Angela?'

'We have, but I think we need a plan of action for tonight. Do you have you two have any idea how we might go about everything?'

'I'm not sure what you mean by a plan of action,' said Simon.

'I know exactly what she means. Tonight, after dinner in the restaurant, we're going to have to say our goodbyes and that's going to be very awkward. But before that I have to decide whether or not I'm coming back and working in the restaurant while Sakis goes off to Corfu.'

Neither Simon nor Angela knew what to say as Carla needed to sort this out by herself, so they sat in silence for a moment, feeling uncomfortable for the first time on the holiday. When Simon's phone beeped they all sighed in relief for the distraction.

'Is everything ok?' asked Angela.

'Yes and no. Polina's messaged. She says she knows it's our last night, but would it be ok to meet up later.'

'That's absolutely fine. Carla and I will be ok in the restaurant. You go and spend some time with her.'

'If I wasn't coming back here to live I wouldn't bother, but I'm now thinking that perhaps I should, both to warn her about my move and to try and make things less awkward now that we're likely to be bumping into one another more often. But not tonight. It's our last night and as we aren't leaving until lunchtime tomorrow I can see her in the morning. I'm not spoiling a lovely evening with you both.'

'Thank you, Simon, you've solved my problem with that idea. I'll invite Lambros here for a coffee in the morning and explain to him how things should go when I come back to visit the island.'

'That's the answer to my problem as well,' agreed Carla. 'I'll meet Nectarios in the morning, too. That gives me time to decide if I'm coming to work in the restaurant while Sakis is away. Now the three of us can go out tonight knowing the difficult conversations have been put on hold and that we can just have a lovely evening all together to finish off this wonderful holiday.'

Chapter 35
Holiday day 13

The table at the restaurant wasn't booked until nine-thirty but the three of them had decided to go down into the harbour around eight so that they could go for a drink first and take in their last evening of the town and the atmosphere.

Angela was first on the terrace after getting ready and she was pleased she'd kept this dress for the last night as it made her feel beautiful and confident. Carla soon appeared in a white dress that she said she had been keeping until her tan was at its very best.

'Don't we all look very smart,' said Simon.

'Yes, very glamorous.'

'I was going for chic, sophisticated, and classy,' said Carla.

'Right, you two, are we heading off or do you both want to find more words in the dictionary?' Simon raised a brow and they all laughed.

Minutes later they were off to celebrate their last night on Vekianos. The walk down was so familiar to them now, all the little streets, alleyways, and cut throughs that took them right down to the harbour.

Every so often Simon would stop and look at something – the rooftops of the buildings, the windows with gorgeous blue washed shutters, steps by a front door with a bright plant pot – inspiration hitting him from every direction.

'How many images have you seen in these last few minutes that you'd like to paint? I would say quite a few,' said Angela.

'Hundreds! Well, perhaps not that many, but a lot. I'm so excited but also scared. It's very exciting and flattering having paintings on a gallery wall, but it means nothing unless they sell and bring in an income.'

'You're right, but the important thing is to have the belief that you can do it, and you have that in spadefuls.'

'Angela's right,' Carla chimed in. 'The last thing you need is to get back to Saltmarsh Quay and start talking yourself out of coming back, which would be so easy to do. It's the thing that worries me about my own situation. I know my mum will say, "Carla, it's only two weeks, just go and have fun," but I'm worried about talking myself out of it. I can hear all the voices of uncertainty and doubt in my head already.'

'Don't forget that you two have each other to support and encourage one another, and at the end of the day you both have homes to go back to in Norfolk. I'm not saying that because I think it won't work out for you – quite the opposite, in fact! – but because I want you to know you don't need to worry too much about the what if's.'

'I see what you mean, Angela, and I appreciate you saying that. Now, here we are. I think I can see a free table. It's not the one you really wanted but if someone in the front row leaves we can just move forward.'

'That's perfect, Simon, go and grab it before anyone else does.'

Once they all got comfortable they ordered some wine.

'Well, this is it! Can you believe the two weeks are nearly up already and this time tomorrow we'll nearly be back in Saltmarsh Quay? I think the second week has just flown by,' Carla marvelled.

'I feel the same. We certainly won't be able to sit outdoors this late in the evening back home. Well, I suppose we could if we put on a hat and a warm coat... Anyway, once we're back you can both start planning your return trips. How exciting that will be.'

'Exciting and nerve-racking. The main thing is to find somewhere to live here because if I don't, I won't be coming back. It's strange but I feel that's the only thing I really need to worry about. Packing will be a breeze and Polina told me she gets her art supplies online from a company in Athens and it's only a couple of days wait once you've ordered.'

'It's good you can be so laid back about it, Simon. My head is already full of all the things I'll be bringing, even though I'll only be coming back for two weeks. But saying that, I guess I'll only really need t-shirts and shorts to work in. There probably won't be much need for dressy clothes.'

Angela wondered if it would really be just two weeks, or if it would turn into the rest of the season – or longer – but she thought that perhaps that was a conversation best saved for when they were back in Norfolk.

'Have you given any thought to when you might come back for a holiday, Angela? Will it depend on when Lambros's house is finished?'

'To be honest, I think it will be next year now.'

'Really? That seems quite a time away.'

'I know, but we'll soon be getting into the lovely summer weather in the UK, and we know the temperature here in Greece will be too hot to be comfortable.'

'I see what you mean. Polina was saying that when she paints in the hottest months of the year she has to be under an umbrella and preferably with a sea breeze.'

'I was thinking as well about the heat working in the restaurant. Nectarios said visitors don't eat as early in the evenings in the hottest months, so that would make for very late nights.'

'But what happens after the two weeks are up? What do you think will be next for you?' Simon asked, voicing the question Angela had tactfully been avoiding.

'I'm not sure. I think I need to address that before I get back to my mum's because I know that will be her first question as well. She won't have a problem with any of this, but she'll want to know that I've thought everything through. At the end of the day, the reason I'm covering for Sakis is because I want to be with Nectarios. Perhaps instead of this short-term plan I should be looking at the bigger picture? For right now though, my priority is food. I'm starving! Should we make a move and head over to the restaurant?'

'I think that's a good idea,' Angela agreed.

As they got closer to the restaurant they saw it was still quite busy, but they were in luck as their favourite table was empty. Alina must have reserved it for them.

Nectarios's face lit up when he saw Carla, and Simon was glad the two had made a connection and Carla's next adventure would bring her back to the island. His dream of working and living on Vekianos was about to come true and it would be lovely to have her there with him.

Alina came out to greet them, Sakis waved from where he was clearing some plates away from a table, and Lambros smiled as he opened a bottle of wine behind the bar. Angela had worried things could possibly be a little tense, but so far so good.

Once they were sat down Sakis came over and said hello, complimenting them all on how gorgeous they looked. Next to come over was Nectarios, who looked so happy. Angela suspected it was because he knew Carla would be back and he wouldn't have to share her with Simon or herself. Then Lambros appeared with the wine, looking just as happy as his grandson.

After lots of chat they ordered their food, each choosing their favourite dishes. Sakis had insisted on serving them and of course he was on good form with lots of funny comments.

Angela couldn't help but notice the way Alina was watching Carla. It was ... curious. yes, 'curious' was the word she was looking for, she thought. Could it be that she was wondering if Carla was capable of doing the job? If that was the case then she needn't worry. Angela knew Carla would give it one hundred percent.

Eventually, as had happened most times they ate at the restaurant, they were the last table. By that point Lambros had pushed the table next to theirs up against the one they were all sat at, so he and Alina could join them. Sakis and Nectarios rushed around finishing everything off before finally coming to sit down as well. Thankfully, the conversation was very lighthearted with no sign of tension. After a while the two chefs came out from the kitchen and came over to say goodbye, and then Alina went to sort out the till.

'Can I get anyone another drink?'

'Could I just have some water please, Nectarios?'

'Of course, Angela, anything for you, Simon?'

'I think I could manage one final glass of wine, thank you.'

'Carla, for you?'

'Yes the same please.'

'Granddad and Sakis, would you both like the usual?'

Lambros opted for a glass of wine and Sakis a gin and tonic. It all went a little quiet for a moment, and Angela reckoned that was because they had all picked up on Simon's use of the word 'final'.

This was it, their last drink before they walked back to the villa.

While Carla got up and headed to the bathroom, and Nectarios went to get the drinks, Lambros asked what time they had to be at the harbour for the trip back to Corfu.

'Not until after lunch, so if you'd like you could pop up to the villa in the morning for a coffee before we leave. Simon is going off to see Polina and I expect Carla will be busy. Shall we say around ten-thirty?' asked Angela.

'I would like that. Should I stop at the bakery on the way?'

'If you didn't, I would be very disappointed.'

Angela's words made them laugh and lightened the mood.

'Are you all packed and ready to go back to England?' asked Alina as Carla passed the bar, heading back to the table.

'I think so.'

'I wanted to say that you're under no pressure to come back and work here if you don't want to. You need to do what's best for you and no one else, so try not to worry about how Nectarios will feel. No, you have to go with your heart, and you need to consider whether the last two weeks with Nectarios were just a holiday romance, or if they were something more, something worth pursuing.'

Chapter 36
Leaving day

Simon had finished all his packing and now it was time for a coffee and one last sit on the terrace before he had to go and meet Polina. He was already thinking about how much he would miss the villa, especially the pool. He had taken it for granted and he knew he would likely not be living somewhere with one when he returned to the island. But it wasn't as though he wouldn't have options for swimming given all the lovely beaches there were to visit.

'That's me sorted. All packed?' Angela asked as she walked out onto the terrace.

'Yes. I was just sat here having a final look at the pool. It really has served us well for the past two weeks.'

'I must agree. I hadn't realised how much I would use it and I know I will miss it... Oh, is that a phone? I think yours has beeped, Simon. I expect it's Carla telling us what time she'll be back.'

Simon looked at his phone but it wasn't a message from Carla.

'It's from Lydia... Oh wow! They've sold one of my paintings at the gallery! How great is that? She says she's here on Vekianos this morning and was hoping to catch me before I leave.'

Ten minutes later Simon was dressed and running down to the harbour to meet Lydia. She'd suggested they meet at the little church, which seemed a strange place to meet, but who cared? He'd sold a painting!

'You were quick!' Lydia called as he approached her a few minutes later. 'Congratulations on the painting! The couple who bought it really loved it.'

'Thank you so much. I'm honestly over the moon and it makes me want to get stuck into the other paintings as soon as possible, but there's a lot to organise first.'

'Have you found somewhere to live yet?'

'No, but hopefully it won't be too difficult. Since being here we've befriended the owners of a restaurant in the harbour and they said they know of people that might have places to rent on the island. Once I'm back in England I'll start the process.'

'I actually might be able to help. It might be easier if I show you what I mean rather than trying to explain, if you have the time?'

Simon nodded.

'Great! Follow me this way,' she said, leading him towards a nearby street.

Simon was confused. Did Lydia know of somewhere to rent here in the harbour? The street they walked down was very narrow and it had lots of little shops on either side. There was a lovely quaintness to the place, and everything was so colourful in the shop windows. Stopping outside an empty shop Lydia got a set of keys out of her bag. She unlocked the door and switched the light on as they went in.

'What do you think?'

He was even more baffled now. It was an apartment he needed, not a commercial space like this. There was no way this could be lived in.

'I've rented this shop as my second gallery, and it has an apartment upstairs,' she explained. She led him back through the shop's front door and walked a couple feet to the right, to another door. Opening it, she revealed a flight of stairs. Simon followed Lydia up and at the top he stepped into a small flat with a little kitchenette in a corner.

'That door in the corner leads to the bathroom and a bedroom, which is equally as small as the main room here.'

He went through to see it, instantly noting that the light in the bedroom would be perfect for painting, though it would mean he would have to sleep in the main room. That wouldn't really be a problem though.

'It's perfect. I'll take it,' he declared.

'Are you sure you don't want to give it some thought?'

'No, it's just what I need. When can I move in? Oh! I suppose I should ask how much the rent is first?' he added sheepishly.

'It's yours then – here are the keys – and as for the rent, there are two ways of doing this: you can either rent it from me for a monthly fee, or, you could work in the gallery I'm opening downstairs in exchange for free board. A sort of swap. I know you might be hesitant because if you're working here seven days a week you won't have time to paint, but there's an easy solution. We just need to find another artist here on Vekianos who is willing to cover, say, two or three days a week, in exchange for their work being displayed in the gallery and a smaller commission than the usual twenty percent.'

Simon was over the moon with that deal, and he knew the perfect person to cover the days where he was painting: Polina. But surely her mum wouldn't allow it? As he was pondering the situation, he thought of something else.

'What time would you want the shop to open in the mornings? I expect it will stay open late into the evenings as the holiday makers walk around until ten or eleven at night.'

'I think the hours should be about the same time as the gallery in Parga, so you'd be open from about ten-thirty. That would allow you to get up early and go off and paint for a few hours.'

'That would work really well, especially as it would be a lot cooler in the mornings with not so many people around at that time of day.'

'So, do we have a deal, Simon?'

'We do. I just can't believe it. My whole life has changed in less than five minutes.'

An hour later, sat on the harbour wall, Simon was still trying to analyse what had just happened. The offer from Lydia was bonkers. Talk about dreams coming true! But the thing that would turn this dream into a fairytale would be if Polina agreed to work in the gallery as well. It really would be the icing on the cake.

'Hi, Simon... Simon?'

'Sorry, Polina, good morning, how are you?'

'I'm fine, thank you. So are you ready to leave? Have you and your friends had a nice holiday?'

'Yes, we have. All three of us have fallen in love with Vekianos. It's such a special island and the people we've met have been lovely.'

'Perhaps you can come back again one day.'

Simon was feeling so many emotions. He was so excited to tell Polina about the new gallery and the apartment above it, but he knew he had to pick his words very carefully so as to not scare her off. He really hoped he would be able to spend time with her when he returned.

'Polina, I haven't got very long, and there's something I need to tell you. Actually, it might be easier if I show you, if that's ok? It will only take about ten minutes.'

'Sure.'

'Ok, we just need to head towards all the little lanes.'

'Do you have some of your art on display in a shop? That's so exciting! I'm really pleased you've been able to do some painting while you've been here.'

'No, that's not it, but you're sort of on the right track. Now, let me think... We should be able to cut through here and then it's just a short walk.'

'I really do love all these little shops in this part of the harbour. In the evenings these lanes get so busy with visitors and the atmosphere is buzzing.'

They were nearly at the new gallery. Simon just knew that once in the empty shop Polina would be as excited as him and she would have the exact same first thought he'd had: what her work would look like on the walls.

'Is this where we're headed? An empty shop?'

'Yes,' he said, fiddling with the keys and opening the door. 'Now, let me explain. First of all, you know the gallery over in Parga?'

She nodded.

'Well, the owner is opening another one here on Vekianos and it's going to be here in this shop. But that's not all. She's also asked me to work here, and the best bit is that I'm going to be living in the apartment upstairs.'

'That's so exciting for you, Simon! I'm so happy for you.'

'But that's not all. Polina, you can also display and sell your art here if you wanted. There would be no more carrying everything to the craft fair every week because it can be on display here seven days a week. Also, if you're willing to work in the shop two days a week, Lydia would take a much smaller commission than usual. It's just what you dreamed of, having your painting in a gallery here on the island.'

Polina looked shocked and didn't say anything, but he wasn't surprised as he knew exactly how she was feeling given he'd felt the same. It took a while for everything to sink in.

'Are you excited? Can you picture it in your head? We could have the wall just here covered with all your paintings. No more being at the mercy of the elements out on the pier, enduring the salty breeze off the sea or baking in the hot sunshine.'

'I'm pleased for you, Simon, but it's not for me.'

'But I don't understand. This is your dream. Why turn it down?'

'Because even though it's my dream, I have to put my mum first and she wouldn't like this. No, my art has to come second to my mum's happiness.'

'But what about *your* happiness? Surely that counts as well?'

'I need to be going. Goodbye, Simon.'

Chapter 37
Leaving day

Carla couldn't believe Nectarios was awake and out of bed before her. It was still early and they hadn't got to sleep until very late. She nipped to the bathroom before going into the lounge, but there was still no Nectarios. He must have gone to get them some breakfast.

She was feeling so much better than she had yesterday morning, when all she'd wanted to do was to get out of his apartment. She wasn't sure if it was what Alina had said last night or something Angela had said, but whatever it was, she felt much more relaxed and had come to a decision. She was going to do it. She was going to come back for the two weeks and see where things went with Nectarios. Making a coffee and going out onto the little balcony, she settled on one of the chairs.

Checking the time on her phone she realised that if Nectarios didn't hurry up, they wouldn't have much time together as she would soon have to go back to the villa to get ready to leave.

Looking over the balcony she could see Nectarios walking up the road with a big bag from the bakery in his hands. There was someone with him – it looked like Alina – and he kissed her goodbye before coming into the building. Carla thought she must be on her way to the restaurant.

'You're up!' he said, stepping onto the balcony. 'I was hoping to be back before you woke up. Sorry I've been so long.'

'Not a problem. I see you bumped into your

mum.'

'Actually, I didn't just bump into her, I texted her to see if she could meet me as there was something I needed to talk to her about and it couldn't wait until later today. Should I put the treats on a plate?'

'You sort the pastries out and I'll make the coffees.'

'Sounds good. We're a good little team, don't you think?'

'I suppose so.'

It was an odd thing for him to say, and he was in a very buzzy mood that was the complete opposite to what she'd been expecting given she was leaving very shortly.

'Pastries are on the table. By the way, how long before you need to be back at the villa?'

'I have enough time to eat a few of those. Here's your coffee.'

'Thank you. Carla, I need to tell you something before you leave and I'm not really sure how to go about it without putting pressure on you, which is the last thing I want to do. But it's about both of us, and it's the reason I had to go and see my mum this morning. Also, I apologise in advance. I shouldn't have left everything until five minutes before you need to go.'

'Nectarios, if it's about me coming back so Sakis can have his holiday, then my answer is yes, so you can stop worrying about it.'

'No, it's not that. Well ... I suppose that *is* part of it. But a small part.'

'You're *not* ok with me coming and working in the restaurant?'

'No, of course I'm ok with it! It's just—'

With that he spilt his coffee everywhere. He was a bag of nerves but why? Carla quickly jumped up and went and fetched a cloth to wipe up the spill.

'I'm sorry.'

'Don't be. You just need to calm down. Take a deep breath and then tell me what you need to tell me.'

Carla could see he was trying to compose himself so she stopped looking at him as she worried that was making him worse.

'Right, I'm ready, here goes... Carla, since meeting you I've gotten to know myself a lot better. I don't need to go back over it all again but suffice to say I've been an idiot for many years and I have a lot to make up to people, especially my mum. That's what I wanted to see her about today. Firstly, to apologise, and secondly, to put things right for her but also me. Of course she didn't want an apology. She said that the way I've been behaving these last couple of weeks was enough of one.'

He paused but Carla stayed silent, waiting to hear what Nectarios would say next. She could see he was building himself up for whatever it was.

'I'm going to put things right by taking on more responsibility for the restaurant. I want to run it and take all the worries and pressure off of her. It's something I should have done years ago but I was too busy having fun and enjoying myself. Actually, let's call it what it was – I was shying away from my responsibilities.'

'I think you're being too hard on yourself, and I know for a fact that Sakis didn't mind covering for you when needed because he was being compensated for it.'

'That's another thing that grates. My mum paid him extra, but she didn't stop paying me as well, even though she should have. Oh Carla, I took so much for granted, and all so I could have fun, go out, and be one of the lads, with everything that came with that. But now I need to put all that behind me and I need to be responsible. My granddad doesn't need to be waiting tables when he pops down of an evening, he needs to be able to sit and have a chat, and my mum needs to be able to take time off when she wants to.'

'I still think you're being too hard on yourself, but I'm pleased you're making this step and I know you're going to be a huge success, and that your mum and grandfather will both be so proud of you.'

'Yes, I want to grow the business and take it to the next level, perhaps even expand and redesign it. I want it to be the place everyone wants to come to eat.'

'That's exciting, and I truly believe you'll achieve everything you want to.'

'Yes but I can't do it by myself. I need help and I need it from someone who has become so important to me, the person who has made me grow up. Carla, I need you by my side. But not just in the restaurant. I want you in my life forever. I tried to convince myself it wasn't that deep but the truth is that I started to fall in love with you the first time we met, and since then that love has just been getting stronger and stronger. Please make your home here with me on Vekianos.'

Carla sat looking at him in shocked silence. She wanted to look away, but her body was frozen to the spot and she couldn't move. Nectarios was waiting for her answer and she knew she had to say something, but nothing would come out.

'Are you ok?' he finally asked. 'Like I said, I'm so sorry to spring this on you just before you're about to leave the island.'

She knew she wasn't ready to answer him so she took the escape route he'd unwittingly offered her, saying, 'Oh my gosh, look at the time! I need to go. Angela will be panicking as I've not packed, and if we miss the boat we won't get to the airport on time and we can't miss the flight... I'm so happy for you and your family, Nectarios, I just know you will make a huge success of the restaurant, it's all very exciting.'

She kissed him quickly, trying not to let herself acknowledge the tears she saw starting to gather in his eyes. He had gone from looking so excited to so sad, but she couldn't answer him. Not yet. Not until she'd had time to think about and process everything he'd said.

'Goodbye, Nectarios. I've had a very special time here on Vekianos and it's all down to you.'

Chapter 38
Leaving day

Once Simon had gone Angela finished off putting her last few things in her suitcase and then she was on a mission to get the villa sorted. She would start with stripping all the beds and then getting all the towels from the three bathrooms. Once that was done, she would tackle the kitchen – not that it was terribly dirty as between the three of them they had always kept it clean – and give the fridge a good wipe down. Even though she knew a cleaner was coming in to get everything ready for the next guests she wanted to leave the place as clean and tidy as she could.

Two hours later she was pleased with her work. The villa was almost sparkling and so all she had to do before they left was to change into her travelling clothes. Time for a coffee and to wait for Lambros to come to say goodbye. She felt different about that today compared to yesterday, when she was still screwed up about him going to all the trouble and expense of doing his house up. This morning, for some reason, she was clear in her head that it had nothing to do with her. Looking at the time, she saw that it was nearly ten-thirty. As Lambros could appear any minute now she put the kettle on and got two plates out ready for the pastries. Then she heard the gate open and close.

'You have perfect timing, Lambros. Coffee?'

'Yes, please. I come bearing gifts, but then you knew I would because you made it clear that you would be very disappointed if I didn't!' He chuckled.

'You know me too well.'

'I'm not sure about that. I think there's a lot more for me to find out still, and hopefully when you come back, and we have the chance to chat more, I can find out what really makes Angela tick.'

'Well, if you promise to keep arriving with treats I'll be back as soon as I can. Now, here are the plates. If you go out onto the terrace I'll bring the coffees.'

Taking the drinks outside she could see there were enough sweet and savoury pastries to feed a family of ten.

'Oh my, are we expecting more people? So many treats! You really are spoiling me.'

'As I was walking to the bakery I was thinking about the fact that the three of you will have a long day of travelling, first taking the boat over to Corfu and then a taxi from the harbour to the airport before your flight home, so I thought you might need these to keep you going throughout the day.'

'They're very much appreciated.'

'Did you enjoy your last evening in the restaurant? I thought it was a fun night. Simon seems very excited about coming back and doing his art, and I've promised to make enquiries for him about accommodation.'

'Yes, I'm so pleased for him. And then there's Carla. The big question is will she or won't she come back.'

'Yes, and I know Nectarios will be very upset if she doesn't.'

'I think she will. Now, tell me how things are progressing with your house. I think you have shocked quite a few people with your plans, especially Alina.'

'Oh yes, you wouldn't believe the number of locals I know who have just happened to be walking by these last few days, most of them going well out of their way. But saying that, I would probably be the same if it was one of my neighbours. There's no denying I am the talk of Vekianos!'

'Well, if they're talking about you that means that they're giving someone else a rest. I'd say someone out there owes you their thanks.'

'I suspect you're right there. First it was "who is the mystery woman out for dinner with Lambros", and now it's "what's he doing to the house? Is he doing it up to sell? Why now, after all these years?" Oh yes, everyone is intrigued.'

'That's my question as well, why do it now, after all these years of refusing to make changes?'

'Several reasons, really. First, there was the conversation we had when you said you didn't want to be just plodding on where you lived. Can you remember? It made me realise that all I was doing was going from day to day, week to week, doing the same old things. I needed something more, a project to get excited about, and what better place to start then with the one thing everyone was nagging me about anyway?'

'And are you enjoying it so far?'

'Strangely, a lot more than I thought I would. I think it's taken me out of a rut that I was in. On a practical level, it was definitely time to do it as things like plumbing and electrics that should have been addressed many years ago are now being sorted.'

'I'm really pleased for you.'

'Thank you. I also wanted the place to be nice when I had visitors, with a nice, comfy guest room with its own ensuite bathroom, a home away from home for anyone who comes to stay. I just want it all done right away though. I've no patience, that's my problem.'

'But there's no rush. It will be finished when it's finished.'

'You're wrong there, as the sooner it's done the

quicker you can come back to visit.'

Before Angela had time to answer, the gate opened and there was Carla. Angela noticed she wasn't her normal bouncy self, like she usually was when she returned from staying with Nectarios. As she started to walk up the path to the terrace the gate opened again, and there was Simon who looked equally unhappy.

Oh dear. Their final morning was meant to be filled with smiles, not frowns!

'Hi, you two, look what Lambros has brought us for our travelling day.'

'Thank you, that's really kind of you. I think I'll nip and have a shower before we leave,' said Carla.

'You'll need to grab a clean towel as I put all the used ones together in a pile for the cleaner.'

'Ok. See you in a bit.'

Though Carla had paused to say hello, Simon had silently walked into the villa and it was clear from his expression that he didn't want to talk.

Lambros gave Angela an uncertain look. 'I'd probably better head off as the three of you have things to be getting on with. Have a safe journey and hopefully it won't be too long until the three of you are back on Vekianos. I won't say goodbye yet as I'll see you down in the harbour in an hour or so, when you catch the boat.'

'That will be nice. Thank you again for the treats.'

While she waited for Carla and Simon to reappear, Angela thought back to what she and Lambros had been talking about. There was no pressure now that she knew for sure that he wasn't remodelling his house specifically for her, and she was actually feeling a little bit excited about coming back to Vekianos. She was glad to know that she had helped him snap out of a rut, and he was doing what was needed to enjoy every moment of the time he still had.

'Are you ok, Simon?' she gently asked as she heard steps behind her.

'No, it's me.'

'Oh, sorry, Carla. We have about an hour or so before the taxi arrives. Can I get you anything?'

'No, I'm fine, thank you. Well ... I'm not, really. Nectarios has told me he's in love with me, and he wants us to have a future together here on Vekianos. He's taking over running the restaurant and wants to grow the business and wants me to be a part of it. What do I do?'

'You already know the answer I'm going to give you.'

'I need to decide for myself.'

'Yes, my darling. Why don't you go into the kitchen and grab the notepad and pen from the bottom drawer. Bring it out here and we'll take it from there.'

Carla wasn't in the mood to do it, but she did it anyway because she knew it would make Angela happy.

'Open up the pad so you have two blank pages, one on the left and one on the right. On the top of the first page, write "against", and on the other one, write "for". I know you think I'm being silly, but it will only take two minutes and you never know, it might work. I'll start you off with the against side: you will miss your mum.'

'What's going on?' asked Simon, joining them.

'I've given Carla a task to do. How did you get on with Polina?'

'It was disastrous.' He quickly filled them in on everything that had happened in his meetings with Lydia and Polina.

'That is fabulous about the job and apartment,

Simon! When will it all happen?'

'In a month or so. I'm very excited ... or, I was, until Polina turned me down because her mum wouldn't like it and she doesn't want to upset her. I can't believe she would say no to an opportunity like this.'

'Neither can I, but it's her choice.'

Before Angela could say anything else she noticed Carla was looking a little happier. Perhaps the pro and con list had helped.

'I've finished. Shall I read out the two lists?'

'Oh no, Carla, that's just for you, to help you decide. Now I think we need to be making a move as the taxi will be here soon. I'll just nip to the bathroom and then get my case and bag.'

'I can get the cases and take them down to the gate. You and Carla just need to grab your hand luggage, and more importantly, the pastries. They need guarding with your lives.'

As she walked to the bathroom Angela thought to herself that it had been a lovely holiday. This gorgeous villa had served them well and not just because of the sunshine and the beautiful views. The three of them had learned a lot about themselves on this trip, and she for one, was going to live every moment of her life going forward to the fullest. She was confident that it would only be a short time before Carla and Simon realised they needed to as well.

The taxi pulled up in the harbour with twenty minutes to spare before the boat departed. Looking out the taxi window Angela spotted Lambros and Nectarios waiting for them.

Once the luggage had been unloaded Simon stood back and looked around, hoping he might spot Polina as she knew what time they would be leaving.

She'd had a few hours to think about the new gallery and perhaps in that short time she could have possibly changed her mind, but sadly she was nowhere in sight.

As Carla stood with the others, she turned to take in the shops, restaurants, and houses. Looking down at the two pieces of paper in her hand, she realised she didn't need them. Tearing them up, she walked over to a nearby bin and discarded them.

'Well, this is it! Thank you all for coming to this lovely island,' said Lambros.

'And thank you to you and your family – and not forgetting your staff – for making the holiday very special. We've eaten the best food ever and I for one look forward to coming back and seeing your new luxury bed and breakfast.'

'No one mentioned breakfast,' Lambros joked. 'Oh, I think they're calling you to board.'

With that Lambros shook Simon's hand and gave Angela and Carla each a kiss.

The three chaps went to pick up the cases to load them onto the boat, but Carla stood motionless.

'Not that one, Nectarios,' she said.

'Sorry?' he asked, confused.

'It seems silly taking my bag all the way back to England just to bring it back again in a few weeks. I think you could take it back to your apartment instead. It would also be nice if you made some wardrobe space for me to put it in.'

'So … you're definitely coming back?' he asked, the hope evident in his tone and expression.

'Yes, and not just to cover Sakis's holiday. I'm coming back to stay. I'm going to make Vekianos my home.'

Nectarios dropped the bags he was holding and swung Carla into his arms while Angela, Simon, and Lambros watched on with huge smiles.

Chapter 39
Six weeks later

Carla was really excited as she waited for the boat to arrive on Vekianos from Corfu. She couldn't wait to see Simon because even though they had chatted on the phone during the past few weeks, she still had loads she needed to tell him. She was also looking forward to having the evening off. It was her first one for weeks – not that she was complaining though, as her life here on Vekianos couldn't be any better. The job was great and she was enjoying it so much, and Alina has said she brought a different and much needed element to the restaurant. The way that Carla, Nectarios, and Sakis bounced off of each other and joked felt so natural, and it was clear that the customers loved the camaraderie between the three of them. Saying that, it was normally her and Sakis piling on Nectarios, but he took it all in good humour.

But the best bit of living here was being with Nectarios, and the time they spent together getting to know each other better and telling stories of their childhood was very special. She was so happy waking up each morning with him beside her, and she couldn't wait for the season to end so she could take him back to England to meet her mum and show him Saltmarsh Quay.

She hadn't noticed the boat arriving in the harbour while she was daydreaming, and it was only when people started to disembark that she spotted Simon in the queue. He spotted her, too, and started waving like crazy.

Once Simon was on dry land there were lots of hugs and laughter.

'Please don't tell me that is the only luggage you've brought!' exclaimed Carla. 'It cost me a small fortune to bring all my things over.'

'Just two cases for me – one with clothes and the other full to the brim with my art things.'

'Madness. You will be forever washing something to put on.'

'I figured it made the most sense to just buy clothes here as what I had wasn't really suitable for living here. But enough of this fashion chat! How are you doing?'

'How do you think? I'm living the dream and now you're here as well, it's even better.'

'We only need Angela to join us and it will be just like our holiday.'

'We did have such a great time, didn't we? And look at us now! Whoever would have believed we would be living here. It's bonkers in the best way. Shall we head off to your new apartment? I can't wait to see it.'

'I'm excited as well. Lydia told me she's bought some furniture – she said only basic things as she didn't want to buy stuff I didn't like – and apparently there's also bedding, towels, cooking utensils, glasses, plates, and cups. So, I should have almost everything I need already.'

'Fab! Let's go and see it.'

'If you could manage wheeling one of the cases, I'll get the other one and my carry-on bag.'

'That's fine by me. You need to lead the way though as I still get lost in all these little streets. To be honest, even though I've been here all these weeks, I haven't ventured very far yet as I just haven't had the time. The restaurant has been manic, but in a nice way.'

'I'm looking forward to hearing all about it. Right, the easiest way to find it is by heading to the church. Can you see the little wooden cross sticking up above the roofs?'

'Yes, I can, but I'll follow you as it might be slow going. These streets aren't designed for wheeling suitcases, are they?'

Simon led the way and they passed through a few courtyards and alleyways, stopping briefly at the church to catch their breath, before continuing on to the gallery and Simon's new home.

'Here we are! By the look of things they've been busy working in the gallery. There are lots of hooks in the walls for the art and I can see a lovely new floor … and I think that's a little counter in the far corner. I'm excited but I now need to produce some art to go on the walls! I'm glad I have ten days before the gallery opens. If I could have three or four paintings done by then I'll be happy. Now, let's take a look at the apartment,' he said, pulling the keys out of his pocket as he led Carla to the entrance. 'Let's just leave the cases here inside the door for now while we head upstairs to have a look at the furniture.'

Simon went first and was pleased to find a sofa and a table with two chairs in the main room. The space looked a lot smaller than he remembered, and though he had been hoping to move the bed into this room, he realised that it wouldn't work. He then walked through to the bedroom, which he had been hoping would be his studio. The bed filled the room and there was no way he would be able to paint in there as his easel just wouldn't fit. It would have to go in the lounge, but the light wasn't as good, and it would be a very tight fit. Oh dear.

'It's lovely, Simon. Perfect for one or even two people to live very comfortably. It really is a gorgeous little apartment, but something tells me by the look on your face you're disappointed?' prompted Carla.

'You're right, it is a lovely apartment, but I was hoping to be able to paint in here and I don't think it's going to be possible. I'll worry about that later though. For now, I'm here and that's what counts. I think that's my phone ringing. Hold on just a moment...'

He pulled his phone out of his bag and answered.

'Hi, Lydia! I just got here a few minutes ago. Thank you so much for the furniture, I love it.'

'I'm pleased and I hope you will be very happy and comfortable living there. Have you been into the gallery yet? I've had loads of work done since you saw it last and am so excited about the spaces.'

'No, I only looked in through the window.'

'I'm looking forward to hearing what you think. For now, I'll let you go and settle in.'

'Sounds great. Bye for now.'

'Is everything ok?' Carla asked once Simon had hung up the phone.

'Yes, it was just Lydia checking I'm here ok. She wants me to go and take a look down in the gallery. I'm not sure why as I've seen everything through the window. It's not as if there's any art on the walls.'

'Perhaps we should go down and get it over with, and then we can have some fun to celebrate your first night living on Vekianos.'

'Sounds like a good plan. I'm looking forward to some food – I'm really hungry!'

Simon picked up the keys and they went down the stairs and out onto the street and then into the gallery. Everything was lovely, all freshly painted and the new floor looking great, but apart from that he couldn't see a lot else.

'Lydia said something about "spaces", but there's only one room. She also said they had done a lot of work, but it's just had a coat of paint and a new floor. Am I missing something here?'

'Perhaps there's something through that door back in the corner?'

'No, that's just a toilet and a storage room.'

'You never know, she might be excited as she has given the toilet a makeover.' Carla laughed.

Simon walked over and opened the door. He stepped through and froze, not sure what to say. He had a lump in his throat and tears in his eyes and he felt as if he was nailed to the floor and couldn't move.

'So have you a posh toilet? Is it your dream toilet?' Carla joked.

'No, not a dream bathroom but rather a fabulous studio. Take a look.'

Simon was blown away. An extension had been built onto the back of the gallery, the little storeroom knocked through to create a studio space.

'Oh, Simon!' Carla gasped, looking around the space with wonder. 'There are even two easels and a long storage unit down the side for all your paints and equipment. How exciting!'

Simon was trying to take everything in but he felt overwhelmed with gratitude. This would be the perfect place to paint while also keeping an eye on the gallery at the same time. No wonder Lydia was so excited.

'Why don't you take a little bit of time to get settled in and then we can go and have a few drinks, something to eat, and a nice catch-up. We can end the day back at Alina's as Sakis and Nectarios are both eager to see you. But first, you need to phone Lydia back and thank her. I'm sure she's sat waiting for your call.'

*

A short while later Simon was down at the sea wall, looking out to the waves while he waited for Carla, who had nipped out to run an errand while he unpacked. He was still a little shell-shocked about the studio and he knew that until he was actually painting in there it wouldn't really sink in. Looking at the boats and the people walking around the harbour he was amazed to think that this was his life now. It felt a bit like an out-of-body experience, but it was real. His dream had come true.

'Sorry I'm late! How did the unpacking go?'

'All done. I also popped into the supermarket and stocked up on essentials.'

'No stop off at the bakery?'

'Of course. I said I had bought essentials, didn't I? And a vanilla slice is definitely an essential. Surely you know that? But I only had the one, so I'm still starving. Lead me to the food!'

'A lovely new pizza restaurant has opened a few streets back. I know it's not your normal Greek cuisine, but it will make a big change for me so what do you say?'

'I thought tonight was all about welcoming me back to the island. Where's my moussaka?'

'You can have that tomorrow. And yes, it *is* all about you, but it's pizza!'

They laughed and Simon agreed, knowing it wasn't a fight worth having because he'd have plenty of opportunity to eat as much Greek food as he liked now he lived here.

Carla led the way and they managed to get a little table outside. Pizza, garlic bread, and – most important of all – wine was soon ordered.

'So, Carla, start at the beginning. I want to hear everything about your last six weeks here on the island.'

'Well, it was hard in the restaurant to start with.

Of course Nectarios and Alina were a big help, but without Sakis we struggled. Thankfully he came back after just a week – his little holiday on Corfu was a disaster and I'll warn you that he will go on and on about it – and I started to really enjoy the job at that point, the four of us working so well together. Alina has been able to take some time off, and she comes in later and finishes earlier on a more regular basis, and once I got it through to Nectarios that I was here to work, and he didn't have to keep doing jobs for me, things started to become great.'

'What do you mean by that?'

'Well, to start with, if a table finished eating he would jump in and try to clear it for me rather than let me take everything back to the kitchen myself, and when customers left he would jump across me to reset the table. Eventually I had to put my foot down and explain that we're a team and I'm capable of doing the job and pulling my own weight.'

'That's very sweet of him, when you think about it.'

'It felt more annoying than sweet at the time.' She laughed and rolled her eyes. 'I also had to get used to Lambros watching everything I was doing. He kept giving suggestions on what I could change and he sort of knocked my confidence, but then one day Alina pointed out that he did it with her as well and it was just something he did because he's struggling to let go of the restaurant.'

'How is his house coming along? Is it finished yet?'

'Nearly, and I have a story about that as well... Oh! Here comes the food. Shall we have more wine, or is that a silly question?'

They both laughed and then got stuck into the pizzas. This had been the perfect place to come to for their reunion dinner.

'Back to Lambros, it must have been about three weeks ago that he asked if I would pop up to the house, saying he wanted some advice. That was a little scary in itself as I wasn't sure what on, but I presumed it could be something to do with decorating. When I got there, there was an interior designer from Corfu. She was lovely and had brought samples of everything from bathroom tiles to rugs, along with paint swatches, and my job was to suggest things that Angela might like.'

'How nice is that.'

'It was scary more than anything else. The bathroom things were easy as I knew how much Angela loved the villa that we stayed in, so I just picked similar things, but when it came to colours for the bedroom I panicked. Thankfully, the woman could see I was struggling and helped out with lots of ideas.'

'So is it finished?'

'Not quite, it should be another week or so.'

'So that's Lambros, Sakis, Alina, and Nectarios talked about, how about you? What's going on in Carla's world, or should I say head.'

'Carla's head is good, but her body is not so good. I have to admit I'm absolutely worn out. How these lovely people manage to work twelve- to fifteen-hour days seven days a week for all these months I will never know. Ok, it's only six or seven months a year, but oh my goodness it's hard, and in the heat as well.'

'But I suppose they know no differently as that's what they've been brought up experiencing. It's just a way of life to them.'

'Sakis and Nectarios make it look so easy.'

'I'm sure you do, too, and you just can't see it. Speaking of Nectarios, how are you getting on together outside of work?'

Simon could see Carla's face light up even more and she didn't really need to answer as he could tell everything was great between them.

'Where do I start? Everything is out of this world and we're both so happy. I could never have dreamt in a million years that I would ever feel the way I do. It's just wonderful. Our life together is perfect.'

'I'm so pleased for you. Once the season is over you'll be able to wind down, relax, and have fun.'

'Yes, and we're heading back to Saltmarsh Quay for a few months. I can't wait to show him Norfolk and introduce him to Mum, which is the most important part.'

'That will be lovely. And then back here for the following season?'

'Exactly. Now tell me, have you been in contact with Polina at all?'

'We have, but only through emails, and there haven't been many. She's made it clear to me that her mum comes before her art, and if she's putting her passion second, where would I stand on the list? I've had to clear my head of her and just focus on my art. Ok, if we bump into one another we can talk about painting, but that's as far as it will go because if I even start to believe we could have the slightest chance of a future together it will screw me up so much.'

'That's so sad, but I really do believe you shouldn't give up hope of having a friendship or a romance with her.'

'No, it's too late for that. If she felt like I do, she wouldn't question that I would be top of her list.'

Chapter 40

Carla's head wasn't good after her night out with Simon. Thankfully for her, Nectarios and Alina had insisted she take the morning off. It had been a lovely night with great food and lots of laughs, and once they got to Alina's Sakis had provided plenty of entertainment, telling Simon all about his disastrous trip to Corfu, and how Trifon introduced him to all his friends who were so boring. Alina jokingly told Simon that they all felt they had been right there with Sakis given the number of times he'd told the story.

Carla messaged Simon to see if his head was as bad as hers. It probably wasn't as he had planned on going out painting early this morning and so had taken it easier with the wine than she had. There was a message right back.

Hi, been up since seven and caught the bus to Thagistri. spending the day here painting. avoiding the harbour as the Wednesday craft market is on today and didn't want to bump into Polina. will see you at Alina's tonight. you can serve me the moussaka! PS I bet you have a bad head today x.

She smiled at the last line but then found herself wondering if perhaps this Simon and Polina situation needed a little helping hand, and if perhaps it was her hand that could do the helping.

After a shower and coffee she was out the door and on the way to the other side of the harbour. It was time to chat with Polina.

The market was really busy and there was a real buzz in the air, though a completely different vibe from the evenings. It was times like this where she really felt part of the community here, locals saying 'good morning' and asking how Lambros and the family were. She felt so accepted by the people of Vekianos.

As she got to the end of the stone pier she could see Polina saying goodbye to a woman Carla realised must be Polina's mum Calliope. This was perfect. With Calliope leaving Carla could go over and chat with Polina without worry of being interrupted.

But then a group of people approached the stand, and started talking to Polina about buying a painting. Polina was showing them different ones and Carla got the sense that this could take a while, so she would have to bide her time. She moved to get out of the way of the crowd and head back down to the sea wall, but then she spotted Calliope in one of the nearby restaurants. Perhaps this was the angle Carla should be taking? She had nothing to lose and though Angela had said the woman was very rude, the key difference between Carla and Angela was that she wouldn't be afraid to be less than polite back.

'Good morning! The market is very busy today, isn't it? Do you mind if I share the table with you?'

Before Calliope could answer Carla had seated herself and ordered a drink from the waitress.

'Aren't you Polina's mum? Calliope, isn't it? I'm Carla.'

'Hello,' said Calliope, her dissatisfaction with Carla's intrusion obvious.

'Polina is so talented and her art is very special. How wonderful for her to have a career that she has such a passion for. You must be so proud.'

'It's her hobby, not a career.'

'Hobby ... career ... whatever.' Carla shrugged. 'It doesn't take away how good she is at it.'

'I've come here for a quiet coffee, not to talk about my daughter with a stranger,' Calliope said pointedly.

'Ok, we don't have to talk about Polina. Instead, let me tell you about a friend of mine who is also an artist. For years he dreamed of doing exactly what Polina is doing, but instead he started a decorating business back in England. It was hugely successful but cutting a long story short, he walked away from it all and came to Vekianos to try to earn a living from his art. It was a huge gamble for him, but there's a new gallery opening here in a week or so and he's gotten a job there and a chance to show his work. It's owned by a lovely lady who has another gallery in Parga. She's expanding her business.'

The mention of Lydia had provoked the expected reaction in Calliope, and she stiffened.

'It's worth saying that if Polina sold her work in the new gallery she would undoubtedly be a huge success, but there is a big but: for whatever reason, you won't let her.'

With that Calliope stood up.

'Please sit back down. This will only take a minute and if you walk away I'll only follow you. I'm determined that you hear me out.'

Calliope sat down.

'I am not trying to upset you, but I just cannot understand why you don't want Polina to be the successful artist she deserves to be. Come to that, why won't you let her have a life of her own at all. Why does everything have to be about you? Ok, your life didn't turn out as you'd hoped and your husband left, and you don't want the same to happen to your daughter because you love her so much. But by protecting her from ever getting hurt like you were, you're not allowing her to have a life at all. Because of your actions, Polina's life isn't turning out how she'd hoped, meaning your attempts to protect her have led her to the exact same unhappy fate you suffered.'

There was a silence and for the first time since she'd sat down, Carla felt bad. Still, she pushed on.

'Calliope, I know Polina loves you, and as much as her art is her passion, *you* are the most important thing in her life. So perhaps you could show her a little love back with one simple gesture: give her permission to move forward with her passion. Now the new gallery is opening she wouldn't even have to leave the island to follow her dreams.'

With that Carla opened her bag and left the money on the table for her drink. Nodding her goodbye to Calliope, she stood and walked away. Had she gone too far? Carla didn't know. Only time would tell.

Chapter 41

Simon had been so busy since he'd arrived back on Vekianos. He'd spent the past three days out painting during the day and in the new studio in the evenings, only stopping to eat late at night. But he wasn't tired; the adrenaline was keeping him going and he was buzzing. Today things would be slightly different as Lydia was coming over with a friend and bringing a lot of the art to put on the walls of the new gallery now they were nearly ready to open. She had told him that he didn't need to interrupt his day for her, so he planned to catch the bus to Thagistri, which was becoming one of his favourite places to paint.

He did a quick tidy around in the apartment just in case Lydia decided to pop in – she probably wouldn't, but he didn't want to be caught out – and once that was done he was ready to nip down to the gallery and fetch his things. As he was sorting through his painting gear he realised he was getting better at only taking the essentials with him. As he closed the door from the studio into the gallery he spotted someone looking in through the window, but as he caught their eye they walked away. But the glimpse had been enough for him to recognize Calliope. Was it just a coincidence that she was walking by, or was there more to it?

Once at the bus stop he took in the long queue. The holiday season had really kicked in and now that schools all across Europe were closed for the summer break, the families had arrived in their masses. The first bus filled quickly and he settled in for the hour-long wait until the next one came. But then another bus appeared, this one off to Zagandros. He had heard the name before, and he knew there was a beach there, so perhaps today was the perfect day to discover somewhere new.

As he got on the bus and sat opposite a young family who were obviously heading for a day of sand, sea, and games, he asked them how long the journey was. They said it could take three quarters of an hour as the bus stopped at lots of villages along the way, but as he was already on the bus and it was on the move, he would make the most of the day.

As he got off the bus in the little beach car park forty-five minutes later, he checked the times of the return buses and worked out that he would have around five hours to paint before he needed to head back. Now to find a piece of scenery he could transfer on to canvas. This was normally the hardest part of the whole day as finding something that had the right proportions wasn't easy. He decided to take a chance and go the opposite direction to all the families, heading into the trees bordering the car park.

He was just beginning to think he might need to turn around when the sea suddenly appeared. The rocky terrain was free of holiday makers, which was just perfect for his needs, and as he found a spot to set up his easel he suspected that this would become one of his favourite places to paint.

An hour later he was well into the work and in a really happy place – it was views like this that gave him confidence and inspiration to paint – and he hadn't realised someone was behind him until they touched his arm.

He jumped in surprise and turned to face...
'Polina!'
'I see you've discovered Zagandros. Are you

impressed? It's very dramatic, this part of the beach, and there's so much character compared to other parts of the island.'

'Yes, the shade created where the sun is hitting the rocks is magnificent. I can imagine it would be completely different being here very early in the morning when the sun first comes up.'

'You're right. It's not a place I usually come to, but when I do, I always ask myself why I don't do it more often. I've come today to take photos – a bit of a research and inspiration afternoon. Have you settled in ok in the apartment?'

'Yeah, it's great. I had such a wonderful surprise as Lydia has created a little studio at the back for me or anyone else working in the gallery to use.'

'That's amazing. So how long now until the gallery opens?'

'Not long, I think. Lydia is over from Parga today with a friend setting everything up.'

'I walked by the other week and I saw men working away.'

'Any chance you've changed your mind about Lydia's offer?'

'No, I'm happy with the weekly craft fair, which is still doing ok.'

'I don't know if I should mention it, but when I was getting ready to leave earlier today I noticed your mum looking through the gallery window.'

'Really? That surprises me as it's a part of the harbour she never goes to and she isn't very well at the moment.'

'I'm sorry to hear that.'

'I can't put my finger on it, but she seems to have gone in on herself the last couple of days. I don't know what happened. She said goodbye to me at the start of the Wednesday market and then, when she came back to help me pack up at the end of the day, she was a different person. She just seems ... distant from me, like she's in deep thought. I can't really put it into words as it's not something I've seen from her before. Take today, for instance. She was more than happy for me to catch the bus here and back, and there was no talk about picking me up. All very odd and out of character.'

'Perhaps she's having second thoughts about the gallery. Wouldn't that be lovely?'

'Yes, it would, but it's unlikely. Right, I'd best let you get on or else you won't have any work to display in the gallery. Sorry to have disturbed you.'

'Not at all. It was really nice seeing you today, Polina. Can I say something? I didn't intend to ... it's not a plan ... actually it's the opposite of everything...'

Simon took a breath as he marshalled his thoughts.

'Before I came back, and even up to your appearance here just now, I told myself not to get involved with you anymore. That sounds horrible, I know, and of course I wanted to see you and speak to you, but I thought it best to keep things professional between us, only really communicating about art and stuff. When I looked at the facts, it was clear to me that your mum comes first in your life, and then your art, and even if something did happen between us, I would always come third, which isn't enough for me, no matter how much I like you.'

'I do understand, and you're completely right, you deserve more than I can offer you. I wish things could be different and I'm sorry.'

'Yes, but now you've turned up here and I'm stood looking at you and talking to you, I ... I want more. I did come back to Vekianos to pursue my dream of being an artist, but to be honest. I could have gone anywhere to do that. The real reason I picked this island is because *you* are here.'

Simon wasn't sure what he expected but it certainly wasn't that Polina would nod silently and then just walk away. Not towards the rocks to take her photos, but back towards the car park. It had been painful to admit exactly how he was feeling, but he was proud of himself and pleased to have cleared the air with Polina, even if it hadn't ended how he'd hoped.

Something told him it was a good time to pack his things up as there likely wouldn't be a lot more creativity in his heart or his hands today. He looked at the time. There was a bus due in twenty minutes, but he was in no rush to catch that one as Polina would probably be on it. No, he would wait for the next one. A journey together on the bus wouldn't be good for either of them.

The bus ride back seemed to take forever with all the stopping and starting. He really didn't have the patience for it, which was so out of character for him. He just wanted to get back to his apartment and forget today had ever happened. But that would have to wait as Lydia would be in the gallery and he would have to go in and say hi. She had done so much for him so he knew he needed to come across just as excited as she was.

After getting off the bus he went to the bakery for some treats, and also nipped into the supermarket to grab a bottle of wine. He wondered briefly if he should be taking Champagne, but no, that could wait until the day the gallery opened.

Right, he was nearly there. Time to put on a smile.

'Hi, Lydia,' he called as he walked through the front door. 'Oh my word!' He almost gasped. 'It's a completely different place to the one I left this morning. There's so much colour, it's gorgeous.

You've certainly been busy and clearly worked hard.'

Lydia laughed. 'I assure you I haven't. All I've done is hang a few paintings. There's nothing hard about that.'

'Let me just put my things back in the studio and then I want you to talk me through everything. By the way, where's your friend?'

'That was actually a little white lie as I knew you would insist on helping me if you knew I was coming on my own – which is lovely of you – but I needed to transfer the images from my head onto the walls by myself.'

'Don't worry, I understand. Now that you're done, I have pastries and wine ... if you're interested?'

'Of course! Once you've put your things away I can show you everything.'

Simon's phone beeped as he poured the wine and put the pastries on a plate but he ignored it.

'You brought some of the olive tree paintings?' he asked, delighted to see them. 'They look stunning on that wall.'

'Yes, I have the five on display – I prefer everything always in odd numbers – and there are another five in a box in the back. That's something I'll need to go through with you as well – the back-up stock... I think that's your phone ringing.'

'It's ok, whoever it is can call back.'

'Right then, let's start by the door and work our way around the room. My biggest challenge is that this gallery is so much smaller than the one over in Parga. Because space is at a premium, we need to be on top of the stock. So, for instance, if that collection of bougainvillaea paintings hasn't sold within the next three months, they need to be taken down so that something else we feel will sell more quickly can go up in their place.'

'Makes perfect sense,' said Simon, nodding.

They started to walk the walls and when they came to a gap Lydia explained that she had left it for his work. He was both pleased and panicked by the gesture, and he quickly moved her on to the next collection of works.

Lydia walked him through each collection and gave him the background on each artist and where they worked. He was a bit worried about keeping all the details straight, but she reassured him that she had back-up notes for him, and he wasn't expected to remember everything off the top of his head.

'Are you happy, Simon?' she asked as they returned to the point where they'd started.

'Happy isn't a strong enough word. I'm blown away by it all, and to think that *my* work will actually be going on a wall in here with all these other fabulous artists, it's overwhelming.'

'You deserve to be here just as much as them. I've got to leave soon to catch the last boat back to Parga so I think that's all for today, but I'll be back the day after tomorrow and we can go through everything from the till to all the codes for each artist and painting. Thank you for the wine and the treats.'

'You're more than welcome, and I promise they'll be here every time you come over from Parga.'

'Thank you. I'm going to head off now as the boat waits for no one. Oh! There's something I forgot to mention. I had a visitor today – your friend Polina's mum. She wanted to know if I would be interested in displaying her daughter's work and of course I said yes. Now I need to fly ... or do I mean sail? See you in two days, Simon.'

Simon couldn't think straight as he locked the door behind Lydia. What had happened to Calliope? What had made her change her mind? With that there was a knocking on the window and he realised he should have turned the lights off. Holiday visitors were always walking by so it was only natural that they would want to come in. He would need to make a sign explaining that they weren't opening for a few days, and put it on the door. The knocking continued so he moved to the door to explain and turn the person away, and when he recognized the figure on the other side his heart jumped and he fumbled with the keys.

'Polina! What's going on?' he asked as he opened the door and ushered her inside.

'I've been messaging you and calling you for the last few hours.'

'I'm sorry, I was with Lydia. What's wrong?'

'My mum sat me down and we had a long overdue chat. She explained that the reason she's always been overly protective is because she was so hurt by my dad, and she never wanted anything like that to ever happen to me. She felt the only way she could guarantee it wouldn't happen was to be like she has been for all these years.'

'And now she's seen the error of her ways, she's going to let you sell your art here?' he asked hopefully.

'Yes! I'm so excited but there's something else that's more important than the art. It's you, Simon. I want you to be number one on my list, not just for today but every day.'

With that Polina put her hand on his face and pulled him into a kiss neither of them would soon forget.

Chapter 42
Three months later

Carla was up early as she couldn't sleep. She took her coffee onto the balcony feeling happy, but also a bit nervous. Today was the last day before the restaurant closed. It was the end of the season for them and from tomorrow both Nectarios and she would have an influx of free time. Well, once they'd finished closing the restaurant down and doing all the necessary deep cleaning and tidying. But once that was done, they'd have four months – sixteen weeks! – off to spend together before they had to get back on the restaurant merry-go-round again.

She was so excited to be taking Nectarios back to England and to let her mum get to know him and of course show him around Norfolk and beautiful Saltmarsh Quay, which would be a shock to him as he wasn't used to a windy and probably very rainy harbour.

The nerves she was feeling stemmed from the fact that they would be together twenty-four-seven without any work to act as a distraction. She was worried things might be different between them or that he might get bored of her, or resent her for taking him away from the usual impromptu parties he was used to in the winter on Vekianos. Just then she heard a noise and turned to see Nectarios stepping outside.

'I hope I didn't wake you! I couldn't sleep.'

'It's fine. I wanted to be up earlier anyway as we have a busy day ahead.'

'Can you believe the day has finally arrived and

we're closing for the winter?'

'Yes and I've never felt so happy about it ever before.'

Carla didn't know what to say to that. What exactly did he mean? She kept telling herself to say something, but she couldn't find any words.

'Is something wrong, Carla? You don't seem yourself this morning with that sad face. Perhaps if we went back to bed for a little bit I could bring a smile to your face.' He grinned cheekily. 'That's actually the one thing I'm looking forward to the most – not having to get up and rush to the restaurant or queue at the bakery for the bread. Not having to look at the clock every day is such a luxury.'

'But won't you miss your normal winter routine this year?'

'You must be joking! Normally I would be going to work on a building site here on Vekianos, or over in Corfu. But this year, thanks to my mum taking on this gorgeous girl to work in the restaurant, we've made more money than other years, so I don't need to do it this coming winter.'

'How about all the parties and socialising you like to do? Won't you miss that? I remember Zeta saying when I first moved here that in the winter all she does is dance.'

'I won't be missing it though because we'll be doing it together. I can't wait for you to meet friends I only see in the winter, and yes, Zeta is right, we dance the winter away. Of course I'm also looking forward to going back to your home and meeting your mum and then planning next year's season back in the restaurant, looking at how we could change things and make things better.'

She loved how he always talked about them as a couple, always factoring her into their plans. She was starting to feel much better about everything and the nerves were disappearing.

'So what's the plan of action for today? All hands on deck? Your mum said the menu will be a lot smaller as the chefs haven't been replacing things this week, so there's not a lot of stock left. It's a shame that the chefs won't be here over the winter to party with us.'

'Yes, but because we close a few weeks before the other restaurant it gives them time to go over to France and work the winter season at the ski resorts. But as for plans of action, I think you need to go and see Simon and make sure he and Polina come to the restaurant for dinner tonight.'

'I can call him. I don't need to have the morning off for that.'

'No, I insist. Go take him out for coffee and have a little walk or something.'

Carla thought the suggestion was a bit odd, and it almost felt as though Nectarios was trying to get her out of the way, but she wasn't going to argue as there were few things she liked more than sitting and chatting with Simon.

She walked past the restaurant, and paused to greet Sakis, who was preparing for lunchtime.

'Good morning! I thought Nectarios said you had the morning off; what are you doing here?'

'Just saying hi. I'm off to meet Simon for a coffee. Last shift for you and then it's holiday time. How are you feeling? Are you excited?'

'Oh yes. The Canary Islands await me, the land of winter sunshine and parties. If you didn't have Nectarios, you could come with me.'

'Maybe next year. We can make plans once you're back.'

'Good plan. If we have as much fun next year as

we've had this year it will be great, and we'll have to make the most of it because there won't be that many more summers.'

'What do you mean?' she asked, confused.

'Well, I suspect it won't be long before little Carla and Nectarios junior arrive. Why are you looking at me strangely? Of course you'll have babies. It would be wrong for two such gorgeous looking people to not produce undoubtedly fabulous children.'

'On that note, Sakis, I think I'll be off!' she said, shaking her head. 'I'll see you tonight. Here come Nectarios – please don't scare him off with talk like that.'

'Scare me with what, Carla?'

'Nothing. Sakis was just being silly,' she said, shooting her friend a glare.

'No I wasn't, I just mentioned that it wouldn't be too long before you two will be having babies.'

'That's not silly. Of course we'll have lots of babies. Before that happens though, Carla has to agree to marry me.'

Carla stood anchored to the spot as Sakis made himself scarce, clearly recognising that Carla and Nectarios needed to be alone.

What had he just said? Before she could form words Nectarios walked over and kissed her.

'This was not supposed to happen like this,' he said, shaking his head. 'I wanted to wait until I met your mum, and she gave me her blessing, but as per usual Sakis has spoilt the surprise.'

Oh my goodness. What had just happened? Had the man she loved proposed to her!? Her heart was racing and her whole body was tingling. She had never been this happy in all of her life and she wanted to scream 'yes!' so many times. Of course she wanted to marry him.

'Yes! The answer is yes for both things. Of course

I'll marry you and then happily have your gorgeous children.'

With that she threw herself at him and they kissed. Carla didn't want to let Nectarios go but after a while he pulled away just enough to say, 'That's what I hoped you'd say. Now go off and meet Simon.'

'I don't want to. I want to stay here with you.'

'No, go on, I have things to be doing and you don't want to be late. By the way, I don't think we should mention this to people until we've talked to your mum.'

'Ok, it's our secret. I love you, Nectarios.'

'And I love you, Carla, more than you will ever know.'

As Carla walked away with tears rolling down her face she felt as though she was in a dream, a very special dream. She then heard her phone beep and looking at it made her smile. Simon had texted.

hi Carla, Polina insisted I take the morning off and meet up with you for coffee.

Carla texted him back.

how about down by the old pier in five minutes?

She so wanted to tell Simon what had just happened, but she wouldn't for the time being. She'd promised Nectarios.

'Hello!' Simon called as she joined him just moments later. 'I told Polina we would be seeing you tonight, but she wouldn't take no for an answer.'

'Nectarios said the same and I was on my way to the gallery when I got your text. There's a table over there. Coffee and pastry time?'

Simon nodded and they made their way over to the restaurant's terrace. Carla realised it was the site of her confrontation with Calliope.

'The last time I came in here I was on a mission and very nervous, but ... well, that's a story for another time.'

They ordered two large coffees and a cheese and bacon pie each.

'So, the last day. You must be ready for a break with all the days and hours you've worked in this heat. And I have to say I'm impressed because you've not complained once. You really do seem to have enjoyed your summer, but then that's probably mostly down to being with Nectarios.'

'It's been hard, but it's been good, and of course it hasn't been a bit boring having a laugh every day with Sakis. And like you say, it's been good being with Nectarios. But enough about me. Is Lydia happy with how the gallery is going? And how are things with you and Polina?'

'I can't believe the gallery has been open for three months already. Lydia is really happy and we've figured out what sells and what doesn't, which is good. Thankfully, my work does sell, which I'm overjoyed about, and I'm not taking any of it for granted.'

'So that's the gallery. Now the exciting bit: you and Polina ... and not forgetting Calliope.'

'What can I say? It's still a shock to Polina how much her mum has changed. It's no surprise that her paintings are bestsellers – visitors love them – and she's had so many commissions from people wanting a second or third piece to add to the original one they bought.'

'That's really good. Is her mum happy with that?'

'She seems to be. She often pops into the gallery on the days Polina is running it. I think she gets pleasure in seeing customers rave over one of her daughter's paintings.'

'Now how about you and Polina as a couple? It's been three months and I know because of Calliope you were both discreet in the beginning. How is it going now?'

'Strangely ok. There have been times when Calliope has come into the gallery when I've been there by myself, and we've chatted about normal things like how busy Vekianos is or the weather, and that's been ok. The odd thing is that she seems to know about me and my past in Saltmarsh Quay. Polina says she hasn't told her mum those kinds of things so neither of us can figure out how she knows.'

'Very strange, but probably nothing to worry about, I wouldn't think.' Carla bit back a smile. 'So you and Polina are openly dating now?'

'Yep. We aren't living together – yet – but there have been nights when Polina has stayed over, and Calliope seemed ok with that. I think the little steps we're taking are working well. Things might change when the gallery closes for the winter though.'

'Have you made any plans for that?'

'Yes, we both want to get ahead with painting as it would be great for us both to have our work over in the Parga gallery next year. Also, I want to go back to Norfolk and spend some time with my family.'

'Will Polina go with you?'

'No, just me for now. We both know that would be a step too far for Calliope and we want to take it slow. We're happy to count our blessings as neither of us could have ever imagined we would be in this lovely situation. Can you believe how our lives have changed in less than six months? And all because we sat down at Angela's dining table and picked this island for our holiday.'

'I think it was fate and meant to be. All three of our lives have changed for the better.'

'How has Angela's life changed?'

'I think now that Lambros's house is completed Angela will come and stay quite a bit. She'll have her own room and bathroom, which I have to say are both gorgeous, and when she sees the guest suite she'll be blown away. Come next spring I think she'll be one of the first visitors to come to Vekianos. In the meantime, I'm looking forward to seeing her when Nectarios and I go back to Norfolk. I know she'll be pleased to see us as she hates the winter and will be glad of the company.'

'Just a sec, Polina's calling me,' said Simon, pulling out his phone and answering it. 'Is everything ok?' he asked his girlfriend.

'Yes, but I need you to come back. There's a customer that wants some help and I think you'll be better at it than me.'

'Ok, give me ten minutes and I'll be there.'

'Can you ask Carla to come as well?'

'Why?'

'I just want to ask her something. I need to go but make sure Carla is with you.'

'Sorry, I need to pop back to the gallery,' Simon explained as he hung up and then signalled to the waiter that they needed the bill. 'Polina would like you to come as well as she needs to talk to you about something.'

'Fine with me. I haven't been in since the week it opened so it will be nice to see what different things you have on display.'

Carla paid for the coffees and the pies, and as they headed back through the little streets to the gallery they chatted about how the island had come to feel like home in just these past few months.

'That's Calliope walking towards us,' Simon suddenly whispered. 'Shall I introduce you?' he asked.

This could be interesting, thought Carla.

'Hello, Calliope.'

'Hello, Simon, and it's nice to see you again, Carla.'

Simon looked between them, confused.

'Polina tells me it's the last day at the restaurant before it closes for the winter.'

'Yes. Please, you must come and join us for dinner tonight with Polina and Simon.'

'I don't think so. They won't want me spoiling their evening.'

'You've got that wrong, Calliope, I think it'll actually make their evening,' Carla said warmly.

'Ok then, I will, thank you. It will be nice to catch up with Alina and Lambros.'

As they chatted about their plans for the coming winter, Simon stood between them with his mouth wide, wondering what was going on and why these two were being so friendly with one another.

'Norfolk. Isn't that where you come from as well, Simon?'

'Yes, that's right.'

'Perhaps once the gallery closes for the winter you might be able to take Polina there and show her around. It would be good for you both to have a holiday as you've worked so hard over the summer. I need to head off now but thank you again for the invitation. I'll look forward to seeing you tonight at Alina's. Yes, thank you for everything, Carla.'

Simon raised his hands in disbelief as Calliope walked away, still lost for words.

'It's a long story for another time. I'm just glad it has a very happy ending,' was all Carla said.

Walking through the open gallery door they found Polina but no customers.

'Are they popping back or did you manage to sort them out?' asked Simon.

Simon could see Polina wasn't herself. She looked nervous. Had something happened or gone wrong?

'No, the customer is out in the studio.'

Now Simon was completely confused. Why had she let strangers into the back and why was the door closed? He walked towards the studio.

'You should go with him,' Polina said to Carla.

At that point Carla also started to wonder what was going on. Simon opened the door and before he had time to walk in someone spoke.

'Hello, you two, I thought I'd best come and have one last meal in the restaurant before it closes for the winter, and of course I needed to see this new, hugely successful gallery on the island,' said Angela, with a bright smile.

'What are you doing here?!' Simon and Carla asked at the same time, rushing forward to hug their friend.

'Like I said, I've come to see you both and hear about what you've been up to since I was last here. And why would I want to be in a cold and frosty UK over the winter when I could be here on Vekianos? Ok, the sun won't be shining that much, but at least it won't be as cold as Norfolk. And, of course, I have a lovely new room to stay in. We started the summer season off here together, so it only seemed right to finish it together, don't you think? A little bit of fun before everywhere closes. Now, come and give this old woman a big hug to finish off the perfect Greek island holiday.'

THE END

Printed in Great Britain
by Amazon